Nuts To You

Michael Marx-Brooks

Copyright © 2009 by Michael Marx-Brooks

ISBN: 978-0-578-00764-9

Acknowledgments

I would like to thank the following people for their help and support:

Samuel C. Crawford for his enthusiastic encouragement. Check out Sam's excellent *Brownwater* novels based on his experiences in the Navy in "the 'Nam."

Nick Terkanian and Derrick Wise for their computer expertise. This book would have never been finished without them.

Nick Rudawski for allowing me to use his name in the book. He was supposed to make only a cameo appearance, but, fortunately for Dewey, it became much more.

Last, but certainly not least, I would like to thank all the Dewey Polpulcionskis out there who have the guts to stand up for what they know is right – regardless of whom they have to stand up against.

Dedication

This book is dedicated to the late Jack Benny – the reason for the 39 chapters – who continues to make me laugh to this day through the magic of DVDs; and to a great entertainer, as well as a truly fine gentleman, Eddie Carroll, whose one-man show "Laughter in Bloom" does much to keep Jack's talents alive. If you ever get a chance, do yourself a favor and see "Laughter in Bloom." You'll be very glad you did!

Chapter 1:   HELLO

I was just about finished with my nine-hour shift for the day. My job was to tail a statuesque blond with hauntin' blue eyes, and legs that apparently went all the way up. Julie Crinn was a 38 year old beauty, and the reason her husband, Joseph, had me tail her was because he hadn't been able to verify the length of her legs for some time, but was certain that someone else could. Part of the problem was that Joseph was also 38, but only if you were dyslexic.

"Just watch her from 8:30 in the morning till 5:30 in the evening," he instructed me. "She's always home by quarter to six, and she's in all night." This seemed awfully strange to me, considerin' that Joe looked like he wouldn't be able to last more than 7:30 on a good night, just about the time Julie would be ready for some action. It seemed like real easy money, so I took the gig

This wasn't the kind of case that I really cared about. Tailin' someone from her house to her office and sittin' there takin' lots of pictures wasn't my idea of havin' fun. After all, if I wanted to be a photographer, I woulda been one. But old man Crinn was payin' seven fifty a day, plus expenses, and the rent was due. Actually, three months rent was due, so snap away is what I did.

I was in my third week of watchin' the luscious Mrs. Crinn drive to work, get out of her car, walk into work, and reverse it in the

1

evening. This chick didn't go nowhere. Not even to lunch. In in the morning and out at night. At least that's what I saw, and that's what I told her husband. If there was a back entrance…hey, a guy can't be at two places at the same time. Can he?

If Legs was doing any cheatin', it was all happenin' at the office. Or maybe it was after the old boy thought she was home, knittin' him some warm woolen socks. Whatever the reason, I think he had a right to be suspicious. After all, Joe was loaded, had himself a real trophy wife, so she had no reason to work. He claimed that he tried to get her to stop, but she insisted, claimin' that she was used to it before she met him, and she liked the routine. Maybe she did, and maybe she didn't. Or maybe the bagel man who came every morning at 9:30 was deliverin' more than bagels.

Like I said, Crinn was payin' seven fifty a day plus expenses for some glossies of his wife comin' and goin' from the office for the foreseeable future, so I wasn't knockin' it. Expenses usually consisted of donuts and coffee for breakfast, fast food for lunch, and a pizza and a few beers after work. Diet conscious I ain't. Also, I don't go near the kitchen except to get a cold one out of the fridge. But tonight would be different. Tonight I was gonna hit old Crinn up for a wine dinner at my favorite restaurant, Sloppy Man's, with a hot little brunette I met on-line, whose lung capacity was nothin' short of the Hindenburg. I figured tonight would be one helluvan evening. Little did I know what an understatement that would turn out to be.

Me? I'm Dewey. Dewey Polpulcionski. Of course, my first name really ain't Dewey, it's David. But nobody's called me David since my eleventh grade English teacher, may her puritanical, bitchy soul rest in peace. I got the name Dewey because when I was growin' up, I had two friends named Howie and Lennie, and we used to sit around all the time watchin' a cartoon show with three ducks named Huey, Dewey, and Louie, and so Howie, David, and Lennie became Huey, Dewey, and Louie. At least that's what I tell people who don't know me very well.

Actually, my last name really ain't Polpulcionski, either. The story I get is that when my grandparents got off the boat from Poland in the early 1900s, their last name was *Polspulcionski*, but since the people checkin' them in really didn't give a shit about a bunch of WOPS, they screwed up the spellin' and it was never corrected. Most people, myself included, didn't know that the first WOPS were actually Polacks, and stood for WithOut Passport.

My grandparents, Anna and Stephan Polspulcionski – now *Polpulcionski* – had my father, David,Sr. a few years before the start of the Great Depression, along with three other sons. Life wasn't easy for the six Polacks, but three of the four boys went to college. Dad was the one who didn't.

Dad ended up marrying Mom, Josephine Gulick, who he picked up at a bar. Dad bein' in a bar I can understand. I never did get the story why Mom was there. Mom and Dad were the strangest couple you could ever meet. I think they got married because both of them couldn't get anybody else. Mom was very straight-laced and prissy, and Dad didn't give a shit about nothin', includin' havin' kids. With everyone else in the neighborhood havin' kids, Mom – Mrs. Keep-Up-With-The Joneses – finally won out, and seven years after their marriage, I was born.

Life was, and wasn't, easy for little Davey. (Eleventh grade was a ways off, and Dewey was still years away.) Easy, because both of my parents worked, and so I got most everything I wanted, although I could never talk them into that horse. Not, because life was pretty lonely without any brothers or sisters. (Dad won that one. One of me was enough.) I had some friends in the neighborhood, but we all had to be in pretty early, so I was a real lonely kid. Hell, even the puppy I had got run over on his birthday.

School wasn't much better. I made it through high school with mostly Bs, and college with mostly Cs, but I was bored as hell. That's when the shit really started to happen. That's when I met Patty.

Patty wasn't much to look at, but she did have big boobs, so we decided to get married when I was 22 and she was 21. What a frickin' mistake that was! I knew somewhere in my head that it wouldn't work out, but I was young, stupid, and thought I could fix anything. Boy, what a real asshole I was!

We had a good marriage for six months. Unfortunately, it lasted for almost ten years. Turns out that after the six months, Patty thought that *sex* came between *five* and *seven*, and one of us was always workin' during that time. Much later I found out that that logic only applied to me, and I guess all other guys. Apparently it didn't go that way for Kathy, Norma, and who the hell knows who else. After ten years, and a real crappy divorce, Patty and I were through. As a side note, Patty immediately went back to her maiden name. Claimed Patty Polpulcionski was just too hard to pronounce one time slow, let alone five times fast.

Last I knew, Patty was a spokesperson for GLAAD.

Chapter 2: UOUTTHERE.COM

After the Patty stuff, I figured it was time to have some fun. I also figured I'd had enough of the real nine-to-five world, and that's when I decided to become a private detective. I was looking for some glamour, some excitement, some action. What I got was a lot of nothin'.

But in a small place like East Arthur, what the hell did I expect. East Arthur is a nice little college town, with tree-lined streets. A lot of churches, a lot of bars, and a lot of good music on the main street almost every night of the week, but not a lot of call for a private detective. East Arthur is about fifteen miles from Queensville, which ain't exactly the biggest spot on the map either.

At first, I got some business tailin' some lawyers' babes who the guys thought were cheatin' on them. A few cases paid pretty good, but that dried up real fast. Not that many lawyers in East Arthur. Soon I was down to livin' hand to mouth, findin' lost cats for little ole ladies, so when old man Crinn showed up, it was like a blessin' from above.

Since I had a lot of time on my hands and not much dough in my pocket, I decided to do the online datin' thing. God, what a mistake that was! To begin with, I got nothin' but the weirdoes, the criers, and the desperates. Let me explain.

The greatest all-time weirdo was Sylvia. Sylvia was the kind of chick that you swear was drunk all the time, but you knew she wasn't.

On the first date, Sylvia was spillin' things all over the table, which made the white tablecloth all the colors of the rainbow. Then she starts yellin', and I mean yellin', about how clumsy she was. Just made things worse. I shoulda known better than to see Sylvia again, but I kinda felt sorry for her, plus the fact that she was an easy lay.

The second date was even better. I tell Sylvia I'd pick her up at one in the afternoon so we could go to Paradise Island and see a show. I get there, and she answers the door, almost dressed. Sylvia didn't have the biggest boobs in the world, but she had no problem showin' 'em off.

"Hi, what are you doin' here?" she asked, looking either high or bombed, as usual.

"I told ya I would pick you up around one, and it's quarter of."

"Oh, I thought it was nine thirty in the morning." Maybe she was crocked after all.

Needless to say, after a roll in the sack, we never did make P.I. So we went to dinner instead. This time Sylvia didn't drop a thing on the floor. This time Sylvia was on the floor. I knew it was time to kiss Sylvia goodbye.

The crier deluxe turned out to be Lulu, and what a Lulu. Had me on the phone for over three hours tellin' me all about some guy she used to live with who died a year ago. Three frickin' hours, for God sake! But bein' the sweetheart that I am, I put up with it. Besides, all the cats were safe and sound, so I had nothin' better to do. Why I ever agreed to meet Lulu in person is beyond me. If I thought the phone call was bad, man, that was nothin' compared to the actual date.

Oh, it started out OK, I guess. Lulu was livin' with a relative in Riten, which is about fifty minutes west of East Arthur, so I agreed to meet her at a restaurant, and that we would go to a movie after. Not bad for a first date, or so I thought! We meet at the place, and have to wait forty five minutes for a table. "Food's really good here, that's the reason for the wait," she tells me.

That was the best conversation we had all night. Once we sat down to eat, it started all over again. "Pete (or was it Paul?) was the best person I ever knew. He had a large house and a lotta land, and a lotta money. Made a fortune creating a new dip for potato chips (or was it a new mustard for hot dogs?), but I really loved him for himself."

When it started again, I just kinda turned her off the best I could, and just nodded and said *Uh-huh* every now and again, just to look like I really gave a shit. Besides, I hadn't eaten anything all day, and the food *was* good.

Once dinner was over, I finally thought, "Good, we'll go to the frickin' movie, and maybe she'll shut the hell up." No such luck! After dinner, she drove us to the movie, since she knew her way around Riten and I didn't. Well, all the way over, it starts up again.

"Jim (or was it Jack? Who the hell knew at this point? More to the point, who the hell cared!) had three kids from his marriage. We got along real well, or so I thought, but once Jim made it big, things started to change. The kids, all grown of course, really never cared about him, or me, but only about his money," she insisted. "They were only after the bucks, and didn't give a damn about me. Once he died, I didn't get a dime. Not that I thought I should have, but I did help him create his kumquat sauce (or whatever the hell it was), but not one dime. But I really did love him." (Sure you did, honey.)

Fortunately, the movie wasn't that far from the restaurant. Good thing, too, that it was a second-run theater, and the tickets were only two bucks each. For some reason, the cats in East Arthur weren't havin' many kittens lately. I couldn't tell ya what we saw if you stuck a gun to my head, but that was OK. For an hour and a half at least I got some peace and quiet.

After the movie, it was back to the restaurant where I left my car. It was more about Bob (or was it Brian?) and I couldn't wait to get back. But, the best was yet to come. When we finally do get back and she parks the car, not only does she go on about What's-his-name, but now she starts cryin', for Pete (or was it Paul?) sake. Bein' the good samaritan that I am, I put my arms around her so she can cry on my shoulder, but all I get for it is a soaked shirt.

I get out of Riten, return to East Arthur, and promise myself never to have anything to do with Lulu again. However, two weeks later I get an email from Lulu tellin' me she's in therapy, tryin' to forget whoever the sonuvabitch was.

The desperates came in all shapes and sizes. After a nice dinner and a good-night kiss – and maybe a feel or two here or there – these babes were ready to walk down the aisle. They really weren't lookin' for me, they were lookin' for anybody who would say "I do." Well, I don't! At least not with somebody the likes of them. The less said about these broads the better.

I was just about to give up on uoutthere.com, when I got an email from Nora.

Chapter 3: NORA

Nora wasn't the greatest lookin' dame I ever saw, but when I saw her picture on the net, I quite frankly couldn't remember who was. A few inches shorter than me, a few years younger, raven hair with gorgeous dark eyes, and, of course, an unbelievable rack. The only problem was, you could never get too excited about the pictures, first because you really didn't know how old they were, and second because you didn't even know if it was them. I swear, some of these broads must have sent in pictures of their daughters, that's how much they didn't look like the picture in person. I learned two things already about online dating. First, never get too excited about the picture; and, second, never respond to anyone who doesn't show a picture or at least says "picture available on request." You're just askin' for trouble if you do. But if Nora looked half as good as her picture, that would be good enough for me.

Nora emailed me first. Said she liked my bio – that's the part where most people, includin' me, lie about themselves. Said I was a top-notch private detective, with a top-notch agency in the greater Philly area. Well, part of that was true, and part wasn't. I *am* a private detective, and I am the best one with my agency. The fact that I'm the *only* one with my agency, and that *my* agency ain't exactly top-notch, I left out. Oh, yeah, it's also in the greater Philly area, like that's gonna help. Nora also told me that I was "kinda cute." Anyone who thought I

11

was cute – "kinda" or otherwise, and had an apparently healthy set of lungs, made my little heart go pitter-patter. Well, to be honest about it, it wasn't my *heart* that I was worried about standin' still.

So, after a few days – you never want to look too anxious about these things – I emailed Nora back. Hit her with the normal first email stuff. You know, "Thanks for the email; great hearing from you; I really like your picture; how ya doin'; wanna get laid on Friday?" Shit like that. Actually, I just made that last one up, but don't think I wasn't tempted.

Nora, apparently not wanting to appear too anxious either, emailed back a few days later, and the online love match was off and runnin'. Typical stuff from her, too. "Thanks for getting back to me; I'm a nurse in a doctor's office; I'm fairly new to online dating, how about you; and, no, I *don't want to get laid on Friday. Friday is too soon, but will Saturday work for you?* I swear, Nora musta been a mind reader, cuz she sure couldn't hear the pitter-patter of my heart, or see the lump in my pants, over the Internet.

Anyway, after a few back-and-forth emails, I thought it was time Nora and I exchanged phone numbers. I really wanted to feel her up – er, *out* – over the phone, and so I felt the time had come where we'd done all we could readin' each other's emails. Nora agreed, and a few days later – never get too anxious with phone calls, either – I gave Nora a buzz.

The phone rang for what seemed like forever, but I guess it was really only four or five times. Finally I heard,"Hello?"

"Hello. Is this Nora?"

"Yes. Who's this?"

"It's Dewey."

"Who?"

"Dewey. You know, from uoutthere.com. Told ya I would give you a call."

"Oh yeah, Dewey."

"Catch you at a bad time? I can call back."

"Uh, no…no. I just didn't recognize the name for a second. So…how are you?"

"Great, now that I'm talking to you. How are you?"

"Well…I've been better, but not bad. Work really sucked today, but that happens a lot in a doctor's office."

The first thing I thought was *Oh, no! Here we go again. Please don't keep me on the phone for three frickin' hours tellin' me how bad your day sucked. No, No, No!* I didn't say that to her, but I was very relieved when she only went on for about ten minutes. A lot of the normal first phone call small talk, and we ended it by saying that I would call her back next Tuesday, which was four days away. So far, so good.

I was really getting worked up over Nora, and couldn't wait to call her back. I was so worked up that I decided to cancel my membership to uoutthere.com right then and there.

The weekend came and went with no surprises, good or bad, and it was Monday again. I was still tailin' Julie Crinn, but it was the same old, same old. Follow her to work at 8:30, snap a few pictures, and follow her home at 5:30. Nothing new with Legs, but hell, it was payin' the bills.

Tuesday came, along with tailin' Julie some more. Only this time, she smiled in the direction of my car. Could it be that she was on to me? Other than that, nothin' unusual happened that day, and I got home around quarter to six to call Nora.

"Hello."

"Hi Nora, it's Dewey."

"Who?" Could she have forgotten me already, or was she just playin' a game?

"Dewey…from uoutthere? Remember, I told ya I'd call back tonight?"

"Oh yeah, Dewey. Sorry. Another bad day at work. A lot of kids in with the flu. So…how are you?"

"I'm OK. Nothin' exciting except talkin' to you."

After a few minutes of the normal small-talk, I figured it was time to get down to business. "So…how about dinner Saturday night?"

"OK, Dew, that sounds nice. Where would you like to meet?"

"How about Sloppy Man's in Queensville? You know the place?"

"No, but I hear it's a great place. Sounds good to me."

"Great! On second thought, they're havin' a wine dinner on Thursday night if that isn't too soon. Wanna meet Thursday instead?"

After I explained to Nora what a wine dinner consisted of, we agreed to meet at Sloppy Man's at 6:45 on Thursday night.

Couldn't wait to see if she looked anything like her picture.

Chapter 4: DINNER WITH NORA

The night of the big dinner was finally here. Nothin' happened since the phone call, except that on Wednesday, Julie smiled again in the direction of my car, and for a second, I thought she was gonna walk over. I was really startin' to wonder whether she was *really* on to me, and was now posin' for the eight-by-tens.

I got home as usual about 5:45 on Thursday night and took a long shower before I got dressed. I was so excited about the evening with Nora that I did somethin' else, too, but to paraphrase the late George Burns, "There might be kids out there reading this who are under forty," so you'll just have to use your imagination.

After I…uh…er…well…you know, I decided to put on my best suit for the evening. It also just happened to be the *only* suit that still fit me. I also decided to splash on a little aftershave lotion. Since I usually didn't go too much for wearing it, and since I didn't particularly like either of the two I had, I came up with the bright idea of combining a little of the two. So, depending on how you cared to look at it - or in this case, *smell* it – I was either wearing HaiVelva or AquaKarate, take your pick. Either way, I personally didn't think it was all that bad.

I got to Sloppy Man's a little early, as I almost always do when I'm supposed to be someplace at a certain time. First, though, a word about the restaurant. While the name certainly doesn't imply it, Sloppy Man's is a great, upscale restaurant, famous mostly for its seafood. The food is fabulous, the service is always first-class, and the waitresses are gorgeous, running around in their skimpy little outfits, showing more leg and cleavage than the frickin' Rockettes. The only complaint I have is that they still need to get the door fixed on the stall in the men's room. I can't tell you have many times someone busted in on me when I was just about to take a dump. But other than that, the restaurant is first class all the way.

The reason that the restaurant is named what it is is that the owner's uncle, whose name escapes me at the moment, was a Broadway star who made a fortune playing Oscar Madison in revivals of the *Odd Couple,* and wanted to help out his niece who wanted to have her own place. In honor of her uncle – since he didn't want his name to be used – she called it Sloppy Man's instead. If you're ever in Queensville, stop in some time if you want a great meal. It's only a block from the main intersection of town. You can't miss it.

Normally, I would have gone right into the bar, but tonight I was just too excited, so I waited in the lobby. I looked at my watch. It said 6:45, when the door opens, and in walks the person I knew had to be Nora. Nora, however, didn't look like her picture. She looked even better.

She walked over to me, and with a beaming smile and gorgeous dark eyes said, "Hi. You must be Dewey. I recognized you right away from your picture. I'm Nora, but my friends just call me "No.""

Well, after sizing up this heavenly creature for what seemed like an eternity, but in reality was only a second or two, I came out with the unbelievably clever remark, "Hi, No. I'm Dewey, but you can just call me Dewey." We both laughed...except for her.

Covering up as quickly as I could I said, "The dinner won't be starting for another fifteen minutes or so, so would you like to go into the bar and have a drink?"

"Okay. That would be great."

We went into the bar, and since it was a Thursday night, Gladys, my favorite bartender of all time, was working. "Hi, Dew. What'll you...oh, I see you brought company tonight."

"Yeah, Glad, this is Nora..er, just "No." No, this is Glad."

"Hi, No. Nice to meet you. I never say '*Glad* to meet you' for obvious reasons. Would you like something to drink? The usual for you Dew?"

No ordered a white wine, while I ordered my usual, a vodka martini, extra-dry, with a twist. Stirred, not shaken. For some reason, the restaurants, including Sloppy Man's were all shaking all their drinks unless you specifically asked. The drinks arrived in seconds, and we were just about to start talking, when I couldn't believe my eyes.

It really couldn't be, or could it? Was that really her? After all these years? I really didn't want to say anything, but I didn't want to go on staring either, so I finally went over to a young lady standing a few feet away. "Uh, excuse me, but are you Geri?"

Geri was a girl who came just after Patty, and right before I started bein' a dick. Geri was what was referred to as a "you buyin,' I'm flyin,'" kinda girl, and flyin' is what she did. Geri wasn't exactly gorgeous, but she wasn't exactly that bad either, and she did have a great pair of…well, you should know my standards by now. Anyhow, Geri and I had some great times together – in *and* out of bed – but we both knew it wouldn't last, cuz Geri would always be runnin' off with the next guy who could do more of the *buyin'*. Last I heard of Geri, she was livin' with some guy in Nevada, or was it New Mexico?

Anyway, about the time this girl was about to say no, she wasn't Geri, her boyfriend said it for her. "Sorry," I said, "it's just that she looks a lot like someone I haven't seen in a long time."

I excused myself and went back to admiring No. I had only taken a sip or two of my martini by this time, when Fred, the manager on duty that evening, came around and said they were now seating people for the wine dinner. Since I had taken only a small sip of my martini, and No still had some wine left, we took our drinks with us.

The wine dinners were held in a sectioned-off part of the restaurant known as the "Bull Pen." It was called this simply because Sue Edgerton, the owner, was not only an expert on the *Odd Couple*, but was also a huge baseball fan. It was in this section of the restaurant that Sue hung her autographed pictures of some of the best relief pitchers in the history of the game – names starting with Joe Black, through Tug McGraw, to Dennis Eckersley, including current greats including Billy Wagner and others, just to name a few – hence the name the "Bull Pen."

The "Bull Pen" was complete with six large, round tables, which could comfortably sit forty-five to fifty people; but because the price of a wine dinner was anywhere from 80 to 125 dollars a person – tax and gratuity *not* included, of course – most of the dinners were lucky to attract 25 people. However, tonight, for some reason, drew a big crowd of 32. Since No and I were the first two in the area, we took seats at a table at the far right corner of the room, so that we could see everything that was going on, without being in the middle of all the action. A few minutes later, a friend of mine from the bar, Larry Holt, came in with one of the off-duty managers, Vanna. "I told them I would come to the dinner if they let Vanna have the night off and come with me," said Larry, "so here we are." I was happy to see them both, since they were both great people, and also because the table was never lacking for conversation anywhere Larry was.

The rest of the crowd was starting to filter in, and in a few minutes the first sampling of wine was being served. This was a dry, white, from the winery that was being the host for the evening. (The whole idea of the wine dinners was to push the wines from different wineries, of course. The one this evening happened to be from around Pittsburgh.) By this time, with the arrival of the first wine, my martini glass – with only a few sips missing – had disappeared. The wine was all right, but since dry isn't my favorite, I only had a few sips.

After the first course, a salad, was finished, everyone started getting up and mingling around the room. There were a few minutes between each course, so we had time to do this. No and I were talking to some other people I recognized, when…I couldn't believe my eyes for the second time that night. No, it was not another old bed partner of mine, but it was my current employer, Mr. Joseph Crinn…*and Julie wasn't the one hanging onto his arm.* Since it wasn't a large group, I couldn't very well ignore the old man.

"Well, good evening, Mr. Crinn," I said. "I'd like you to meet my date, Nora." I really didn't feel like giving him the "No" speech about Nora, since I didn't want to spend any more time with him than I had to, so I just skipped it.

"Uh, hello Dewey." (He never called me Mr., and besides, he couldn't pronounce Polpulcionski, so he always called me Dewey.) "This is…uh…er…my…uh…*secretary,* Miss Roberts. I've been really working her hard with late hours lately, so I thought she deserved a nice dinner."

"Hello Dewey, hi Nora," said Miss Roberts. "You can call me Sally."

I had to give the old guy credit. I thought it would be just about time for dreamland for him, but I guess I had him pegged wrong. Sally was a real knockout, with long red hair and gorgeous blue eyes, and a figure that was nothing short of perfect, including…well, you know. Joe was nothin' great to look at, but I guess when you're a multi-billionaire, you don't exactly have to be. Also, that story about his uh... er...*secretary,* was just a bunch of bullshit. Joe, from what I understand, wasn't really active in anything in years; so, if he had a secretary, it wasn't to take dictation. Also, it looked to me like he was having me tail Legs so that he could keep her hoppin' while he was playin' on the side. Like I said, I had to hand it to the old man.

Nora was being very quiet all this time, but did manage a barely audible "Hi," but the way she and Joe were looking at each other made me think they had met before. Nora quickly excused herself and appeared to be going to talk to someone that she thought she recognized.

By the time the second course, along with the second sampling of wine, came along, No and I were starting to get fairly chummy. "So tell me, Dewey, what's your last name?" inquired Nora.

"It's Polpulcionski," I replied, "but most of my friends just call me 'Dewey P,'" I said, setting her up with the straight line.

"Dewey P?" she asked, as I hoped she would.

"Well, I do, and if you don't on a regular basis, you're gonna be in big trouble," giving her the answer I give everybody else. This time everybody laughed, including No.

As the evening wore on, No and I were becoming even chummier. At one point, we even discussed going to Paradise Island on the upcoming Saturday, just two days away. "Why don't I give you my cell number," said No at one point. "You already have my email address, but my computer is down, and someone is supposed to come and take a look at it in a day or two."

By the time the fourth course came along, things were really moving quite well. And when there was a brief lull, Larry was still there to fill in the void. "Great dinner," said Larry, "and, of course, the girls look absolutely gorgeous. I assume everyone is having a wonderful time."

Even though Larry was always a big-time schmoozer, everyone did seem to be having a wonderful time. Joe Crinn and his…uh…er… *secretary,* Sally Roberts, were on the other side of the "Bull Pen," and it looked like everyone wanted to keep it that way. By the end of the fourth course, complete with a tasting of another white, dry wine – which I wasn't particularly fond of, so I only had a sip or two – I thought it was time to make my move. Since No was wearing a skin tight black leather skirt, which didn't hide much of anything from her feet to her waist, I reached under the table for a little action. Since there were two empty seats on both sides of us at the large table, with Larry and Vanna directly across, I knew no one else would notice.

Nora, fortunately, didn't say anything, but she instantly moved my hand away. *You little tease, I thought. Get me all hot, and then… nothing.* I didn't say anything, either, but I was beginning to understand why most people just called her "No."

By 10:45, the dessert and the last samples of wine had been served. Nora and I, and Larry and Vanna were having a very interesting conversation at this point – with Larry doing most of the talking, of course – about really nothing in particular. I looked across the room, but there was no sign of Joe and Sally, so they must have left the second it was over.

"The night is young," I said to Nora, like it was really frickin' original or something. "Wanna go into the bar for a nightcap?"

"Sure," she said. "But only one. I have a long drive home, and I have a very long day at the office tomorrow."

We went back into the bar a few minutes later, and I ordered my usual after-dinner sipping drink, B&B neat, but in a rocks glass, not a snifter. They usually served B&B in a snifter, but I found out years ago that the snifter kept bumping into my sniffer, so I found a rocks glass a lot easier to handle. Nora's "one" was a glass of water – on the rocks.

After a few minutes of small talk, I saw the jazz duo finishing up, so I knew it was a few minutes after 11 o'clock. I don't know who was playing bass that evening, but my good friend and piano teacher, Tommy Adirondack, was on keyboards. Tommy, or just "Tom," (or sometimes "Addie," or "Ron," or "Dack" – he answers to almost anything you call him) had his coat on, with his check in his hand. I knew he was always in a rush to get out of there once the gig was over, since he had a great marriage to a little Italian dish named Angela, but I had to stop him and introduce him to No.

"Tommy, I'd like you to meet Nora. Nora, this is my good friend, and the greatest jazz pianist in the Philly area, Tommy."

They both said a quick "Hi. Nice to meet you," but I knew Tommy was itchin' to get the hell out of there, so I only kept him a few seconds without going into the "No" story. I knew it had to be around 11:05 without checking my watch.

A minute or so later, I finished most of my B&B, No finished her water on the rocks, and I paid the check. I walked her out to her car, a shiny new BMW, which the valet attendant had just brought up, and said goodnight.

"Don't forget to call me about PI," No reminded me. "I'm looking forward to it."

I bet you are, you little tease! I thought to myself, but said, "So am I," thinking I would never see Nora again.

I held the door, she got in, and drove away. I didn't even get a "thank you" or a good-night kiss.

Now I *knew* why everyone called her "No."

Chapter 5: THE LONG RIDE HOME

All the way home I kept rehashing the evening that was just completed. *What a frickin' waste that was,* I told myself. *Two hunderd and fifty frickin' bucks – tax and gratuity* not *included(not to mention the before and after dinner drinks) – and not so much as a good-night kiss or a frickin' "thank you."* It really pissed me off about the frickin' money, even though this would be going on old man Crinn's expense account. I knew goddamm well he wouldn't say anything about it, knowin' that I could blow the whistle on him at any time to Julie.

Even though my old Dodge Omni practically knew the way home from Sloppy Man's by itself, I was still taking it real easy. And although I knew that with the combination of drinks I had – the two sips of the vodka martini, the few ounces of wine (mostly dry or semi-dry white, which I didn't particularly care for), and the one shot of B&B - added up to only a little over three actual drinks in over four hours, I knew I still had a little over fifteen miles to go between Sloppy Man's and home.

The cops, local and state police, would be all over U.S. Route 408, which was the first step in my trip home. I made damn sure I was doing the speed limit, which was fifty-five, as cars whizzed past me in both lanes, probably doing seventy-five and better. I would normally be doing sixty or sixty-five myself, but because I had alcohol on my breath, and didn't want to be stopped, I kept it at the limit.

I got to the East Arthur exit without any problems. One step down, and two to go.

The next step was a few miles on Business Route 45. This was one lane in both directions, and again I kept it at the legal limit. Two steps down and one to go.

After just a few miles on 45, I finally turned right onto my street, Jasper Road. I was now within twenty minutes walking distance of my apartment, and since I traveled the road every day, I knew it *very* well. I also knew two other things. First, that the speed limit was 25, and second, that the local assholes who thought they were the second comings of Barnard P had their not-so-secret hiding places.

Since Jasper Road was a twenty-five mile speed limit, I kept a sharp eye on my speedometer. You could easily be doing 35 to 40 without even knowing it, and the local yokels were only too glad to pull you over and write you out a ticket. Especially if it was getting near the end of the month, which was only a week away. Whoever said cops don't have quotas must have very brown eyes, cuz they're really full of shit. Besides, I was stopped in the parking lot of my apartment complex for going 38 on Jasper; but the cop, acting like he was God's gift or something, let me go with a warning. I guess he had his quota for the month.

Like I said, I knew the cops had their not-so-secret hiding places, but because it was close to 11:30 at night, I couldn't see them. I was less than a block from home when I saw the flashing light and heard the siren, so like the law-abidin' citizen that I am, I pulled over to the side of the road, figurin' they were goin' after someone down Jasper Road, and would drive past me.

When they pulled up behind me, I couldn't believe it. Two cops – at least I thought they were, since they were *both* dressed like cops – came up to the car and I rolled my window down. "Hello, officers. What can I do for you?"

"Could I see your driver's license and registration, sir?" said one of the officers.

"Certainly," I said, as I pulled them out of my wallet.

"Could you step out of the car, sir?" said the same cop.

Thinkin' that bein' cooperative was the smart move, I got out. Later I realized that this was my first mistake.

"Have you been drinking, sir?" said the other person in a police uniform.

"Yeah, I'm coming from a wine dinner, and I live right there in the apartments. I had three drinks."

Again, another frickin' mistake on my part. *Ain't they supposed to read me my rights, or somethin'?* I thought to myself.

"Could you breathe into this, sir?" said, what I thought was the lower ranking cop, since he wasn't the one who drove the car.

At this point, I should have answered, "No," or at least "Why?" but I know what I had to drink, and I knew damn well that I wasn't anywhere near drunk.

So I breathed into the machine, and the cop doing the test just looked at the other cop and shrugged, as if to say, "He passed. What do I do now?"

"Have him do it again," said the one in charge.

At this point, I should have blatantly refused, but having nothing to fear – or so I thought – I did it again. What a dumb-ass mistake that was.

After I did that, the cop in charge said, "We're taking you in for DUI."

I said nothing.

The "head" cop – that's the one with the dirty knees – put handcuffs on me and put me in the back seat. Once in, the "junior" cop said, "Mike, are you alright back there?"

I didn't answer, first of all because my name wasn't Mike, and second, because he was reading my license wrong. My middle name is Michael, but I wasn't about to help this SOB out, so I just sat there.

A few seconds later, the boss whispered to him, "His name's David," like I was too frickin' drunk to hear that or somethin'. I kept quiet.

"You OK back there, Dave?" the other cop asked again, getting my name right this time, at least.

"Just fine, officer," I replied, even though I didn't like bein' called Dave. If it wasn't Dewey, I preferred David.

I didn't look at my watch, but we couldn't a been at the car more than ten or fifteen minutes tops, so I knew it had to be around quarter to twelve. They drove me to the hospital, which, when I timed it later, was no more than seven minutes away during normal traffic. It was now almost midnight, and there were very few cars on the road.

When we got to the hospital, the cops made me stand up, instead of having me sit down.

"Hey, can I go to the restroom, please?" I asked. It was about five after eleven when I left Sloppy Man's, and I couldn't remember when it was that I used the restroom there.

"No, not yet," I was told. I guess they thought that if I took a leak, that would lower my already-legal blood alcohol even more, so they weren't taking any chances.

As we were standing against a wall, I noticed that we were the only people in that part of the hospital. *What the hell are they doing?* I thought to myself, but didn't say anything. *If they're gonna do a frickin' blood test, why the hell don't they do it. No one else is in the goddamm place.*

While we were standing there, Cop Junior finally does do something. He takes my frickin' temperature with an ear thermometer. I expected him, at any moment, to ask me if it hurt and had a temperature, just like on the old TV commercial, but he didn't.

He seemed like an OK guy – for a cop – so I asked him why I was stopped.

"You were driving all over the road," is *all* he answered. I knew that was just more copshit (Why insult a bull? No bull ever did nothin' to me.) But I just stood there and kept my mouth shut, and besides, I was tired, *very* tired, and I still had to take a wicked piss.

Finally, someone came from the hospital and had me sign a form allowing them to take some blood. I signed, they took, and I heard – what else? – nothing! A few minutes later, I heard someone at the other end of the room say, "Point one-four," but I knew they couldn' a been talkin' about me. Or was this just more copshit, or maybe hospitalshit? I really couldn't see who was doin' the talkin'.

Well, after all that was completed, they finally let me take my long-awaited, much-appreciated piss, and it was time to get the hell out of there, compliments of the East Arthur Keystone Kops.

We rode in silence back to my apartment complex, which suited me just fine. I'd been up since six o'clock the previous morning, and I still had to get up to tail Julie Crinn. When the cops let me out of the car, they had yet another surprise in store for me.

"We need someone who can vouch for you," said the cop in charge. "Do you know any of the neighbors?"

While I really didn't *know* any of the neighbors, I did say hello to the people who lived next door, and they seemed like real nice people, so I said, "Yeah, I know the people next door."

So the cop in charge rang the doorbell and waited for a few seconds. No answer. He then pounded on the door, but got the same results. I didn't know what time it was, but it was late, and it was a Thursday night – now a Friday morning – before a long holiday weekend. Maybe they were away, or maybe they didn't want to get out of a nice warm bed, or maybe they were getting it on, or who the hell knew what other *maybe* was happening. Anyway, what did this son of a bitch expect?

We went over to my apartment, and I let them in. I looked at the clock on my wall, and it read three minutes to two. It had been almost two and a half hours since I was stopped. Since it was only a fifteen minute round-trip ride to the hospital, the cops had farted around for two hours and fifteen minutes. *What the hell were you guys doin'?* I thought to myself. *Was it a slow night, or wasn't that a rod you were packin', and you were just happy to see me?* But I thought better of it and said nothing.

"Is there someone you can call?" asked Boss Cop. "We have to release you to someone."

Not wanting to wake anyone up at two in the morning, I asked, "What happens if I don't?"

"Well, in that case, I'm afraid you'll have to spend the night in jail," said Boss Cop. I didn't understand why, but he seemed to be doing all the talking since we left the hospital.

So I called my cousin, Janet, who lives just outside of Scranton. Fortunately, after a few rings, she answered the phone. I explained the situation to her, Boss Cop talked to her for a few minutes, and then we let her get back to bed.

As they were leaving, Boss Cop left me his name and the number of the police station. It was Sergeant Walter Hanley. The other cop was still silent, not even saying good night. I knew there was something strange about him.

It was now 2:15 a.m. I'd now been up for over twenty hours, and tomorrow being Friday, it was another day of tailin' Julie Crinn.

Or so I thought.

Chapter 6: A NEW CLIENT

By the time I got to bed, it was nearly three a.m. This meant that with any luck, I would get about four hours of sleep. This was between three and four hours less than what I was used to, but it was better than nothing.

When the alarm went off at seven, it felt like I hadn't slept at all. I had no sign of a hangover when I got up, but because I had only four hours of sleep out of the last 25, tailing Julie Crinn was the last thing on my mind.

Just then, the phone rang. Not only was I surprised to get a phone call this early, I was surprised to get one at all. Usually, I was the one to make the calls.

"Dewey Detective Agency," I answered. I didn't want to call it Polpulcionski Detective Agency. I figured business was bad enough the way it was.

"Hello? Is this Mr. Polp…Mr. Popple…(I usually gave them three tries before I helped them out) Mr. Poppa…?" a sexy, but frightened, female voice purred.

"Polpulcionski. But you can just call me 'Dewey P'."

"Dewey P?" she asked, as they almost always did.

"Well, I do, and if you don't on a regular basis, you'll be in big trouble real soon." I could never help myself. I just loved that line, and used it as often as I could. "But, seriously," I continued, "what can I do for you?"

"My husband...he's dead. They just came and took him away. Said it looked like a heart attack, but I don't think so."

"Well, I'm awful sorry to hear that Mrs?...uh, Mrs?" Now she had me at the disadvantage, and I was wondering how many times I had to say *Mrs.* before she would come to *my* rescue.

"It's Crinn. Mrs. Joseph Crinn. Julie Crinn. We've never talked before, but I'm sure you know who I am."

For a few seconds, I thought that maybe I was actually still asleep, and that the alarm hadn't gone off at all. Maybe this was just a dream I was having because of last night.

"Hello? Dewey? You still there?" let me know this was no dream. It had now become a nightmare.

"Yeah, I'm still here. So, how did you happen to call me, and what can I do for you, Mrs. Crinn?"

"First of all, you can call me Julie; and second of all, you can cut the bullshit right now. I know damn well that my husband had you spying on me. It didn't take long to figure that out, especially when you show up in front of my office every day in that rust bucket of yours. I got your license number, and had it checked."

"OK, *Julie,* so if he's dead, where do I come in?"

"Like I said, I know he hired you to spy on me, because he thought I was cheating on him. I guess you found out that wasn't true."

"As far as I could tell, that would be correct. But I still don't see where I come in now."

"Well, even though I wasn't cheating on *him*, I know damn well *he* was cheating on *me*. I want to hire you to find out who *they* were. I knew for a long time he had more than one on the side."

"But if he's dead, I don't see why that matters now."

"Look, Dewey – are you sure your name isn't Dummy? – do I have to spell it out for you? Like I said, they told me that he probably had the big one, but I have a hunch that he didn't. If I'm right, I know I didn't kill him, which means that someone else did. I want you to find out who he was screwing around with, and anything else you can find out. I'm the only heir he has, and they'll probably tie up the estate until after the autopsy, so I'm sure I can't pay you as much as he was, but will a thousand a day plus expenses do?"

That cheap son of a bitch, I thought to myself. *Pays me 750 a day, while his widow is now going a grand.* Instead, I said, "That sounds just fine, but you sure you can afford it?"

"Oh, I can afford it alright. You know that building you were pulling up to everyday?"

"Yeah."

"Well, not only do I own it, but I also own the business, and I happen to be the CEO."

"Wow! *Very* impressive."

36

"Thanks. Yes, Petunia's Peanut Pieces. Named it after a puppy I had when I was a little girl. Best peanut candy in the whole country, maybe the world. Funny thing was, Joe had a very serious allergy to peanuts. Two or three nuts would have done him in."

"I see. So how'd you hook up with him?"

"Well, Joe might have been allergic to peanuts, but he wasn't allergic to money. He knew a money maker when he saw one, and he kept after me to sell him the business. I never did sell – the company's still in my name – but we had a number of meetings – some over dinner – one thing led to another, and eventually we got married. He got me, but he never did get the company, or any part of it."

"I see. But if you knew the old guy was cheating on you, why stay with him?"

"Well, I'm not exactly allergic to money either. I'm 38, I'm his only heir, and at 83, he wasn't going to last forever. I thought I would stick it out. The billions he had made the millions I have look like chump change, and with the pre-nup I signed, I wouldn't have gotten a dime. I certainly didn't kill him, but I certainly had the patience for someone else to. So…how about it? You in, or do I look for someone else?"

"When would you like me to start?" was my only reply.

"Why don't I give you the weekend off. You can start on Monday. OK?"

"Fine with me."

"Oh, and Dewey, just one more question."

"Yeah, what's that?"

"How *did* those pictures ever come out?"

Chapter 7: PARADISE ISLAND

Since it was Friday, and I now had the weekend off, courtesy of
Julie Crinn, I decided to make two phone calls. The first one would be
to my attorney, Susan Bradley, of Borneman and Bradley. I liked Susan
a lot, especially since her motto was "Never screw with a lawyer named
Sue."

Susan handled all my legal issues, including the two previous
DUIs I got over the last twelve years. I wasn't any guiltier of them than
I was of the current one, so Susan had no problem defending me. The
two previous DUIs, however, were the real reasons for the nickname
Dewey. See, D-U-I, when pronounced, is a homonym for D-E-W-E-Y.
That's something that I learned in a remedial English class I was forced
to take in college.

English 000, commonly called "zip English," because that's
how many credits you got for the course. This was for all those high
school students – mostly "jocks" and guys like me who didn't give a
shit – who scored under 400 on the English part of the SATs. We had
to pass "zip" before we could get into a "real" English course. "Zip"
was taught by a little hottie by the name of Paulina Mousskowsky, who
all the guys in the class wanted to screw. (Or should that be *whom* all
the guys in the class wanted to screw? Whom the hell knows?)
Actually, it was *Dr.* Mousskowsky, and I don't think anyone ever got
close to her – I know I didn't – but at least all of the guys in the class,

except one, had perfect attendance. We were never quite sure about the one who didn't. The book was called somethin' like *English for Idiots Who Think They Know English But Really Don't.* It was written by someone by the name of Francoise Bourget. It figured. Only in America could a Polack take an English course taught by a Russian, using a book written by some French dude.

Anyway, it was in "zip" that I learned that a homonym was a word that sounds like another word but is spelled different, and usually has a different meaning – or somethin' like that. Up till then, I thought a homonym was some gay guy who had a dangling participle. What did I know?

Waitin' for the phone to be answered, I expected to hear Brenda's voice on the other end. Brenda was Susan's secretary. Instead I heard, "Borneman and Bradley. This is Barbara Rhodenbaum. How may I help you?"

Figurin' she was someone new who was workin' for Susan, I said, "I'd like to set up an appointment, please."

"Certainly, sir. May I ask what this is about?"

"Yeah, I'm Dewey Polpulcionski. I was stopped for DUI last night. I thought I would talk to Susan about it."

"I see. Well, tell me, did you get the actual summons last night?"

"No, the cops told me I should be receivin' it in the mail in about eight to ten days."

"Well, mister *Popelskinski"* – since she got a lot closer than most people, I didn't bother correcting her – "I suggest that you wait until you get the actual summons, and then call back. We can set something up at that time. It's possible that you just ran into cops who were having a bad day. Maybe they'll forget the whole thing."

"I certainly hope that's the case. I'll call back if I hear anything more."

"Thank you, mister Pollupski." At this point I told myself *Why bother?* and wished her a good morning.

The second call I made was to Nora. I thought since No wasn't all that friendly at the dinner, and that I would probably never see her again, I figured the number she gave me was probably to the public library, or maybe the local police station. But I figured, what the hell. I told her I would call, so I'll call. I've got a steady client willin' to pay more than my dead one, and since I have nothin' better to do on Saturday, I'll give it a shot.

The phone rang three or four times, and just as I was expecting to hear a voice message, I heard,"Hello?"

"Hi, No, it's Dewey. How ya doin'?"

"Fine, Dewey, I'm really glad you called. I was afraid you wouldn't." I still got the feeling that No was long on talk and short on action.

"I told ya I would call about PI, so…you still wanna go?"

"That sounds great, Dew. What time would you like to pick me up?"

After deciding on a time, and getting directions to her house, I figured I owed myself a nice brunch, so out I went. I came back and spent the rest of the day in bed – alone.

Saturday came, and while I was happy to be goin' to PI with Nora, I was now looking at her as someone I should keep tabs on for Julie.

When I picked No up at 9 o'clock, I hardly recognized her. Oh, she still had the gorgeous raven hair and the beautiful dark eyes, but now she was dressed differently. Instead of the tight black skirt and the revealing top, No was dressed in jeans and a U of P T-shirt. Of course, the T-shirt didn't do a thing to hide her outstanding pair of boobs.

"Wanna stop for some breakfast first?" I asked her.

"Fine by me. I was running late, so I didn't have time for anything."

Normally, I would have stopped at a fast-food place, being as health-conscious as I am; but instead, No directed me to a diner only a few blocks from her place. Since she had a fantastic figure, I was sure that she would order a low-cal, phony-egg kind of breakfast.

"I come here quite a bit," No told me. When the waitress came, Nora ordered the lumberjack breakfast, without looking at the menu.

Not wanting to look like some kind of wimp, I told the waitress I would have the same. The lumberjack consisted of three eggs – real ones – three pancakes, two pieces of bacon, two pieces of sausage, and a six ounce steak. I couldn't imagine where No was going to put all that, but finish it she did, along with a large OJ and three cups of coffee – regular, not decaf. Since we were busy wolfing down the banquet, we didn't get to talk at all. By the time No was finished with hers, I couldn't eat another bite, so she finished mine.

"Haven't you eaten anything since the wine dinner?" I asked. "How can you possibly eat like that and still look the way you do?"

"Oh, it runs in the family, I guess. Very good metabolism. I've been eating that way all my life."

After plunking down 25 dollars for breakfast, we were on our way to PI. At least this time, the tip *was* included.

After consuming the breakfast-and-a-half, No slept most of the way to Paradise Island. It was too bad, because I wanted to pump her – in more ways than one. But the second way would have to wait. I've heard of people doing it while flying down the highway, but it just wasn't gonna happen in my 1987 piece of junk. Since she was sound asleep, the first way would have to wait, too.

When we got to just outside of PI, No finally woke up. "Oh, I'm sorry, Dewey," she said. "I must have dozed off. How long have I been asleep?"

"'Bout an hour-and-a half. You conked out before we hit the expressway. Any particular casino you'd like to go to? We're just about there."

"No. Anything is fine with me. Why don't you pick it."

I was glad she let me make the decision. My favorite place was the Lucky 7s, since I seemed to do real well there, and because I'd heard that it was the closest casino in PI that compared to Vegas. Oh, yeah, also because the cocktail waitresses had the skimpiest outfits; but then, what did you expect from me?

When we got inside the Lucky 7s, for some reason, I expected No to head for the slot machines. Instead, she headed straight for the craps tables. Being a poker player myself – both live and video – and blackjack, but wanting to hang around No, I stayed at the craps table, just watching.

"So, craps is your game, huh? Kinda figured you for a slots player. Ya never know."

"Used to play slots," she said. "But then an ex-boyfriend taught me how to play craps and showed me his system. Got really hooked on the game, and usually do pretty well."

Well, at least on this day, was an understatement. The first time No got to be the shooter, she held the dice for over 20 minutes before she "crapped out." After another 40 minutes at the table, No was up over $1500.

"I need a break," No said. "Let's go get some lunch. My treat."

I was still stuffed from breakfast, and couldn't help wonder where she would have room for lunch. But since she was sound asleep the whole way down, I thought now might be a good time to pump her – the first kind. Hopefully, the second kind would come later.

We found a nice little food court on the second floor. Nothin' too fancy, but combined, the places had just about anything you could want. When Nora ordered a half-pound cheeseburger, an order of large cheese fries, and a large root beer – regular, not diet – I was totally amazed. Me? This time, I wimped out and ordered a Caesar salad and a diet iced tea.

"Where do you possibly put all that?" I asked.

"Like I said," she replied, "it's the metabolism thing. Besides, you know the old saying: 'Eat breakfast like a king, lunch like a prince, and dinner like a pauper.' It's always worked for me."

This sounded great to me, since I figured that she picked up the lunch, so I would be stuck – again – with the dinner.

Finally we had our chance to talk.

"So, whadya think of the wine dinner the other night? Didn't look like you were too thrilled with it," I said.

"Oh, no Dew, it was great. Sorry I gave you that impression. It was just that I had a bad day at work, and I had a lot on my mind."

"Well, I'm glad to hear it. I thought it was me."

"Not at all. It was very nice. Honest. Tell me, who was the old man you introduced me to?"

At this point, I wasn't sure who was the pumper, and who was the pumpee. Not wanting to tip my hand, I said, "Oh, that was Joseph Crinn. Had me tailin' his wife cuz he thought she was cheatin' on him."

"Was she, cheating I mean?"

"Not by the looks of it. From the dinner on Thursday, it looks like it might have been the other way around. I didn't totally buy that secretary story he was telling about Sally Roberts."

"Neither did I," said Nora, seemingly just a bit annoyed. "So, are you still tailing her?"

"No need to now. He's dead."

"What!?" No said. I really couldn't get a read on her face.

"Yeah. Died either late Thursday night or early Friday morning. Officials said it was a heart attack, but they won't know for sure till after the autopsy." I didn't want to tell her that I was now working for *Mrs.* Joseph Crinn, and that Julie was sure that it *wasn't* any heart attack.

"So, why are they doing an autopsy?" No asked.

"Well, when there's that much money involved, they usually want to make sure there ain't any foul play involved. Ol' man Crinn was a billionaire, you know."

"Right. Now I remember the name. Joseph Crinn. Made most of his money in real estate, if I'm not mistaken?"

I wasn't sure at this point if I bought No's story or not. "The one and the same," is all I replied.

"So, who do you think the money will go to? Any family?" Again, I felt more like the pumpee than the pumper.

"Probably to the widow. I don't think there were any kids. Big age difference between Joe and his wife."

Since we were now done lunch, and since I thought that *I* had been pumped enough, I thought it was time to change the conversation. I still couldn't figure Nora out.

"So, you wanna go play some more?" I suggested.

"Sure," No replied. "This time you pick the game."

With that, we headed to the blackjack pits. Since it was a Saturday, most of the tables had higher minimums than I usually liked to play; but since it was still early, we did find a $15 table that had an empty seat. This time, No decided to watch.

On the first hand, I was dealt a 20, an automatic "stand" hand. The dealer's up card was a 5, so I thought I was in pretty good shape. When the dealer turned over a 10 for her hole card, I figured it was money in the bank. The dealer's next card was an ace, giving her 16, meaning she had to draw again. I was really feelin' pretty smug now. If the dealer drew another ace, or a 2 or 3, she would have to stand, and I would win with my 20. If she drew a six or more, I would automatically win, since she would bust. If she drew a 4, it would be a push; but as they say at the tables, "A push beats a pull any time." Then she flipped over another 5, giving her a 21, and beating everyone at the table except the one player who was dealt a blackjack. When this happens on the first hand you play, it's usually not a good sign.

The next two hands I busted, and the one after that I was a dealt a hard 17. A 17 is what I refer to as a "stand and hope" hand, because you can't hit it, but you usually won't win with it either. When the dealer turned up a 10 to go with her up card of 9, No and I left the table.

"Well, where to now?" I asked. "This doesn't look like it's gonna be my day."

"Why don't we find the poker room," No suggested.

With signs everywhere, the poker room wasn't hard to find. Still being fairly early in the day, a 2/4 limit Texas Hold'em game wasn't hard to find, either. We sat down and both bought in for 100.

No and I both folded our first two hands, but then No started getting hot again, just like she did at the craps table. She won the next four hands in a row, with nothing less than trip bullets. At the end of an hour, I was down about 25 bucks, but No was up over 350. Apparently she could do no wrong.

"Same boyfriend teach you how to play poker that taught you craps?" I asked, as we left the table.

"No, different guy, but just as good of a system."

"Wanna grab some dinner? We haven't eaten in at least three hours, so I know you must be starved," I said, laughing.

"OK, and don't be a wise guy. What do you feel like having?"

"I don't know. Nothin' too big, but nothin' too small, either. I think some kinda sandwich would be good."

We found a nice little sit-down place to have dinner. I ordered a Reuben sandwich with a diet cola, and No ordered just a salad with water. "Dinner like a pauper," she said, when I gave her a funny look.

I was really enjoying my Reuben, and I really wasn't in the mood to try to get any information from her about Joe Crinn, so we said very little during dinner. After dinner, we walked around, checking out the Lucky 7s Casino.

During our walk, we passed the box office, and noticed that there was a comedy club starting a 10 o'clock. We checked at the office, and there were plenty of tickets left, so we decided to go. The show started at 10, with seating starting at 9:15.

Since it was only 7:30, we walked around some more, until we came to a section of video poker machines. "We got some time to kill. Wanna play some?" I asked. "My luck can't get any worse."

"Fine with me."

No and I were playing dollar machines for about a half hour, breaking about even. On the next hand, I was dealt an ace, king, queen, and jack – all hearts – plus a four of spades. "Hey, look what I got," I said to No. "I'll dump the four, and maybe I'll get another heart for a flush. My luck's gotta change some time."

So I held the four hearts, and pushed the draw button. Finally, my luck did change. And did it ever! Not only did I get another heart, but I got the 10 of hearts, giving me a royal flush, paying $4000 on a dollar machine. Bells and whistles were going off, so much to the extent that No and I were tired of hearing them. Finally, an attendant came over, congratulated me, and wrote down some numbers. More importantly, he turned the damn sound off. "We'll be right back with your money, sir, and congratulations again from the Lucky 7s."

Well, in case you've never hit a jackpot at a casino, "right back" to them usually means another 15 or 20 minutes. They're real quick on taking your money, but not nearly as fast when they have to give it out. Also, since you have to sit there, they figure you might just play the machine next to the one you hit on while you're waiting. I didn't play, but watched Nora, who continued to break even for the next 15 minutes.

The attendant finally came back with the money, but asked to see my ID, and had me sign a tax form first. Even though the casino doesn't deduct any taxes, any winnings on a machine have to be reported to the IRS. Uncle Sam'll get ya one way or another. After signing the tax form, getting my winnings, and tipping the attendant, I figured I was up over $3500 for the day. Not bad for an afternoon's work. Sure as hell beat findin' cats in East Arthur.

No cashed out about $80, and since it was now 8:45, we decided to take a slow walk to the comedy club. When we got there, there wasn't much of a line, but we still had about 15 minutes to wait until they opened the doors.

"So, what about this guy who died after the wine dinner? What was his name, John Crinn?"

"*Joe. Joe* Crinn, I answered." Again I felt like the pumpee, rather than the pumper.

"You said he died of a heart attack?" she said. "So tell me again why they would do an autopsy."

"Well, first they want to make sure that it was a heart attack; and second, since the guy was worth billions – with a capital B – they want to make sure nothin' funny happened, if you get my drift."

"Oh," she said, and let it go at that. But Nora seemed too concerned about the fate of one Joseph Crinn to sit well with me.

At that point, the doors opened, we walked into the comedy club, and took our seats. A waitress came by, and No and I both ordered drinks. No ordered a white wine, and since this was my first drink since my DUI, I decided to get a drink I could nurse, so I ordered a Scotch on the rocks. The show started a little after 10, with the three comedians being the standard fare for a comedy club at the shore. No one that either No or I had ever heard of, but we did get quite a few laughs. No one was really dirty, but it wasn't a kid's show, either; and after a few drinks, they all seemed a lot funnier than they probably really were.

When the show ended a little after 11:30, I said to No, "So, are you ready to drive home?"

Expecting her to agree, I was extremely surprised when she answered, "Oh, I'm very tired. We both came out way ahead, so why don't we get a room for the night and leave tomorrow."

Not wanting to risk having her change her mind, we went immediately to the hotel registration desk and got, not a room, but a suite. I figured if we were gonna do it, we might as well do it in style. When we got to the suite, No wasted no time in disrobing.

I knew that we would be leaving tomorrow, and that on Monday I would start reporting to Julie Crinn, but at that moment those were the farthest things from my mind. Now it was my turn to be the pumper.

Chapter 8: LEG WORK

We drove home around noon, after having a breakfast fit for a king. There was a little discussion about the money we had won and the show at the comedy club, but nothing about the activity in the suite. We both had very little sleep, and were totally exhausted. It was the first time since I'd known her that Nora didn't say No.

When we got back to No's place, I walked her to her door, but I didn't go in. I wouldn't have, even if she had invited me. I told her I would call her, which I knew I would have to do, even if it were only to keep an eye on her for Julie. There was still something very strange about this girl that I couldn't quite put my hands on, although I did have my hands all over *her*.

I drove right home to East Arthur after dropping No off, knowing that I would just crash for the rest of the day. After all the food I had over the weekend, I certainly wasn't hungry; and after having No Saturday night into Sunday morning, I really wasn't in the mood for anything else, either. Knowing that my detective work would start for real on Monday, I just wanted to get some sleep.

I called on Julie bright and early on Monday morning – 10 a.m. At least that was bright and early for me. "Hi, Dewey, ready to go to work?" Julie asked.

"Well, Julie, I already have. And you don't even have to pay me extra."

"What do you mean?" asked Julie. "And don't worry, I *never* pay extra, but if you play your cards right, the fringe benefits just might make up for it."

I thought about that for a few seconds more than I probably should have, but decided not to comment – at least for now. "I actually think I might have a suspect, assuming that your husband was murdered," was how I answered.

"Really! Who is it, and how did you find this person so fast?"

"Well, her name is Nora, and I was at a wine dinner on Thursday night with her, and we spent the weekend in PI. All in the name of doing my job, of course. Does she sound familiar to you?"

"I'm not sure. I actually know a couple of Nora's. What's her last name?"

"You know, I met her on an online dating service, and I never did bother to ask. Maybe that's why I was voted the 358th best private eye east of the mighty Manatawny last year."

"Oh great! And I'm paying you a thousand a day!? Well, can you at least tell me what she looks like?"

"Yeah, let's see. She's about 5 feet 8, has long dark hair, very dark eyes, a great figure, and a really nice pair of...er...uh"

"Boobs, Dewey. Boobs. Most people call them boobs these days."

"OK, a real nice pair of boobs."

"For some reason she sounds familiar. Sounds like someone Joe had some business dealings with."

"I kind of thought there was a connection," I said, not filling in any details.

"Really. What makes you say that?"

"Oh, I don't know. That's the way I always talk. But, seriously, you'll never guess who else showed up at the wine dinner Thursday night."

"Let's see. George Bush? Bill Clinton? Richard Nix...no, it couldn't be him. He's dead. How the hell should I know, Dewey?"

"Well, I'll give you a clue. The guy that showed up is now dead, too."

"You mean Joe? Why that sonofabitch. And he didn't even ask me."

"Yeah, well...I was surprised enough to see him there, but I really would have been surprised to see him going for a *ménage a trois.*"

"Really. Who was that bastard with?"

"His secretary, Sally Roberts. At least that's how he introduced her. Joe and Nora seemed like they knew each other, but neither one of 'em let on."

"His *secretary,* my ass. If Sally's his secretary, then I'm his great-grandmother."

"Well, that's what I thought, too, but I didn't want to say anything. Want me to keep an eye on her, too?"

"Yeah, I guess you might as well, although I can't see Sally as the one who bumped him off. She might be a gold digger, but I don't think she's a murderer."

I told Julie I would be in touch with her just as soon as I had any new information about the case. I also asked her for my first day's pay of a grand. I didn't tell her about the money I'd won over the weekend in PI. "Will hundreds be OK, or would you like something smaller?" is all Julie said.

"No, hundreds will do just fine, thank you."

With that, Julie handed over 10 C notes, and added, "And Dewey, try not to get too involved in your work, if you know what I mean. I get awfully cold at night, and I might just have another job for you."

I left the lovely Legs without saying another word.

The rest of the day I spent planning how I would handle the investigation. This was certainly going to be more challenging than tracking down some lost pussies. Besides, it was starting to look like I was going to wind up with more pussy than I would know what to do with.

I realized that tomorrow would be too soon to get back to Nora-No-Last-Name. I didn't want her to think I was getting serious or anything, and besides, I'd already pumped her enough for the time being. I thought it would be a good idea to try someone new, so tomorrow I figured I would try to track down Sally Roberts. At least I knew her last name.

With a thousand dollars in my pocket, not to mention the money I'd won at PI, I decided I had done enough work for one day, and besides, I was finally getting hungry. I went out for a pizza and a few beers.

Like someone once said, old habits do die hard.

Chapter 9: THE UH…ER…SECRETARY

The next morning I got up bright and early – 8 o'clock. When I'm not tailin' anybody that seems like the middle of the night to me.

I figured since I didn't have to worry about No for a few days, and since I could usually smell a rat (and Julie didn't smell like one to me), I figured it was time to check out Sally Roberts. The first place I decided to look was Joe Crinn's old office building, appropriately enough named the Crinn Building. Even though the old man wasn't really active in business before he died, he still had an office, so I thought his uh…er…secretary might be cleaning out his things. But when I got there, the office was locked up tighter than an illegal whore house after a raid. The only difference was that this place wouldn't be opening again any time soon, since the local cops and politicians weren't being paid off to do so.

Since Joe and Sally had apparently left the wine dinner the second it was over, I didn't get a chance to talk to Sally again that night. The only thing I could do now was check the local phone directories and hope I got lucky.

The first one I checked was the East Arthur book, since that's where the Crinn Building was located, but I didn't have any luck. There were no Sally Roberts listed, but there were three S Roberts. When there's just an initial with the last name it's usually a good indication that it's a female living alone. However, today apparently was an unusual day. The first S Roberts was Sam, the second was Sheldon, and the third was Salvatore. Sal, however, did tell me that he thought he had a cousin living in Tucson by the name of Sally, but he wasn't sure she was still there since he hadn't seen her in over 20 years. I thanked him and hung up.

The next book I checked was the Queensville directory, and it looked like I might get lucky. There was a listing for a Sally Roberts, so naturally I called. When Sally Roberts answered the phone, I quickly realized that she wasn't the one I was looking for. When I asked her if she happened to be at the wine dinner at Sloppy Man's the previous Thursday, she politely told me, "No, young man, I'm afraid I don't get out too much late at night. You see, I'm 87 years old, and besides, I was babysitting my great-granddaughter that night." She then added, "But if you let me know when the next one is, I'll be glad to go with you. You sound like a very nice young man." I told her I would let her know if they were having another one and wished her a good day.

The third book was from the next town over from Queensville, the Manatawny directory. After seeing no listings for Sally Roberts, and after striking out with the first four S Roberts in the book, I was about to give up. I only had one S Roberts left, so I thought I would give it a shot.

On the third ring, I heard, "Hello."

"Hello. Is this Sally Roberts?"

"Yes."

"Hi, Sally. This is Dewey. We met the other night at the wine dinner at Sloppy Man's."

"Oh, yes. I remember you, Dewey. What can I do for you?"

"Well, I really hate to bother you at a time like this, but I'm sure you know by now that Joseph Crinn died either late that night or early the next morning, and you being his secretary (naturally I didn't throw in the uh...er...) I was wondering if we could get together and talk about him. I don't know if he told you or not, but I was doing some work for him when he died."

"Yes, I read in the paper that he died, but I really don't know how I can help you, Dewey. If he owed you money or something, I have no access to that, so you'd probably have to check with his wife."

"Oh, it's nothing like that. It's just that sometimes I do some articles for the *East Arthur Gazette* on the side, and the editor thought that a story about Joseph Crinn would be a good idea, him bein' a billionaire and all, and his wife really isn't in the mood to cooperate. Since you were his secretary, I thought you might be able to help." I figured if I was gonna lie, I might as well make it a good one, and I wasn't about to tell her that Julie thought that he had been murdered. At least not until I had a chance to talk to her and feel her up...uh...I mean *out*. Like I said, old habits really do die hard.

"Well, OK, if you think it will really help. It doesn't surprise me at all that his wife isn't cooperating. When would you like to get together?"

I decided to ignore the comment about Julie not being cooperative, but kept it in the back of my mind. "Since we both know where the place is, would you like to have dinner at Sloppy Man's tonight at six, if that's convenient for you?" I figured that since I still had the grand from Julie and most of the money I won at PI, I could afford another good meal. And besides, who knew what might develop. Sure beats chasin' pussies around East Arthur.

"That's certainly convenient for me, but isn't that place on the expensive side?"

"Oh, that's OK. Besides, the *Gazette* will pick up the tab." Lying to me was like eating potato chips. Once I started, I just couldn't stop at one.

"Well, OK then. I'll meet you there tonight at six."

"I'm looking forward to it, Sally." This time it was no lie.

The rest of the day was totally uneventful. Nothing to report to Julie, I wouldn't call No for another few days, and all the cats in East Arthur were safe and sound. I decided to go home and take a nap. Getting up at 8 a.m. really had me bushed.

After I got up at 5 p.m., I took a shower and splashed on a little of the aftershave I splurged on before going to PI with No. It was called Midnite Madness for Men, guaranteed to drive your partner wild with desires. Well, maybe it would do that at midnight, but if I couldn't do that without its help before then, I figured it was a lost cause. And besides, my own concoction of HaiVelva or AquaKatate smelled a whole lot better to me, but by the time I realized it, it was too late to take another shower to get rid of the smell.

Since I only have the one suit that still fits, and since Sally saw me in that less than a week ago, I decided to put on a nice pair of dress pants and a comfortable sweater. Nothing too classy, but nothing to sloppy, either, even though we *were* meeting at Sloppy Man's.

As usual, I arrived at Sloppy Man's ten minutes before I was supposed to meet someone. Only this time, I headed for the bar. Since it was a weeknight, Gladys was working the bar.

"Hi, Dewey," she said with a smile. "The usual?"

"No, Glad, I think I'll just have a diet for now."

"What? Are you on the wag?" But before she could finish saying wagon, she started sniffing the air. "What *is* that I smell?"

"Oh, that must be the new aftershave I have on. It's called Midnite Madness for Men. Doesn't it make you wanna do something wild and passionate?"

"Yeah, it sure does. It makes me want to make sure I'm out of here by at least 11 o'clock."

"That bad, huh? Quite frankly, I ain't exactly too crazy about it myself, but it was too late to take another shower."

"Well, maybe if you stand down wind of people, no one else will notice. You're not meeting anyone tonight, are you?"

"As a matter of fact, Glad, I am. She was here at the wine dinner last week."

"Oh, the girl you brought to the dinner? What was her name? Sara, wasn't it?"

"No, her name was Nora, and no, I'm meeting someone else. She should be walking in any time. Her name is Sally Roberts, and she was at the dinner with Joe Crinn."

"You mean his uh…er…secretary?"

"I take it you were introduced?"

"Yeah. Say, didn't I read in the paper somewhere that Crinn died shortly after the wine dinner? I hope it wasn't something he ate here," she said, half sarcastically.

"The coroner put the initial cause of death as a heart attack, either late that night or early the next morning, but we still won't know for sure until after the autopsy. I'm havin' dinner with Sally to see what I can find out about the old man."

Just as I was finished telling that to Glad, I looked up and saw Sally standing at the entrance to the bar. "Don't mention anything to Sally about what we were talkin' about, OK, Glad?"

"No problem, Dewey."

I saw Sally before she noticed me, so I got up and walked over to her. To say she looked ravishing would have been a complete understatement. She looked fabulous at the wine dinner, but tonight she really outdid herself. I just wished that I could somehow take a two-second shower to get rid of the triple M.

Sally was wearing a *very* low-cut top, and a skirt that revealed more leg than the outfit the waitresses were wearing. Her long red hair looked fantastic, coming down just to below her shoulders, and the perfume she was wearing made me forget all about Midnite Madness for Men. Well…almost. All of the workers in the bar just stopped and gave me a stare that I'd seen a few times before. Even though no one said a word, their looks told me loud and clear, *She can't possibly be with you!*

I walked over to Sally and extended my hand. (I always start off slow, but I almost always end with a bang – if you get my drift.) We shook hands for a moment, and then I said, "Wow! You look fantastic!"

"Do you really think so? I didn't have to go into work today, so I thought I would get dressed up for our dinner. Actually, I won't be going to work for a while, now that Joe is gone, but I will have to start looking soon." Even though Sally was a real doll and all woman, she really seemed like a very sweet kid.

"Well, I'm sure you won't have any trouble getting a new position," I said, wondering to myself what position she preferred. "Would you like to have a drink at the bar before dinner, or would you just like to go into the dining room? I'm sure our table is ready."

"Why don't we go right in, if that's all right with you? I haven't had much to eat all day, and I'm starving."

"That's fine with me," I said, while thinking about No's eating habits compared to Sally's. Totally different styles, but as long as they produced the same results, who was I to argue.

Even though the restaurant was almost empty since it was the middle of the week, we were given a table in the far corner so we wouldn't be disturbed. Being a regular at Sloppy Man's does have its advantages.

After we were seated, Rick, probably the best waiter in the place, came over for our drink orders and left two menus. To my surprise, Sally ordered a beer and so I did too. I could tell right away that she was my kind of girl.

We exchanged a few pleasantries until the beers came, but then Sally wasted no time getting down to the main topic of conversation. "So, Dewey, what can I tell you about Joe Crinn?"

"Oh, I don't know. For starters, how did you happen to go to work for him, and how long did you know him?"

"Well, I applied at his real estate office eighteen years ago, right out of high school. I never did go to college, and took the secretarial course."

"I see. So real estate was where he made all his billions, I suppose?"

"Yes. That's where he made most of his money. Say, shouldn't you be taking notes or something?"

"No, actually I have a photographic memory," I lied, for the first time that evening. "You were saying…"

"Oh, yeah. Real estate was where he made most of his money, but he was involved with a lot of other businesses when I first went to work for him."

"Uh-huh. Like what?"

Just then, Rick came back to take our dinner order. Sally decided on the shrimp cocktail for an appetizer, a 32-ounce steak medium rare, green beans, and a baked potato. I decided that this was going on my expense account with Julie Crinn.

"Oh, and could I have a glass of red wine with dinner, and could you bring me another beer, now, please?"

"And for you, Dewey?" Rick asked.

"I think I'll just sit here and watch her eat," I jokingly told Rick. "Actually, I think I'll have the lobster bisque, prime rib medium rare, a baked potato, and a wedge with vinaigrette. I'll have a glass of red wine, too. On second thought, why don't we make it a bottle." I figured, *What the hell. Julie's payin' for it.*

"Very good," said Rick. "I'll put your order right in," and he left us alone.

"Now, you were telling me about Joseph Crinn."

"Oh, yes. Well, like I was telling you, he was mostly – are you *sure* you shouldn't be writing this down or something?"

"No, pornograph…I mean *photographic* memory. Remember? (Another lie, with the first part being closer to the truth than the second.) Go ahead."

"Well, Joe, uh…Mr. Crinn, that is, made most of his money from real estate, but he was involved with some other businesses."

"Like what?" I repeated from before.

"Well, I know he had a few car dealerships, he owned a few minor-league sports teams, and, of course, he had Petunia's Peanut Pieces. He also had some other businesses that he never discussed, but I could tell there were other things going on."

Leaving the part about Petunia's Peanut Pieces go for the moment, I questioned her about the "other things." "So, why did you think there were some other businesses that he never talked about?"

"Well, within two months I became his confidential secretary – and don't give me that look. I'm a great secretary, and I *earned* the position. I certainly wasn't playing bed sheet bingo with the old man."

"Hey, did I say anything?" realizing that I was giving her *that* look.

"No, but I recognize the look you were giving me. I used to get it all the time. Anyway, being his confidential secretary, I was at all of his business meetings, except the ones he had when certain men showed up."

"Really. Can you tell me anything about these certain men?"

"Well, like I said, I wasn't at any of the meetings, but I came to recognize the guys when they showed up. Expensive suits, slick talkers. You know the kind I'm talking about?"

"Yeah, I get the picture. Did these suits have names, by any chance?"

"Let's see. There were usually three of them. I didn't get their last names, but if I recall, their first names were Vinny, Angelo, and Oscar."

"Oscar?!" I said, quite surprised. "Must be related on his mother's side."

"What?"

"Oh, never mind. I'm *really* starting to get the picture now."

Just then our dinners arrived, so we made some small talk about how great the food was.

After we finished the meals, I asked Sally if she would like dessert or an after-dinner drink.

"Another drink would be nice, but not here. I know this great place we can go where we can be all by ourselves. Why don't you follow me in my car."

Things were really starting to shape up with Sally. More and more she was becoming my kind of girl as the night went on. I paid the bill – compliments of Julie Crinn – Sally got in her car, I got in mine, and I let her lead the way.

I knew the area fairly well, but when Sally turned down some back roads, I had no idea where we were headed. Finally, she went down a residential street, and pulled up into the driveway of one of the houses. I parked on the street.

"So, why are we stopping here?" I asked.

"I told you I was taking you to a place where we can be all by ourselves. Well, this is it. This is where I live."

I was so excited that I couldn't think of anything to say, so I just followed her inside.

Once inside I reached for Sally, but to my surprise, she pushed me away. "Hey, what's goin' on here?" I asked, totally confused.

"That's what I'd like to know, Dewey. It's time we were honest with each other. I think we're probably after the same thing."

Well, I certainly knew what *I* was after, but I just said, "Whaddaya mean by that?"

"Look, Dewey, you're a writer for the *East Arthur Gazette* like I'm a shortstop for the New York Yankees, so let's just cut the bullshit. Your name's Dewey Polpulcionski, and you're a second-rate, no offense, private detective who was tailing Julie Crinn for Joe before he died. My guess is you're now working for Julie. How else could you afford the dinner at Sloppy Man's? And by the way, what *is* that aftershave you have on?"

Not only was I surprised at what just happened, but I was really surprised that someone could actually pronounce my name correctly. I was also very flattered knowing that I had moved all the way up from 358 to number two. At least that's how *I* took it. "OK. You win. But how did you know all of this so soon?"

"Well, Dewey, for one thing, my real name isn't Sally Roberts, it's Teri Smallings. Second, I *was* Joseph Crinn's confidential secretary, but I was planted there by the F.B.I. We're pretty sure Crinn had some real high connections with the Mafia. But we can discuss that stuff later. Third, you can smell that aftershave a mile away. Why don't *we* go take a shower and I'll help you get rid of the smell. Then we can pick up where *you* left off when we first walked in the door."

"You know, I'm really beginnin' to like you. But could I ask just one question first?"

"Sure, what do you want to know?"

"Who the hell is Oscar?"

We were both laughing as I carried her into the bathroom.

Chapter 10: THE AUTOPSY

The next morning I left Sally's place bright and early – and this time it *was* early. *Five* a.m., to be exact. Maybe I shoulda said it was just early. At 5 a.m., it wasn't bright yet. And just in case you're thinking that I can't keep my own characters straight, I *know* that Sally's real name is Teri. We just decided to stick with Sally so no one would ask any questions when I called her by her real name.

"I'm sorry we have to get up so early," Sally said, "but I have to drive to D.C. to report my findings, now that Joe is dead."

"Oh, that's OK," I lied. "I'm usually up around this time anyway." I wondered what my second lie of the day would be. "So, who do you report to, J. Edgar Hoover?" Sally just laughed, but I thought *OK, if you don't want to tell me, be that way!* (Go ahead, Smartie Reader, *you* tell *me* the name of another director of the F.B.I. without looking it up on the Internet!)

"Call me?" she asked, as she gave me a big kiss.

"Of course I will." No, this *wasn't exactly* the second lie of the day. I told her I would call her, and I certainly would. I just never mentioned *when.*

We got into our cars and headed in opposite directions. Sally for the turnpike, and me for East Arthur – and some more sleep.

I got home a little after 5:30, and was really looking forward to another eight hours or so of sleep; so you can imagine how pissed I was when the phone started ringing at 8:15.

"Dewey Detective Age…"

"Cut the bullshit, Dewey," interrupted Julie. "I just got a phone call from some people I know downtown. They're doing the autopsy this morning at 9 o'clock. I haven't gotten the official word on this yet, and I'm certainly not going, but I want you to snoop around and see what you can find out. After all, I *am* paying you a grand a day to do more than wine and dine the current selection from the Bimbo of the Week Club." My pissed came in a very distant second to Julie's.

"Sure, boss. Whatever you say. And, oh yeah, by the way, that's a grand a day *plus* expenses. I'll get back to you as soon as I have anything." I was gonna add that I was very insulted by her last remark, but thought better of it. How dare she refer to anyone as "of the Week."

Julie was in no mood to talk, but she was still very considerate. I'm pretty sure I heard her say, "Luck to you, Dewey," right before she slammed the phone down in my ear. At least that's what I *thought* she said.

Getting the dirt on the autopsy wouldn't be that hard. Julie wasn't the only one with friends downtown, you know. My friend wouldn't be able to get me into the morgue for the slice and dice show, as we called them in the business, but for a couple of bucks he would be able to let me know when it was over. Bill and I were friends since our high school days, an' up until the time I started workin' for ol' man Crinn, I was extremely envious of him. He was the head custodian at the morgue, and he was making a helluva lot more dough than I was.

At 9:30 I got the call.

"They just finished up, Dew."

"Thanks, Bill. You catch anything anybody was sayin' about it?"

"Nah."

"Know why they did it so fast? I expected it to be a few days yet."

"Nah."

"Know anything else about it?"

"Yeah, they just finished up."

"You already told me that. Oh well, wha' do I owe ya?"

"Twenty five oughta cover it, Dew, beins how we're pals and all."

Normally the stuff he gave me wouldn't be worth five, let alone 25, but I figured, *What the hell. Another item on my expense account for the grieving widow.* "OK, Bill, I'll see you this afternoon."

When I went downtown in the afternoon to pay Bill, I figured that I would see another old friend of mine, Sheila. Sheila was the

M.E.'s secretary, an' I woulda called her before Bill, but she didn't go on duty till noon.

"How ya doin', beautiful?" I asked. And she was, too, only she was married and had three kids. Strictly friends all the way.

"Oh, hi Dewey, what brings you down here, as if I didn't know?"

"Aw, can't a guy just drop in an' say hello to his favorite girl once in a while?"

"Oh, Dewey," she mockingly purred, "I'm like putty in your hands. Only you better watch it, cuz putty can get awfully messy."

"Well, Sheila, actually I do have another reason for being here, other than to see you, of course."

"Uh-huh. I knew it."

"Word is they did the autopsy on old man Crinn a few hours ago. Hear anything interesting?"

"Nothing official yet, but just between you and me, I heard they found something in his system that shouldn't have been there. Looks like it wasn't a heart attack after all."

"Any idea what?"

"No, they're keeping that under wraps for now, but I suspect it will be released pretty soon."

"Thanks, kid, I owe you one. One other thing. Any idea why they did it so fast? I thought it would be a few days yet."

"From what I heard, this was a real rush job. Somebody wanted things wrapped up in a hurry."

"Any idea who?"

"Well, I know it wasn't his wife. I think it was a business partner of his, but I don't have a name."

"Thanks again, Sheila. I owe you one."

"You're welcome, Dew. And Dew…"

"Yeah?"

"You owe me about six."

I blew her a kiss as I walked out. On the way, only one name came to mind.

Oscar.

It was time to report back to Julie. But before I went back, I went out for a sit-down lunch at a nice restaurant. My tastes were really improvin' since Legs was footin' the bills.

It was a little after 2:30 when I got back to Julie's. Since I didn't have a key – at least not yet – I rang the doorbell. When Julie answered the door, she let me in without saying a word, but I could tell she was still pissed from our conversation that morning.

"Well, good afternoon to you, too," I said, trying to sound serious, but smiling at the same time.

"OK, Dewey, did you actually find out anything, or were you with one of your little floozies again?"

"Gee, my taste in women must be getting better. I'm pretty sure a floozy is a grade above a bimbo, ain't it? But if you must know, and I guess you must since you're the one who's payin', I got some dope on the autopsy."

"Really? So what did you find out?" She seemed to lighten up a bit, but *just* a bit.

"Well, for starters, it looks like you were right. Wasn't a heart attack after all. They found somethin' in his system that shouldn' a been there, but they ain't releasin' what, or how it got there. I'm sure they know the *what*, but they probably don't know the *how*."

"Second, it looks like one of your husband's business associates got some pull, cuz somebody wanted the work done real fast. No name on who it might be. I take it it wasn't you, was it?" I didn't tell her Sheila already told me it wasn't.

"Of course it wasn't me."

"I didn't think so."

"So tell me, how did you get this so fast?"

"Sometimes it helps to know a lot of bimbos in the right places," I said sarcastically. "On second thought, she ain't no *bimbo*, I'd say she's a first-class *floozy*."

"Oh, Dewey, I'm really sorry. It's just that with everything that's been going on, I've been under a whole lot of strain lately. Can we start over?"

"OK, boss, apology accepted. It'll probably be a day or two before I get anything else, but I'll let you know as soon as I have somethin'." I didn't add that I hoped it wasn't peanuts they found in the old boy's body. Hate to lose a great meal ticket.

"OK, Dew. But right now I have another assignment for you."

"Yeah, what's that?"

"How are you on massages?"

"Giving or getting?" I replied.

"Both," she said. Then she took me on a guided tour of the house, with one particular stop along the way.

Chapter 11: THE SUMMONS

After getting the guided tour of the house – not to mention the one I got of Julie – we had a little somethin' to eat. (Admit it, you expected me to say somethin' like, "I was gonna say *nibble on*, but I already had that," now weren't you?) Just a little wine, bread, and cheese. Kinda like the old saying, "A loaf of bread, a jug of wine, and thou," only I already had the *thou*. (See, if you woulda only waited a few more sentences you wouldn' a been disappointed. But nooooo, you had to go and spoil it. Well I hope you're satisfied.)

The next morning I actually did get up early, mainly because Julie was still going into the office despite everything that was going on. Plus, I didn't want anyone to think I was gettin' the grand a day – *plus* expenses – because I was sleepin' with the boss. Geez, what kinda self-respectin' private eye would want to do that? (That one's *way* too easy, so feel free to make up your own jokes. Besides, with everything bein' inneractive these days, I can't supply all the ennertainment, ya know.)

Julie headed off to work, and I headed off to home to get some *actual* sleep. I would've offered to drive her to work, but with the car I had I didn't want people to think that she was broke now that Joe was dead.

I got home around 8:00, so I only slept until 2:00, and then went and had lunch at my favorite fast-food place. I know my tastes are getting better, but I gotta wean myself off the junk a little at a time. When I got back home, there was a notice of a registered letter waitin' for me at the post office. I knew damn well what that was.

I got to the post office just before they closed. When I got home, the first thing I did was call the law offices of Borneman and Bradley. Once again, Barbara answered the phone.

"Borneman and Bradley. This is Barbara Rhodenbaum. How may I help you?"

"Oh, hi Barbara, it's Dewey Polpulcionski."

"Yes, Mr. Popple...uh, Pollup...uh"

"Look, why don't you just call me Dewey P. Everyone else does."

"Dewey P?"

"Well, I certainly do, and if you don't on a regular basis you'll be in trouble real soon."

I still loved that line, and hadn't had a chance to use it in a coupla days.

"I see," she said. "Uh...why don't I just call you Dewey." Apparently she didn't get the joke.

"Suit yourself." I figured I had a real live one here.

"So, what can I do for you, Mr...uh, I mean *Dewey*?"

"Remember last week I called you about bein' stopped for DUI, and you said maybe the cops were just havin' a bad day?"

"Oh yes. Now I remember you."

"Well, I guess they weren't havin' a bad day. I just got back from pickin' up the summons."

"Oh, I 'm sorry to hear that. Well, would you like to set up an appointment to come in and discuss it?"

"Sure."

"OK, what's good for you?"

"Actually, I'm self-employed, so any time's good." I didn't tell her that I was a private investigator.

"OK. Let me see. How about next Monday at 10:30. Will that work for you?"

"Yeah, that'll be fine."

"I'll see you then."

Monday was still four days away, there was nothing new to report to Julie, and I assumed Sally was still in D.C. reporting to J. Edgar. I decided to give No a call.

"Hello?"

"Hi, No, it's Dewey."

"Oh, hi Dewey. What's new?"

"Not much. Just callin' to see if you'd like to go to PI tomorrow. I'm kinda slow and was wonderin' if you'd like to take the day off."

"You know, I could use a day off. Haven't had one in a long time. Sure. Sounds like a good idea to me."

"Good. I'll pick you up about 8:30, OK?"

"Fine. See you tomorrow."

The rest of the day I just relaxed and had a pizza and a few beers at home for dinner. Like I said, gotta break away from the junk a little at a time.

The next morning I got out of bed at 6:00. I think I beat the sun by about 30 minutes, but it was a good hour to No's place from mine, and I had to allow for rush-hour traffic since this was a work day for most normal people. But traffic was light, so I made it to her place by 7:30. Fortunately, No was up.

"Hi," she said, opening the door. "I thought you said 8:30. Did I miss daylight savings time or something?"

"No, No, you didn't. (Who says you can't have a double negative in the same sentence?) I got up a little early, traffic was light, so here I am."

"Good. Well since you're here, you can help me with something."

"Sure. What can I do?"

No led me into the bathroom, disrobed, and said, "You can wash my back."

"It will be my pleasure," I said, taking my clothes off. After all, I didn't bring a change of clothes with me, and I certainly didn't want to get the stuff I had on wet. Needless to say, it took quite a while before I actually got to wash her back.

At 9:15 we finally got out of No's place and were on our way to PI. Along the way we stopped at the same diner for breakfast, only this time I wasn't taking any chances. While No ordered the same breakfast she had the time before, I settled for scrambled eggs, bacon, and coffee. I still couldn't figure out where she put all that food.

By 10 o'clock we were on our way to PI.

"So, what's new with the Joe Crinn case, anything?" No asked the second we were in the car. Once again I felt like the *pumpee*, only this morning I got to be the *pumper* first.

"Not much so far," I answered. "They've already finished the autopsy, and from what I've heard they found something strange."

No's answer seemed to indicate that she was just a little too interested in what was going on. "Oh really. What strange thing did they find?" I couldn't tell if she was interested because she worked in a doctor's office or had a more personal reason.

"Well, apparently it wasn't a heart attack. They found something in his system that didn't belong there, but they're not disclosing what it is, or how it got there. I'm sure it will come out in a few days."

"Oh, that poor man. Do you think it was some kind of poison?"

"That would be my guess," I said, not wanting to add that I hoped it wasn't some form of peanuts that they found.

"Well, let me know when you find out anything, OK?"

"Sure," I said. "You'll be the first to know." That was my first lie of the day. I wondered what the next one would be.

The rest of the trip was spent mostly in silence, with the music from the radio being the only sound we heard, other than the traffic. We arrived at the Lucky 7s Casino a little past noon.

Once inside, we headed straight for the craps tables. Since it was early afternoon on a Friday, the place was almost deserted, so it was just the two of us and one old guy at the table.

"So, you gonna work your magic system again?" I asked. "I think I'll just watch."

"Oh no you don't," said No. "We're both going to play."

Since he was there before us, the old guy held the dice; but he crapped out real fast.

Next it was No's turn to roll. After hitting a few numbers "the hard way," No crapped out, too. At least she was up a few bucks.

Now it was my turn. Since blackjack and poker were really my games, I hadn't played craps in years; but it must have been my lucky day, cuz I held the dice for over 20 minutes and was up over 200 when we left the table.

"Let's get something to eat," said No. "I could really go for a pastrami sandwich."

"OK. Since I didn't have much for breakfast that sounds good to me too."

We found a small restaurant in the casino, and even though it was lunchtime, the place wasn't very busy. As soon as we were finished ordering, No started up again.

"I still can't help thinking about that man that died the other day. You really think he was murdered?"

"It sure looks that way," I said. "From what I heard, it wasn't a heart attack, and there wasn't any note, so it doesn't look like he did himself in. I guess we'll know more in a few days when they release what they found in his body."

"Some kind of poison, huh?"

"Well, it sure looks that way, but we'll find out soon enough. But, tell me, why all the interest in the old guy?"

"Well, I guess I should tell you. Before he met Julie, he was a patient of the doctor where I work. One thing led to another, and we had a little *thing* going."

I didn't say it, but now I *really* had to hand it to the old guy, only I couldn't. Now he was dead. Instead I just said, "Really. How long ago was this?" not knowing how long Joe and Julie had been married.

"About five years ago," she said. "That was before he was married to Julie."

Well, at least that answered that question.

"And so I suppose you also knew his *secretary*, Sally Roberts? What do you think of her?"

"She's OK, I guess, only I really didn't buy that *secretary* story. Somethin' funny was goin' on there."

"Why do you say that?" I asked, not telling No that Sally really was his secretary; and I certainly didn't tell her that Sally was *really* with the F.B.I.

"Oh, I don't know. When he met Julie and dumped me, he said Julie was *the one,* but from what I understand, Sally had been with him a number of years, and he was always buyin' her things and taking her places. It just didn't add up."

"Well, maybe he needed a secretary with him when he traveled on business, and maybe he was just showing his appreciation for all her hard work."

"Yeah, and maybe I'm Miss Universe. Are you kidding me? Joe probably had her on the side for years."

I didn't tell her that Julie suspected the same thing.

After lunch, we went back into the casino to play poker for a few hours. We both did OK, but nothing big like the last time, so we decided to beat the rush-hour traffic home.

When we got back to No's place she asked, "What do you want for dinner? Are you up for a pizza and a few beers?"

No was really turnin' out to be my kind of girl.

The next morning I left No's bright and early. Even though it was a Saturday, she had to go back to work and so did I.

When I got back to my apartment, the light was blinking on my answering machine. "Dewey, it's me, Julie. Call me when you get this message." Legs sounded pissed again.

Since it was still only a little after 7:00, I decided to take a shower before calling her back. When I finally did call, she answered the phone and snarled, "So who was she this time?" I really hated caller ID.

"Well, and a good morning to you too, boss," I said in the most pleasant voice I could come up with.

"Cut the bullshit, would you, Dewey? Where the hell were you and who was she?"

"Gee, Jules, I must really be comin' up in the world now. In only a week I've gone from a bimbo to a floozy, and all the way up to a *she*. Next thing you know, I might actually be seein' somebody with a name."

"Would you cut the crap? I just got a call from my friend downtown who told me what they found in Joe's body. I'm getting

86

more info out of them than I am out of you. What the hell am I paying you for?"

"Well, if you must know, I was busy pump…uh…I mean *getting* information from someone I consider a prime suspect in this case. Remember the girl Nora I told you about?"

"Yeah, well what about her, and did you at least find out her last name?"

"Oh, shit, I forgot to ask again. But what can you expect from the 358th best private investigator east of the mighty Manatawny? Actually, I found out something more important."

"Yeah, and what is that *Mr. 358th best private investigator east of the mighty Manatawny?*"

"Well, for starters, she works in the doctor's office that Joe used to go to before he married you. And second, according to Nora, they were playin' bed sheet bingo before you came along."

"Now I know who she is," said Julie. "Remember I told you I knew a few Nora's? Well, her name's Nora Klause. Joe mentioned her once or twice when we first started seeing each other."

I didn't want to mention it, but it seemed real funny to me. No's last name is Klause, huh? Even if I did say something to Julie, she probably wouldn't have gotten it – and I bet you don't either.

"Think she could have bumped him off?" I asked.

"I don't know," said Julie. "I've never met her, and besides, why hold a grudge that long?"

"Oh, I can give you about a billion good reasons," I answered.

"Maybe, but what good would it do her now?"

"Who knows? What's the old saying, 'Hell hath no fury like a woman scorned?'" (That's one thing I learned from personal experience and not my zip English class.)

"Well, who knows?" said Julie. "See what else you can find out from her, and Dewey…"

"Yes?"

"More information and less *pumping*, if you don't mind."

"Yes ma'am. So, whadya find out about the autopsy?"

"Oh, Dewey," she said, almost in tears. It was the first time I heard Julie get upset. I thought she was one tough broad. "Oh, Dewey, it doesn't look good, but I swear I had nothing to do with it."

"What are you talkin' about, Julie?" I asked, seriously concerned.

"What they found in his body was traces of peanut oil."

"You're right. That don't look too good. I'm sure the cops'll be around any time now, but just hang in there. We'll get this figured out."

"Oh, Dewey, do you promise?" asked Julie, now definitely sobbing.

"Of course I do," I said. This was my first lie of the day, and it wasn't even noon yet. "Just hang in there, kid."

That afternoon I did nothing but relax at home. I knew Julie was in big trouble, but there was nothin' I could do about it on a Saturday afternoon. I just wondered how long it would be until the cops paid Julie a visit.

It didn't take me all that long to find out. Around seven that evening, I got a call from Julie's lawyer.

"Dewey detective agency. How may I help you?"

"Hello. Is this Mr. Popple...uh, Mr. Polper...uh, Mr. Pollup..." I really should think about changing my last name to somethin' easier. Czyxtrmpanovanitchky, perhaps? Whadya think?

"It's Polpulcionski, but you can call me Dewey P. Everyone else does."

"Dewey P?" she asked.

"Well, I certainly do, and if you don't you'll be in big trouble real soon." It's almost automatic now, but I still love it.

"Well, OK...uh...*Dewey P.* I'm representing Mrs. Julie Crinn. She asked me to give you a call. I'm her lawyer, Mary Payson." (Hey, if you're gonna do a spoof, ya might as well pull out all the stops.)

"Yes, Ms. Payson – or should I call you *Mary P?*- what can I do for you?" I asked, although I was pretty sure I already knew the answer.

"Julie, Mrs. Crinn, that is, just called me. She was just arrested for the murder of her husband, Joseph Crinn. The bail hearing has been set for Monday afternoon at one o'clock, and she would like you to be there. Can you make it?"

"Absolutely. I have a little business to take care of Monday morning at 10:30, but one in the afternoon won't be a problem at all. Tell her to hang in there, and I'll see you both on Monday."

"That's fine, Dewey. I know she'll really appreciate it. We'll see you then."

"I'll be there," I said, wished her a good day, and hung up.

The next day was Sunday. I did absolutely nothin' except sit around all day and drink some beer. I told myself, *What the hell. If God can rest on the seventh day, so can I.*

I knew Monday was gonna be quite an interestin' day, so I got up at 8:30 and had my favorite breakfast. Two bowls of Frosted Flakes, four Twinkies – the regular ones, I don't like the strawberry – and a can of Jolt. I figured with all that sugar, it should keep me goin' till about Thursday, but I knew I was gonna be busy. The first stop of the day was the law office of Borneman and Bradley.

I walked into the office not really knowin' what to expect. After all, I hadn't seen Susan in over two years, and every time I called, this new girl answered the phone instead of Brenda. The office still looked the same as I remembered it, but no one was sitting at what I assumed was still Brenda's desk.

"Hello, may I help you?" I heard.

"Yes. I'm Dewey Polpulcionski, and I have an appointment at 10:30," I said, still thinking that I was going to be seeing Susan.

"Oh yes, Dewey. We spoke on the phone. I'm Barbara Rhodenbaum. Why don't you come into my office and have a seat, please."

Your office, I thought, but just thanked her and sat down.

"Now Dewey, why don't you tell me exactly what happened."

"Oh, are you working for Susan? Are you gonna be handlin' my case?"

"Actually, I bought the practice a little over a year ago. I still have the right to use the name of Borneman and Bradley for a while yet. Susan and her partner, Pete Borneman (his middle name is Timothy in case you're interested) moved right after they sold it to me."

"I didn't know that. I haven't seen Sue in over two years. So where'd they go?"

"Saskatchewan, I think, but I'm not really sure. They just wanted to get away."

While this conversation was goin' on, I was studyin' Barbara. She was OK, I guess, but not really my type. Too short, too flat, an' I think she was wearin' a wig. I thought maybe she really was bald. (Hey, what the hell did you expect? Purple? I already have a blond, a brunette, and a redhead in this case.)

"So tell me what happened, Dewey."

91

Instead of telling her what happened, I had everything typed up for her; from the time I left my place for the wine dinner, until the time the cops escorted me home. I handed it to her, and waited a few minutes while she read the papers.

"I see," was all she said when she got finished reading.

"So you see, I know I ain't..."

But before I could say "guilty," Barbara hit me with, "You screwed up, so shut up and take ARD."

Glad she ain't my type, I thought. *Great bedside manner.* But since it looked like she wasn't gonna pull any punches with me, I figured I wouldn't either. "Susan always handled my other cases real easy, cuz she knew I wasn't guilty. So what the hell's this ARD stuff?"

"ARD stands for Accelerated Rehabilitative Disposition. It means that you don't plead guilty, but you don't fight the charges, either. You accept their findings, pay your fine and costs, and give up your license for a month or two. I think it would be two in your case. It saves you a lot of time and money and the courts a lot of time."

"ARD, huh?" I said. "Sounds like a rip-off to me, and like I was gonna say, I know I ain't guilty, so thanks, but no thanks."

"Well, Dewey, from my experience I think you're making a big mistake. DUI cases are very hard to win, you know."

"Well, Barbara," I said as sarcastically as possible, "from my experience Susan didn't seem to have any problem winning my other cases. So...do you want the case or not?"

"Under the circumstances, *Mr. Polupski*" – when they butcher it they *really* butcher it – "I think it would be better if you would find someone else to represent you."

"I assume that means no?" I asked.

"Yes."

"Fine." As I was leaving the office I added, "Tell Susan I said hello if she ever comes back from Saskatchewan," without turning around.

Chapter 12: JAIL TIME FOR JULIE?

When I left Barbara Rhodenbaum's office, I still had enough time to grab a bite to eat before my meeting with Julie and her lawyer. More importantly, it gave me time to do some thinkin'. Things were unravelin' real fast now. Julie was under arrest for the murder of her husband, and I needed a new lawyer for my DUI case. I finished my lunch and headed over to the courthouse.

As I got closer to the building, I spotted Julie walking with two other women. I assumed one was her lawyer. I had no idea who the other one was.

"Hey, Julie, wait up," I yelled.

"Hi, Dewey, I'm glad you could make it," she said. It appeared that Julie hadn't had much sleep lately, but it seemed like the old Julie was back. No sobbing or sniffling, just the tough broad that I'd come to know over the last few weeks.

"Dewey, I'd like you to meet my attorney, Mary Payson."

"Nice to meet you, Mary. We talked the other day on the phone."

"Yes, very nice to meet you, too, Dewey. Thanks for being here."

"No problem. Glad I'm here. Anything to help. But I gotta ask you one question, Mary."

"Certainly, what is it?"

94

"You must get kidded a lot about your name, bein' a lawyer and all. Right?"

"Well............(here she was taking a long deep breath), yes." To the lady next to her she said, "Now where did I put that damn inhaler?"

"Dewey P," Mary said, I'd like you to meet my secretary, Stella DeRita." (Who the hell were you expectin' the secretary of Mary Payson to be?)

I didn't say anything as I extended my hand, but I was kinda surprised. I thought for sure her name would be Bella Lane.

"Pleased to meet you, Dewey. Tell me, what does the P stand for?"

Damn! I couldn't use my favorite line on her. I guess we had a smart one here.

"Nice to meet you too, Stella. And the P stands for Polpulcionski," I said, still tryin' to salvage the joke. "That's why most people just call me Dewey P."

"I see," she said, looking at me like I had 14 heads or somethin'. "I think I'll just stick with Dewey."

I certainly hoped the rest of the day would pick up in a hurry.

Around quarter to one we walked into courtroom 12. Mary had Julie and Stella take seats at the table on the left side of the aisle as you face the judge. Mary walked over to the assistant DA handling the bail hearing. I took a seat in the visitors' section, but close enough so that I could hear everything that was going on.

"It looks like we'll make bail," Mary said, "but it's going to be pretty......(another long breath) steep. I've got to find that damn inhaler."

Just then the judge came into the courtroom. We stood, he sat, and the show was about to begin.

"Your Honor," Mary began, "my client, Mrs. Julie Crinn, has been an upstanding, law-abiding citizen......in this...... comm....Excuse me, Your Honor, but could I possibly borrow your inhaler?"

The judge, the Honorable Abraham J. Moses, looked like he should have been somewhere else either takin' a nap or playing with the grandkids. If this guy wasn't 90, he was leanin' all over it; but with the courts backed up, they were pullin' the retired judges out to handle these kinds of cases. "Certainly, Ms. Payson. Here you are. Would you like a short recess, Ms. Payson?"

"No, thank you, Your Honor," said Mary, after using the inhaler. "I'll be fine now."

I looked at the judge and thought, *My God! This old coot's gonna decide bail in a first-degree murder case?*

Mary continued. "As I was saying, Your Honor, my client, Mrs. Julie Crinn, has been an upstanding, law-abiding citizen of this community for many years. Mrs. Crinn has never been arrested before, she owns her own very profitable business, and certainly would not think of leaving the area. We therefore request that Mrs. Crinn be released on her own recognizance."

"Your Honor," started the assistant DA, "and may I say you're looking very dapper today, Your Honor…"

Now I recognized the assistant DA. She was the ever-unpopular Suzy K. Sukumupi. I tried to ignore her babble the best I could, but it was no use.

"…and we understand and agree with everything Ms. Payson has said, Your Honor, but this is a first-degree murder case we're talking here. Therefore, your honor, we believe that bail should be set at one million dollars."

The judge didn't say anything for quite some time. I wasn't sure if he was thinking, meditating, or…could he have possibly died on the bench? After a few more seconds, the bailiff went over and gently nudged the judge. Apparently he was just sleeping.

"Well, uh, yes…a-hem," the judge started to speak. "I realize that Mrs. Crinn is a very upstanding member of the community – oh, by the way Mrs. Crinn, I just love Petunia's Peanut Pieces. You don't by any chance have some on you, do you?"

"Sorry, Your Honor, but I didn't bring any with me," Julie answered. She gave me a very quick look that said *What the hell's going on here?*

"Oh, that's too bad. Yes, well, as I was saying, uh…what was I saying?"

The bailiff once again went over to the judge and whispered to him what he was saying before his candy craving kicked in.

"Oh, yes. As I was saying, I know Mrs. Crinn is an upstanding member of the community. But we must keep in mind that this is a first-degree murder case. However, I feel that one million dollars is quite excessive, even for someone with Mrs. Crinn's financial ability to pay, so I'm setting bail at 250 thousand dollars. You may pay the bailiff on your way out, and please don't leave the area. Your trial is scheduled to start in two weeks from today. Court is adjourned."

He rose, we rose, and he walked out of the courtroom. I really didn't think he could make it under his own power.

"Well, Julie, at least you're out on bail. You wouldn't look good in stripes anyway," I said, trying to lighten up the situation. "Can I give you a lift home?"

"No thanks, Dewey. Mary and I have some things to discuss. Tomorrow is the funeral. You are coming, aren't you?"

"Certainly I'll be there," I said, all the while thinking *Are you kiddin'? I wouldn miss this cast of characters that are gonna be there for all the money in the world. Well,* maybe all *the money in the world.*

"Good. I'll see you then. Give me a call if you find out anything before then."

I left the courthouse, headin' for home, with just one stop along the way. If you guessed a pizza and a six pack, go to the head of the class for payin' attention.

The next day, the viewing was held for old Joe Crinn. The funeral parlor handlin' it was none other than the immortal – hey look, if you're gonna boo, come up with your own puns – Graves and Graves. With a name like that, I fully expected Herman Munster to be workin' there, but I didn't see him. Maybe it was his day off.

The viewing was gonna be from 9 to 11, and then a quick stop at the cemetery to lay old Joe to rest. (It was probably the first time he'd gotten laid in a long time.) Julie and Mary were already there when I arrived a little after nine.

"How ya holdin' up?" I asked.

"Not bad," she responded. "I actually got some sleep last night."

One guy came in a few minutes later and paid his respects to Julie. He then went over to the casket for a few seconds to be near Joe, obviously for the last time.

"Who was that?" I asked Julie.

"I don't know. He didn't introduce himself. Just said he hadn't seen Joe in a long time, and just heard that he died. Seemed like a nice guy."

"An' you talk about me not gettin' names. At least I get their first names," I said, smiling all the time.

"OK, Dewey. You win." I was glad that she was finally beginning to lighten up a bit.

Then three guys came in together. They said a quick "Sorry" to Julie and went up to the casket. Looked like they were there to make sure Joe was really dead. They didn't stay long, and I didn't get their names – first *or* last – but I had no problem tellin' which one was Oscar just by lookin' at 'em.

That left only Sally and Nora left to show up. I really wasn't sure either of them would show, and I still ain't, so I'll tell ya all about it tomorrow at the readin' of the will.

At 11 o'clock we put Joe in the back of the hearse, and headed out to the cemetery. A priest was out there who said a few words about Joe. The fact that he never met Joe in his life didn't slow him down one bit. Sounded like he used the all-purpose speech he always used for just these kinds of occasions.

Julie had me reserve the "Bullpen" at Sloppy Man's for lunch. I guess you could say that things had gone full circle. The only problem with that was they were just gettin' started.

After spendin' a few minutes for lunch, and tellin' Julie that I would see her tomorrow, I headed home for some rest and a few beers.

It had already been a long day.

Wednesday was the reading of the will at the law offices of Covet and Urdo. It was supposed to start at 9, so I got there at 10 of.

Julie and her lawyer, Mary Payson, along with Mary's secretary, Stella DeRita, were already there sitting in the first row. Sally and Nora were up front, too, even if they weren't at the funeral. I would talk to them later. Oscar and his two cohorts didn't show, but the guy whose name we didn't know was sitting in the second row. I sat two seats over from him, and close enough to hear what Julie and Mary were saying.

At exactly 9 o'clock, a door to the office opened, and in walked someone who had lawyer written all over him.

"Good morning, ladies and gentlemen," he began. "My name is William Covet. I'm sure you're all here for the reading of the last will and testament of Mr. Joseph Crinn. And before we begin, Mrs. Crinn, let me offer my sincere condolences on the death of your husband from everyone here at Covet and Urdo."

Julie just nodded.

"Well, as I was saying," he continued, "I am the executor of the will of Mr. Joseph Crinn. We shall now begin."

"What's going to happen, Julie?" whispered Mary.

"I don't know," Julie answered. "We never discussed his will."

The executor started reading. "I, Joseph Crinn, being of sound mind and body, do solemnly swear this to be my last will and testament. To my wife Julie, I leave half of my monetary estate, which as of today, comes to a little over 3 billion dollars. Along with this, I leave all of the property which we owned either separately or collectively."

"Well, at least I won't starve," I heard Julie whisper to Mary.

Covet continued. "To my dear friend, and the best nurse a man ever had, Nora Klause, I leave the sum of 1 billion dollars."

I thought for a moment that Nora was going to faint, but she just turned around and winked at me.

"To my faithful secretary, Sally Roberts – I thought *What, no uh...er?* – I also leave the sum of $1 billion."

I could see a little smile come over Sally's face, but it actually looked more like a smirk.

According to what the old man left Julie in cash, there should have been $6 billion, and that only accounted for five. Where was the other billion?

Covet quickly answered that. "And finally, to the only blood relative I know of still living – he's either my second cousin three times removed, or my third cousin two times removed – I leave the sum of $1 billion to my distant relative, Nick Rudawski."

Nick was obviously the guy at the funeral. He was the only person left at the reading, and I swear I heard him mumble a barely audible "All right!" after learning what Joe had left him. Since he realized that I heard him, he tried covering up by saying, "Poor Uncle Jim. Oh, poor Uncle Jim."

I leaned over and reminded him that the dead guy's name was Joe, not Jim; that he was his cousin, not his uncle; and that Joe wasn't anywhere close to bein' poor, and now he wasn't either.

Covet then concluded, "In the event that any of the other heirs predecease Mr. Rudawski, that heir's share will also go to Mr. Rudawski. In the event that Mr. Rudawski predeceases any of the other heirs, Mr. Rudawski's portion will go to my favorite charity, the ASPCA."

Just like Joe, I thought. Still thinkin' of the pussies. Even in death.

Covet was going on about something else that I didn't catch, and the readin' was over.

There were people I definitely wanted to have a talk with.

The first person I wanted to talk to was Nick Rudawski, one Polack to another.

"Hey, Nick," I started, "how does it feel to be a billionaire?"

"I'm still in shock," he answered. "I didn't think Uncle Jim... uh, Joe, would remember me. Didn't he leave you anything? I saw you in the room."

"No. Actually, I work for Mrs. Crinn. She's out on bail. Accused of his murder, ya know."

"No, I didn't. I didn't even know that he was dead until I got the call a few days ago from Mr. Covet, informing me that I was in his will. By the way, I don't think we've been introduced."

"No, you're right, we haven't," I said. "My name's Dewey Polpulcionski, but most people just call me Dewey P."

"Dewey P, huh?" I was just about to hit him with the punch line when he continued, "I bet when they say 'Dewey P' you say something like, 'Well, I do and if you don't on a regular basis, you'll be in trouble very soon.'" He then started laughin' at what he thought was his original joke. It was gonna be another long day.

"So, tell me, Nick, what did you mean when you said that you didn't think that Joe would remember you?"

"To tell you the truth, I only remember seeing the man once, and I was either five or six at the time. It was at a family funeral. He came over and patted me on the head."

"So, how did you remember him from that? I still don't get it. Lots of little boys get patted on the head."

"Yeah, but do lots of little boys get folding money with a picture of Ben Franklin on it? You can bet I never forgot Uncle Joe after that."

"OK, but why do you call him *Uncle* Joe? I thought they said he was some kinda cousin of yours?"

"Well, technically he was, but because of the age difference he wanted me to call him *Uncle* Joe," Nick replied.

"So, Nick," I asked, "what you gonna do with all that money?"

"I guess once the money is released, I'll go back to Tucson and quit my job. If I kept working, I might just as well send my paycheck to the government, with all the tax I'll be paying. No sense in working for the government, right?"

"That's for sure," I said. "By the way, what do you do now?"

"Oh, I work for the government," he said.

I should have known better. With his new-found wealth, Nick asked if I'd like to join him for lunch. I thanked him for the invite, but said that I had some business to attend to.

Although he didn't seem like the type that would murder *Uncle* Joe, I made a mental note to keep an eye on Mr. Nick Rudawski, just in case.

I saw Nora and Sally walking out, separately, of course. I told Sally that I would give her a call tomorrow and quickly caught up with No.

"I didn't see you at the funeral," I said. "Didn't feel like payin' your respects, or what?"

"Not with the grieving widow there I didn't. If she was behind bars where she belongs I would have gone. I know she's out on bail, but I bet you anything that she bumped him off, or had someone do it for her. I wouldn't be here today, only I got a call from Mr. Covet saying that I was in the will."

"You really think Julie did it?" I asked. "What makes you say that?"

"Well, first of all, I know she only married Joe for his money," she said. "Second, I bet she was fooling around all over the place. After all, there was a *huge* age difference, and with her money and looks I bet she had guys all over the place."

I didn't remind No that I had been tailin' Julie for Joe right before the old man was bumped off and that I saw nothing to indicate that Julie was foolin' around. I let her continue.

"And third, who else knew that Joe was allergic to peanuts? That's what killed him, wasn't it?"

"Yeah, but how did you know?"

"Don't you read the papers, or watch TV, or anything?" she asked. "It's been all over the news. The biggest thing to hit East Arthur ever since the guy that the town was named for, Jeremiah P. Arthur, paid a visit in the year 1938, right before he died."

"I, of course, knew that he was allergic to peanuts, but that's only because I worked in his doctor's office. You don't suspect *me,* do you?"

"No, of course not," I answered. It was my first lie of the day.

I told No that I had some important things I had to do – this was the second lie of the day – and said that I would be in touch with her.

I went home and took care of the important things I had to do, namely, have another pizza and a six pack.

Chapter 13: A NEW MOUTHPIECE

While Julie was still going to stand trial for the murder of her husband, she seemed to be in pretty good shape. She was out on bail, she still had Petunia's Peanut Pieces, and she would inherit half of Joe's money and all of his property – assuming that she wasn't found guilty of murder. And with Mary Payson as her attorney, how could she possibly lose?

I, on the other hand, needed a new mouthpiece. No, I was not going back to playing football, although I was a very versatile player in high school. When I wasn't holding down the left end position, I was holding down the right. Unfortunately for me, and lucky for the team, it was either the left end or the right end of the bench.

I did, however, manage to get into one game. It was the last game of my senior year and there were five seconds left to play. Our coach, Knute Klemens, called time out and designed a play for me. Our quarterback, A. Y. Yabolinski, threw me the ball for a five-yard gain. (Hey, I can honestly say that I averaged five yards a play for my high school career.) Since I knew this was going to be the last play of the game, I tried to lateral the ball back to our halfback, Jim Brown (no, not *that* Jim Brown. *This* Jim Brown went into the car business after high school. *Stealing* them, if I remember correctly.); but some hot dog from our arch-rival Felix Frankfurter High (hey, what did I tell ya before about booin'. Let's not have it happen again. OK?) got in the way and intercepted the lateral and ran it back for a touchdown. We still won the game 56-6, and Frankfurter was celebratin' just like they'd won the frickin' Super Bowl or somethin'. It was the only touchdown they scored all year.

If you believe any of that, you still think I got my nickname from a duck on a cartoon show. But I still needed a new lawyer since Susan was in Saskatchewan, and Barbara apparently didn't have the guts to defend me. I didn't want to ask Mary Payson because I wanted her to concentrate on Julie's case. And besides, I'm sure that a DUI case would be well beneath her standards.

I talked to a friend of mine, Chip Milton, who owned a bar and had lots of experience with DUI situations. Chip recommended that I contact Benjamin Loller, so I called Mr. Loller and set up an appointment for the following day.

Later on in the day, I tried giving Sally a call several times, but all I got was her answering machine. "Hello. This is Sally. Please leave your name and number after the beep and I will get back to you as soon as I can. And Dewey, if this is you, where the hell have you been? You damn well better call me soon!"

After the third time of listening to the message, I left my own message. "Yes, ma'am. It's Dewey. I'll call you tomorrow right after lunch." Women! Sheesh!

At five minutes to ten on Friday morning, I walked into the law offices of Benjamin Loller. His ad in the phone directory read: "If you don't want to holler, have Loller for your lawyer." (I tried saying it five times fast, but you really don't want to know how it came out.) Maybe it was better when lawyers couldn't advertise.

His receptionist buzzed him to let him know I was there, and she took me back. Ben Loller was a dead ringer for the comedian Lenny D. Vinky, and thought he was twice as funny. The second I stepped into his office, he greeted me with, "You ain't a gonna holler now that you've got Loller for your lawyer." He thought it was hysterical. I just stood there.

"Yes. Well…have a seat, have a seat," Ben said. I sat, I sat.

"So, what can ol' Ben do fer ya?" At this point I wondered which one of us really needed the zip English course.

"Well, ol' Ben," I started, "you don't mind if I call ya ol' Ben, do ya?" He just nodded and grinned. "Well, ol' Ben, it's like this. A few weeks ago, ol' Dewey here – I was really gettin' into this – ol' Dewey here got himself (I was gonna say *hisself*, but even I couldn't go that far) arrested for DUI, an' ol' Dewey here knows that he ain't guilty."

With that I handed him the same type-written sheets that I gave to Barbara.

Ol' Ben quickly read the papers and said, "Well…what ol' Ben recommends here is that ya take what's called ARD. This is yer first time, right?"

"Well, ol' Ben, it's my first time since they've had ARD. I was stopped twice a number of years ago, but I was found not guilty both times. I know I ain't guilty, an' I know all about ARD. If you ain't guilty and still take ARD, it should stand for Another Ridiculous Decision. So I ain't takin' ARD."

I expected ol' Ben to laugh or at least grin, but he just sat there and stared at me. Finally Ben said, "So why ain't ya using the same lawyer, then?"

"Well, ol'Ben," I replied, "I woulda, but she moved to Saskatchewan."

"In that case, Dewey, by the way, what is your real first name? We certainly don't want to call you Dewey in court for a DUI case." Ol' Ben had disappeared, and Benjamin Loller, hot-shot attorney, was now in his place.

"My first name is David," I replied.

"Good. Then I better start calling you David. Do you know when your hearing is set for, David?"

"The preliminary's supposed to be next Wednesday."

"Oh, I'll get that waived. No point in wasting time with that. Nobody wins those anyway."

"I see."

"And David, my fee is $300 an hour. You OK with that?"

"Sure," I said, thinking all the while, *Julie better not be guilty. Not enough cats in East Arthur to cover that.*

"Good. I'll give you a call and let you know when your hearing will be set for. If you hear anything before I call, you call me."

"No problem. Thanks for takin' the case."

"Ol'Ben's only too happy to help." He just winked, and I headed for home.

That afternoon I gave Sally a call and finally got through.

"Hello."

"Hi Sally, it's Dewey."

"Dewey. Where the hell have you been? I saw you Wednesday at the reading of the will, but why haven't you gotten in touch with me?"

"I called you three times yesterday, Sally, but I kept gettin' your answerin' machine. I was at the funeral on Tuesday, but I didn't see ya there."

"No, I didn't go. I didn't want to be in the same room as Julie. I only went on Wednesday because Mr. Covet called and said I was in the will."

"You're the second one to tell me that," I barely mumbled. I was wonderin' if I should start wonderin' about Julie myself.

"What was that?" Sally asked. "I couldn't hear what you said."

"Oh...nothin'," I replied. "So where were you yesterday when I called?"

"Well, with Joe gone, I'm supposed to be reassigned. I had some personal things I had to take care of."

"I see. We really need to get together on this and compare notes. When's a good time for you?"

"I think I'll be out of here sometime next week, so why don't you come over tonight. I'll make dinner and we can talk then."

"That sounds good to me," I said. "Is six o'clock good for you?"

"Fine. I'll see you then," said Sally.

Right after I finished talking to Sally, I decided to give Julie a call.

"Hi Julie, it's Dewey."

"Oh, hi Dewey. You have some good news, I hope?"

"Nothing yet. I'm just calling to let you know that I'm havin' a talk with Sally Roberts tonight. I didn't know she would be in the will, so I think I'm gonna keep an eye on her."

"Sounds like a good idea. You might also want to keep an eye on the distant relative of Joe – what's the guy's name, uh...Nick something or other? I had no idea Joe had any blood relatives left."

"OK. I found out that he's stayin' at the Sheraton in Queensville, so he won't be goin' anywhere until the trial's over and he gets his share. He won't be hard to find."

"Well, let me know if you find out anything new. And Dewey…"

"Yeah?"

"Just make sure your *eye* is the only thing you're keeping on Sally."

Before I could answer, Julie hung up.

Women! Sheesh!

I got to Sally's about quarter to six. I had no idea what she was makin' for dinner, so I took along a six pack and a good bottle of wine, just to play it safe. She must have been lookin' out the window, waitin' for me to show, cuz the second I got out of my car she came runnin' out.

"Hello, stranger," she said, and gave me a big kiss. Fortunately I hadn't gotten the beer or wine out of the car yet, or it would have been all over the sidewalk. "Why don't we go inside?"

"Wait one second," I replied. "I bought a six pack of beer and a bottle of wine. You didn't say what we were havin' for dinner."

"I made spaghetti and meatballs," said Sally.

"In that case, either will go real well with dinner."

Once inside, I reached for Sally. After all, Julie never did give me a chance to answer after she told me to just keep my *eye* on her, so she couldn't accuse me of lyin' to her, now could she?

"Later," said Sally. "Let's eat first."

The dinner was good, not the best I've ever had, but not out of a can, either. We polished off the wine and saved the beer for later.

"From what you said on the phone," I started, "I suppose you think Julie killed the old man, huh?"

"Damn right I do," answered Sally. "It's been all over the news that they found traces of peanut oil in Joe's body, so who else could have done it?"

"Oh, I don't know? Maybe his secretary who knew him before Julie came along?" I tried to make it sound as funny as I could, but wonderin' how funny it really was. "You had to know about his allergy after all those years."

"Well…yes, I knew. But you don't really believe that I had anything to do with it, do you? I didn't even know I was in his will until Covet called me the other day."

"Of course not. I'm only kidding," I said. This was my first lie of the day. "Just the same, you bein' his secretary and all, I'm sure the cops'll have some questions for you. I'm kinda surprised they haven't been here already."

"To be honest about it, that kind of surprises me too. But I'll just explain to them who I really am, and that should take care of the situation."

"I certainly hope so, but just in case, you still might need a good attorney. Ever hear of Benjamin Loller?" At this point, I didn't know how good – or bad – Ol' Ben was, but I figured if I drummed up some business for him, he might take a little off my tab.

"Never heard of him," Sally replied, "but I'll keep him in mind, just in case."

"I figured Julie would get the bulk of Joe's estate, assuming she is out of jail to collect it; but what about leaving a billion to his nurse? And what about his second cousin, or third cousin, or whatever the hell he is? What's the guy's name? Nick somethin' or other?" (I thought maybe Nick should consider changin' his name to somethin' easier to remember, too.)

I was about to ask her why she thought *she* should get a billion, too, but thought better of it. I was also gonna tell her that Nick seemed to just come out of the woodwork, but said instead, "Yeah, he's from Tucson. I had a talk with the guy. Seems legit to me, but I think I'll keep an eye on him just to be sure." (And in this case, when I said an *eye*, I *really* meant an *eye.)*

"I saw Joe's three business partners at the funeral. They looked like they were there to make sure Joe wasn't goin' anywhere except six feet down. I didn't talk to 'em, but I had no trouble tellin' which one was Oscar."

Sally just laughed, but I could see her give me a weird look out of the corner of her eye. "Well, I guess I won't be seeing those characters again," she said.

"You never know. With the trial supposed to start in 10 days, who knows who'll be in the courtroom."

"So... what do we have so far?" asked Sally. "Let's see. I still think Julie bumped him off, but let's look at the other possibilities.

"First, there's Nora the nurse," she said. "She could have slipped some peanut oil in his drink or on his food. After all, she was at the wine dinner that night."

"Yeah, that's a possibility," I answered. "But why would she do it? According to her, she didn't know she was in the will any more than you."

"Well...maybe that's true and maybe it isn't. And maybe she took advantage of her opportunity to get back at Joe for dumping her for Julie. Being his nurse at one time, she had to know about his allergy."

I didn't tell her that Nora was the number one suspect on my list. I also didn't tell her who number two was, either.

"Then there's cousin Nick," she continued. "He could have been at the wine dinner, too. No one would have recognized him at the time."

"I guess so," I said, "but how would he know that Joe would be there that night? I know that all that money would give him a good motive, but that just doesn't add up. I think he's pretty harmless."

"Well," said Sally. "That leaves just three other possibilities then, doesn't it?"

"Yeah, Oscar and his two buddies," I said. "Maybe Joe was into 'em for somethin' and thought he could get away without payin'."

"No, I don't mean them. Two of the other three possibilities are right here in this room, and the third…"

"Hey, wait a minute. Why would I bump him off? After all, he was payin' me to keep tabs on his wife. Why eliminate my meal ticket?"

"Maybe you liked what you were tailing and thought you could have it all for yourself," she said.

"You know," I said, "I never thought of that. But, nah, I didn't do it. Now you, on the other hand…"

"Me? Why would I bump him off?"

"Hey, don't get sore at me," I answered. "You're the one who brought it up, and bein' his secretary for all those years, just maybe you got a look at his will."

"No I didn't," she practically screamed, sounding really pissed.

"Hey, look what we're doin' here," I said. "You mentioned a third possibility?" Although that's what I said, I knew we were both now more suspicious of each other than ever before.

"The third possibility," said Sally, "is that someone we don't even know bumped him off for some reason we know nothing about."

I had to agree with her on that one. (But be honest, don't ya just hate it when you get to the end of a murder mystery and find out that the murderer is someone who ain't even in the book until the last 20 pages? I think that really sucks.)

All through our conversation we were finishing off the six pack, and my eyes – at least the one I was keeping on Sally – were getting very tired. It was time for the rest of my body to pick up the slack.

Chapter 14: DO DEWEY KNOW TOO MUCH WITHOUT EVEN KNOWIN' IT?

It was barely 7 a.m. when Sally and I got up on Saturday. She claimed she had to drive back to D.C. and report in.

"Another meeting with J. Edgar?" I asked.

"Something like that," she answered, although she gave me a look that said, *Hey, it was cute the first time, but don't push it, OK?*

Sally's car was parked on the driveway and mine was on the street in front of the house. I walked Sally to her car, kissed her goodbye, and waved as she drove down the street. I walked out to my car, and there they were – two flat rear tires. I wasn't sure whether somebody did it deliberately, or whether the retreads I bought for my piece of junk had finally given out.

I bent down to look at the tires and got my answer. There was no glass or nails that I could see, but it was obvious that both tires had been cut on purpose. Was I followed? Was this some kinda warning? Do bears really shit in the woods?

I was pretty sure I knew the answer to that last question, and I was almost as certain that I knew the answers to the first two, too. The only question was – Why? Was I getting too close to the truth? Did I already know something and not even know what I knew? Will Debbie finally tell Brad that the baby she's carrying is not his, but is really... Sorry, but once in a while I watch this soap opera called *Debbie and*

*Brad and John and Bill and Sam and...*It's really quite entertaining, but I guess Debbie must get real tuckered out. Maybe that's why they've had four actresses play her in the last four months. Anyway...

I could wait till later to figure out the answers to all those questions, but first I had to have my car taken care of. Fortunately, that wasn't going to be a problem. While other people had other car services, I had one that was not quite as good, but very reasonably priced. Free! Double Z Auto Service.

Yeah, Zeke Zembrowski and I were old friends from high school, and it was usually Zeke who was holdin' down the other end of the bench on the football team. I gave Zeke a call.

"Double Z Auto Service. This is Zeke speakin'."

"Hello, Zeke," I said. "It's Dewey. How's it hangin'?"

"Ah, lower than ever, Dew. Wuzzup wit you?" (Zeke and I also took zip English together.)

"I got a job for ya, Zekey. Somebody decided to take a little air outta my back tires last night. Actually, all the air."

"That's a real shame, Dew. An' such a real classic car, too." I'm sure Zeke would have known a great car *if* he would have seen one, but with the customers he had, there was no possibility of that ever happenin'.

"Yeah... well...could you come over and bring two of your best retreads for my car?" I gave him the address.

"Sure, Dew," he said. "You always did go top drawer, din' ya? I'll be right there."

While waitin' for Zeke to get there, I decided to give Julie a call.

"Hi, Dewey," she said, even before I could say hello. Damn. I really hated caller ID. "How did it go with Sally, and where the hell are you calling from? You damn well better not…"

"Hey, hold on there, boss. I think we might be gettin' close to somethin'. I'm callin' from my cell phone. Somebody must be awful scared that we're on to somethin', cuz the two rear tires on my car are flatter 'n a pancake. I'm waitin' for my auto service to get here." I didn't lie, but I didn't tell her I was callin' from in front of Sally's house, either.

Julie quickly calmed down and said, "OK. So what did you find out from Sally?"

"Well, first of all, you're her number one suspect, but she ain't rulin' out other possibilities."

"Why that little bitch," Julie said. "So, who are her other possibilities?"

"Well, let me see. There's me – I didn't go into an explanation as to why. Then there's Nora, because she was gettin' back at Joe for dumpin' her for you. Then there's Cousin Nick, because somehow he knew he was in the will. Then there was her last possibility."

"Yeah, and who might that be?" Julie asked.

"That might be somebody we don't know who bumped Joe off for some reason we don't know either."

"Oh, don't you just hate that when it happens in a good mystery? Spoils the whole damn thing." Apparently Julie and I had the same taste in mysteries, too.

"I see my service guy's here. I'll give you a call in a day or two. And don't worry, everything's gonna be all right." My first lie of the day.

Zeke pulled up with the two new retreads. (Well, they were new to me!) "Such a beautiful car," he practically purred. Zeke really surprised me with that. It wasn't often that I heard him say a word that had three syllables in it.

Once Zeke was finished changin' the tires, I slipped him a five for his troubles – hey, if he was happy with that, so was I – and headed for home.

When I got home a little after 11, I decided to have lunch and then give No a call.

"Hi, Dewey," she said, even before I could say hello. I guess everybody has caller ID.

"Hello, No," I replied. "How you doin', now that you're gonna be a billionaire after they figure out who bumped Joe off?" Of course I didn't mention that she wouldn't be if she happened to be the bumper.

"I'm doing OK, I guess. I'm just so shocked I really don't know what to think."

"Well...how 'bout thinkin' about buyin' me dinner tonight. There's a new place in East Arthur called Charlie's Chop House. Wanna give it a try? I'm kinda gettin' tired of Sloppy Man's." From the location, I just assumed Charlie's was a restaurant, and not someplace that dealt with stolen car parts.

"OK. Why don't you pick me up around 5:30 and we'll eat about 7, if that's good for you?"

"Sounds fine with me. I'll see you then."

I needed some sleep after last night, and I had to decide how I was gonna pump Nora.

I got to No's place right at 5:30 and saw a note on the door. "Dewey, I had to step out for a moment. I'll be right back."

No was back in less than five minutes, but she definitely looked a bit shaken up about something. I decided not to push it – for now.

"How ya doin'?" I asked. "Ready to go try Charlie's Chop House?"

"What? Oh...yeah...sure."

"You OK?" I asked. "Somethin' the matter?"

"Huh? Oh...no...everything's fine," she answered, but I knew that wasn't the truth.

We said very little on the way back to East Arthur. I could tell there was definitely something on No's mind. Something that was really bothering her. Still, I thought I would let it go till later.

When we got to Charlie's Chop House, the place was packed. Since it was a Saturday night and it was a fairly new place, the hostess said it would be about an hour before we could get a table. No and I headed for the bar.

"White wine, right?" I asked.

"No, I think I'll have a Scotch on the rocks," No answered, "with a twist."

I told the bartender to make it two, only to skip the twist with mine. We sat there for several minutes in silence, just sipping our drinks. Finally, it looked like No was more relaxed.

"How've you been, Dew?" she started. "Anything new on the case?"

Here we go again, I thought. *Looks like I'm gonna be the pumpee.* "I had a talk with Sally, Joe's secretary, yesterday. She seems to think that Julie's the one who bumped Joe off."

"Yeah, well, I'll certainly go along with that. Who else would have done it?"

"Well, Sally thinks there might be some other candidates, if Julie didn't do it."

"Oh, really? Who else did she mention?"

"Let's see," I said. "First of all, there's me." Again, I didn't go into any explanation. "Second, there's you. She said that…"

"What!? Why would I kill the guy? I didn't even know I was in his will."

"I mentioned that to her, but she said that you were just gettin' even for Joe dumpin' you for Julie. Said you were pissed cuz you coulda had it all."

"That's ridiculous! We fooled around some, but there was never anything more to it than that. Besides, what about her? I still don't buy that secretary stuff. Maybe she did it. She was in the will, too, and she had the opportunity to slip something in his drink that night."

"That's what I told her. But she said she had no idea she was in his will, either. She also mentioned Joe's cousin Nick, and she mentioned one other possibility."

"And who was that?" No asked.

"She said it coulda been somebody we don't know who bumped him off for some reason we don't know either."

"Oh, don't you just hate that in a good mystery? Makes for a very disappointing ending." At least No, Julie, and I were on the same page there.

"I'll say," I said. "Other than that, there's really nothin' new to report."

Just about that time, the hostess came and said they had a table in the dining room ready for us. We went into the dining room, and were seated at a table right next to Mary Payson and her secretary, Stella DeRita.

"Hi, Mary, hello Stella," I said. "Mary and Stella, this is Nora. Nora Klause (I still thought it was funny, even if no one else did), Mary Payson and Stella DeRita."

"*The* Mary Payson?" No said, almost gushing. "Well, this really is quite an honor. Nice to meet you, too, Stella."

Mary extended her hand and was just about to say something when she had another attack. At least this time she had her inhaler with her.

"So, what are you two doing here?" asked Stella.

"Just a night out, getting something to eat," I answered. "I've heard this place is supposed to be really good, so we thought we would give it a try. You been here before?"

"No," said Mary, now recovered from her attack. "This is our first time, too."

"If you'll excuse me, I have to go powder my nose," No said.

When No left the table, this gave me the chance I needed. "This is great bumpin' into you two," I said. "I need to talk to you as soon as possible, Mary. I know tomorrow is Sunday, but would it be all right if I gave you a call?"

"Sure," Mary said, and wrote down her number.

In a few minutes, No returned from the ladies' room. The waiter came over and took our orders. I figured, since it was Charlie's *Chop*

House, I would order the lamb chops. No ordered scallops, Stella had prime rib, and Mary ordered surf and turf. It didn't take a rocket scientist to figure who had the money at our tables.

There was a little small talk during dinner, but nothing about the case. I needed to talk to Mary and Stella without No, and No still looked too shook up with whatever was bothering her to ask Mary any questions.

Once dinner was over, we had a drink and talked about the food. We all agreed that it would have been better if Charlie's Chop House *had* dealt in stolen car parts. To say that the food was not good would have been paying it a compliment, and we knew that Charlie's wouldn't be in East Arthur very long.

Mary and Stella left a few minutes later, while No and I finished our drinks. It was time to drive Nora home.

Nobody said anything for quite a while, so I decided it was time to find out what was goin' on. "You really haven't been yourself tonight, No. Wanna tell me about it?"

"Oh…it's really nothing, I guess. Right after I talked to you this afternoon, a guy I used to see called up and said he had to see me right away. Said he was very upset about something. I asked him if we could discuss it over the phone, but he said no, he wanted to talk in person. That's where I was when you got to my place."

"I see. So…did you get it straightened out?"

"I hope so. Like I said, I used to date this guy, and he found out that I was seeing someone else, and wanted me to stop."

"Oh, you mean *me*?"

"No, Dew, I don't mean you. There's someone else I've been seeing for a while now."

"Oh," I said, and couldn't think of anything else to say, but what I was thinkin' was *How dare she! It's a good thing I have Julie and Sally, or I'd be real upset.* I was also thinkin' *Stella's lookin' real good, too. Wouldn't mind checkin' her out.*

We rode in silence all the way back to Nora's, and I thought about just walkin' her to her door and sayin' goodnight. But you know how the old song goes…uh…oh, yeah…*If you can't be with the one you love, honey, love the one you're with!*

It turned out to be great advice.

Chapter 15: SUNDAY WITH STELLA

I left No's house right after 9 a.m. She didn't bother walking me to my car; and, as a matter of fact, she was still in bed asleep as I slipped out the front door. When I got to my car, I checked all my tires, but they looked good to me. Maybe my retreads had just given out.

As I got closer to home, I stopped at a fast-food place for a fast-food breakfast. Eating all this normal stuff – whether it tasted good or not (like Charlie's last night) – was startin' to play tricks with my system. I knew it was time for some good old-fashioned junk food.

I checked my answerin' machine the second I got home, but there weren't any messages. There was no point in givin' Julie a call cuz there was nothin' new to report. I knew I wanted to give Mary a call, but it was only 10:30 when I got in, so I decided to wait till after lunch. It was time to take a nap.

I got up at 1:00 and dialed the number Mary gave me.

"Hello." Either Mary didn't have caller ID, or she wasn't quite awake yet.

"Hi, Mary, it's Dewey. Sorry to bother you on a Sunday, but I think we really need to talk. I'm gettin' real concerned about Julie, and maybe we can compare notes."

"Certainly," said Mary. "I'm at home right now, but can you meet me at my office in about an hour? I'll give Stella a call so she can meet us there, too. Do you know where my office is?"

I told her that I didn't know where the office was, so she gave me the address. It was only gonna take about 15 minutes to get from my place to hers, which gave me plenty of time to get my notes together about the case.

When I got to the office, Stella was already there waitin' for me. "So, how are you, Dewey? Mary called and said she would be here in a few minutes. Can I get you anything? Coffee? Tea?"

"No thanks," I answered, "but how about dinner later on tonight? There's a new place over in Tigerton?" What the hell. If No was seein' somebody else, why couldn't I? After all, Julie and Sally were strictly in the line of business. And, by the way, remind me to tell you about the time I made a 40-foot hook shot to win...

"Thanks, Dewey, I'd love to. Any place but Charlie's."

"How 'bout I pick you up at 6. Why don't you give me your address and phone number?"

Right after Stella finished doing that, Mary walked in. "So, what's so urgent that you need to see me on a Sunday, Dewey?"

"Well, with Julie's trial starting a week from tomorrow," I started, "I think we need to compare notes. I guess she told ya that I'm workin' for her."

"Yes, she did. I also have a detective working on the case by the name of Saul Swann." (Thanks for not booin'. They can't all be winners, ya know.)

The Saul Swann Detective Agency was the biggest in the area. He was involved in all of Mary's famous cases, and I really had to look up to the guy. After all, he'd been voted the number one detective east of the mighty Manatawny for the last five years in a row – that, plus the fact that I was five foot eleven, and he was six five.

"I sorta figured that. He's worked on all your big cases, hasn't he?"

"Yes," said Mary, "but he's thinking of retiring after this year. Said something about moving to Saskatchewan. If that happens, I could use a good man very soon."

I immediately thought, *Well, I've already got Julie and Nora and Sally, and maybe Stella. Oh, wait. I think she means a detective.* "Well, if you do, keep me in mind."

"I certainly will," she said, a lot more seductively than I imagined. "But what have you discovered so far?"

"What I've discovered so far is that just about everyone thinks that Julie is guilty. And, quite frankly, it doesn't look too good that they found traces of peanut oil when they did the autopsy. I'm wonderin' if the authorities are holdin' back any information till the trial."

"Many times they do," said Mary. "I'm having Saul check that out, but so far he hasn't been able to come up with anything. So what have you been working on?"

"Well, for starters, I've been keepin' tabs on Nora, Joe's one-time nurse, and Sally, his confidential secretary."

"I bet you have," Mary and Stella said at the same time.

"Hey, this is part of what Julie's been payin' me to do," I answered.

"*Sure it is,*" said Mary. "So, what have you found out from those two that you're keeping an *eye* on?"

"The one thing they both seem to agree on is that Julie's the one who killed Joe. They figure she had to know about his allergy, that she was tired of his runnin' around, and that she wanted all his money without him. But they also figure that there are other suspects if she didn't do it."

"And just who might they be?" asked Stella.

"Well, they both think that the other one had good reasons to bump him off, considerin' they were both in his will. They also think that I could have done it, cuz I was tailin' Julie for Joe when he died, and maybe I liked what I saw enough to go for it myself. Then there's Joe's cousin, Nick. They think that maybe he actually knew he was in the will. And, finally, there's one last suspect."

"And who would that be?" Stella asked again.

"Oh, that would be the mystery person that we don't know who killed Joe for some reason we don't know, either," Mary answered before I could. "Don't you just love a good mystery where the murderer doesn't even appear until the last 20 pages?" I reminded myself not to invite Mary to any of my book signings.

"So Dewey, if you were a betting man, who would your money be on?" Mary continued.

"Well, right now it's a toss-up between Nora and Sally. I know I didn't do it, and I'm pretty sure Julie didn't, either. Unless it's the mystery person, it almost has to be one of them."

"What about Cousin Nick?" asked Mary.

"He just doesn't seem like the type," I answered, "although there's somethin' about him I can't quite figure out. I know where he's stayin', and he ain't goin' anywhere until at least after the trial, so I'll keep an eye on him."

"Let me know if you find out anything more," said Mary. "I know right now it doesn't look too good for Julie, but I just can't believe she did it."

"I'll let you know the minute I hear anything," I said to Mary. To Stella I said, "And I'll see you tonight about 6?"

"And is Julie paying you to keep an eye on *her*, too?" Mary said. I couldn't really tell if she was hurt, bein' cynical, or just jokin' around.

Women! Sheesh!

***

After leavin' Mary's office, I took a little drive just to clear my head. Of course, many people over the years have told me that I wouldn't have to do much to clear my head. Can't clear somethin' that ain't there.

I just had to be missin' somethin'. Was it Nora or Sally, as I suspected? Was it Cousin Nick? Could Julie be guilty and be really pullin' one over on me and her lawyer, Mary Payson? Or could it possibly be the unknown suspect? Things were just movin' around in my head way too fast.

I would have to sort it all out later. Right now I had to go home and get ready for my date with Stella. Oh, and in case you missed it, Debbie *did* tell Brad that the baby wasn't his, but said she was sorry, so Brad had to console her, one thing led to another, and now Debbie's expectin' twins – by two different guys. (Hey, it *is* possible, ya know.) But Debbie doesn't know it yet, so she can't tell Brad about the baby that *is* his. I can't wait to see what happens next. I bet that honeymoon'll be real interestin', with the three of 'em – not includin' the babies – and all.

When I got home, I got cleaned up for my date with Stella. I took a shower and shaved, but I didn't splash on any HaiVelva or AquaKarate, and I certainly didn't put on any Midnight Madness for Men. Matter of fact, I'm pretty sure I threw that out. I put on a nice shirt and pair of pants, but I really didn't go to too much trouble gettin' ready. After all, Stella was OK, and while she was definitely a cut above most of the women I'd met on uoutthere.com, she wasn't any match for Julie, Nora, or Sally.

The more I thought about it, the more I wanted to call Stella and tell her that somethin' came up and so I'd have to cancel our date. But when I looked at the clock, it was already 20 minutes to 6, and even I ain't that much of a rat.

When I got to Stella's place, I rang the doorbell, and heard, "Come in. The door's open." I stepped inside, and heard from another room, "Is that you, Dewey?"

"It's me," I said. (I did pass that zip English class, ya know, but who the hell ever says, "It's I?")

"Good. I'll be out in just a minute. I'm just about finished getting ready."

Oh, goody! I thought to myself, wishing I were someplace else. Instead, I said, "That's OK. Take your time."

I was walking around the livin' room, when I heard from behind me, "So…how do I look? You won't be embarrassed to be seen in public with me, will you?"

A second before I turned around, I figured this would be my first lie of the day. But when I finally did turn around, I couldn't believe what I was looking at. "Hello," I said, totally serious. "My name's Dewey. Stella said she would be right out."

"Don't be silly," she said.

Then it hit me. *She* was Stella. Gone were her secretary glasses. Gone, too, was the nice-looking, but overly-professional pants suit that revealed absolutely nothing. In its place was a stunning low-cut dress that revealed practically everything, and a pair of legs that belonged to a top movie star. Now I wanted to be somewhere else but going to dinner, only *with* Stella next to me.

"Wow!" was what came out. "Maybe we'd better get going to dinner while I still want to." There was no way I was gonna shake hands with the beauty that was standin' in front of me, so I gave her a light kiss on the cheek. I was sure the evening would improve as it went along.

Thank God I decided to toss the Midnight Madness for Men.

It was only a few minutes from Stella's place to Tigerton, so we rode over with just the radio on. "I hope you like Chinese," I said. I hadn't had Chinese in a while and was looking forward to it.

"Chinese is fine," Stella answered. "I haven't had Chinese in quite a while."

When we got near where I thought the restaurant was, I saw a sign that said Chinese, but I couldn't read the name under it. We got out of the car and walked inside.

"Table for two?" asked the host. "Right this way."

As soon as we were seated, our waiter came over and said, "Weccome to Charrie's Chop Suey House. Would you like to start with drink?"

Stella and I looked at each other and both started laughing. "Well, we're here," I said, "so we might as well give it a try."

"Might as well," said Stella. "It can't possibly be as bad as last night."

"Something matta," said our waiter.

"No," I said. "It's just that we were at a place last night called Charlie's Chop House. Is that Charlie by the door?"

"Oh, no sah, that not Charrie."

"Well, tell me then, are you Charrie…uh, Charlie? You don't look very Chinese to me?"

Our waiter lowered his voice, "Actually, sir," he said in a voice that reminded me of Arthur Treacher, "my name is Reginald. I'm just doing this so that I can practice my Chinese accent for when my next acting job comes up."

"I see. So, *Reginald*, who's this Charlie fella that owns these restaurants?" I asked, even though he didn't look very British to me, either.

"I believe, sir," said Reginald, "that Charlie doesn't exist. I think it's the name of the corporation that owns the restaurants."

"They don't have a Charlie's Chopped Liver House, do they?" Stella asked. We both laughed. Reginald waited until we were through.

"No, ma'am," he said. "Now, may I take your order?"

Stella and I both ordered some chicken, along with a bottle of wine.

"Very good, sah, you order be righ ow." Reginald just winked and walked away.

Once we were alone, I couldn't keep my eyes off Stella. "You look fabulous," I said. "I really didn't recognize you for a second when you came out. Uh...not that you don't look good other times."

"Thanks," she laughed. "I know what you mean. It's just that I have to look very professional around Mary, and I don't get to dress like this and go out very often."

"I really can't believe you're not seeing anyone? Too busy with work?"

"Actually, no," Stella answered. "The truth is that I was seeing Saul Swann for a long time, but we decided to call it off. I really didn't want to wind up in Saskatchewan."

"Why not?" I said. "Everyone else seems to be going there."

"What?" said Stella.

"Oh...nothing," I replied. "Oh look, our dinner's here."

All through dinner, Stella and I talked about many things, but we never discussed the case. After all, we both knew everything there was to know about it at this point.

I found out that Stella was into needlepoint, cooking (I wonder if she has a Radar Range?), and bobsledding. Bobsledding!?

Stella found out that I was into Stella – at least for the evening.

Dinner was certainly better than it was at Charlie's Chop House the night before, but it still wasn't great. When we got outside, we agreed that we wouldn't go to another restaurant that had the name Charlie in it for quite some time.

"Would you like to go someplace for a nightcap?" I asked.

"How about my place?" she replied.

"Fine with me."

When we got to Stella's, she said, "Why don't you fix us some drinks? I guess you saw where the bar is earlier. I'll have a Scotch, neat. I'll be right back."

Stella came back in a few moments. While she was gone, she had slipped into somethin' as comfortable as you can get.

Nothing.

I handed her the Scotch and said, "A toast."

"A toast," she said.

"To us," I continued.

"To us," she replied.

I don't think we ever finished the drinks.

Chapter 16: A LITTLE TRICK WITH (COUSIN) NICK

Stella had to meet Mary at the courthouse at 9 a.m., so we had to get up early. Mary was defending another client who couldn't possibly lose having Mary Payson defend him. Stella had on another one of her overly-professional pants suits, complete with her secretary-style glasses. I almost didn't recognize her again, but I kissed her goodbye and wished her luck with the case. I told her that I would be in touch and headed for home.

It was only a little before 9 when I got there, so I decided to take a nap. This detective work can really tire a guy out, ya know. I checked my answerin' machine first, but there weren't any messages, and my favorite soap opera didn't come on until one in the afternoon, so I had about four hours to get some rest.

It was some dream I was havin'. The girl in it had Julie's eyes, Sally's hair, Stella's legs, and No's boobs – although that last one was a pretty close call. So I was real pissed when the phone woke me up at 10 o'clock.

"Dewey Detective Agency," I said. "This is Dewey speakin'."

"Hello, David," the voice said. It didn't take me three guesses to figure out who was callin'. "It's Ben Loller."

"Well, how the hell are ya, ol' Ben?" I asked. "Ol' Dewey here's doin' jus'…"

"Cut the shit, will you *David*," he said. "And remember, until after your trial it *is* David."

"Sorry, Ben…uh, Benjamin…uh, Mr. Loller. What can I do for you?"

"Ben is fine for now, David, but when we get to court, please refer to me as Mr. Loller."

"All right, Ben, what can I do for you?"

"Well, I've got some good news, and I've got some bad news," said Ben. "First the good news. The good news is that I got your preliminary waived without any problem. The bad news is that they want to get this over with in a hurry, so your trial starts this Wednesday. I tried to get a continuance, but the judge wouldn't go for it. That doesn't give us much time. I want to see you in my office tomorrow afternoon at three. Do you have a problem with that?"

"No, Ben," I answered. "That won't be a problem at all."

"Good. Oh, and David, there is one other problem."

"What's that?" I asked.

"We drew Judge Roy B. Osbourne for your trial."

"Is that bad?" I wondered.

"Well, for starters, the B stands for Bean. This guy is the great-great-grandnephew of Judge Roy Bean. You know, the guy they called the law west of the Pecos?"

"OK, so what's the problem with that?" I asked, not gettin' the connection.

"Well," Ben said, "the problem with that is that Judge Roy B. Osbourne thinks that he's the law *east* of the Pecos."

"Oh boy!" was all I could say.

"Oh boy is right," said Ben. "I'll see you tomorrow at three o'clock."

I just hoped ol' Ben was up to the challenge.

I went back to sleep, hoping that I could continue the dream where I left off before Ben rudely interrupted it, but it was no use. I started havin' a dream about my ex-wife. She was a chariot driver in the old days, and guess who the horse was who was pullin' the frickin' chariot. I had no idea what that meant, but I'm sure that Freud would have come up with one helluvan explanation for it. But it was like goin' from the penthouse to the outhouse in terms of dreams. I didn't stay in bed too long.

I got up about 11 and had my favorite breakfast. Two bowls of Frosted Flakes, four Twinkies, and a can of Jolt. (If they ever start puttin' pictures of detectives on the Jolt cans, I bet I'll be the first one.) I was just about to get into the shower when the phone started ringin'. I thought about lettin' the machine take it, but with everything that was goin' on, I figured I better pick it up.

"Dewey Detective Agency," I said. "This is Dewey speakin'."

"Hello, Mr. Polpulcionski," someone said. This was startin' to bother me. This made two people in the last week that could actually pronounce my last name.

"Yes, hello, who's this?" I asked.

"It's Nick Rudawski. I'm staying at the Sheraton in Queensville. I need to see you about something. I think it's very important. Can you come over here at 1 o'clock?"

I thought a minute and said, "Could we make it about 2:30? I have something to do around one." I didn't want to tell Nick that I *had* to watch the soap opera. Couldn't wait to see who Debbie was sleepin' with this week. "Say, Nick, would it be OK if we met over at Sloppy Man's? It's right around the corner from where you're stayin'. Ever been there? I'll buy ya lunch. We can talk then."

"No, I haven't been there, but I've seen the place from the outside. I'll meet you there at 2:30."

"Good. I'll see you then." I didn't think Nick was lyin', but this way I could make sure. I still didn't think that he bumped Joe off, but there was still somethin' about him that I couldn't quite figure out.

At one o'clock I turned on *Debbie and Brad and John and Bill and Sam and...* Today, Debbie was going for her doctor's appointment, not knowing that she was now havin' two kids by two different daddies.

"So, how are you feeling?" asked Dr. Steven Fix. I was wonderin' if Fix was the ... in the title.

"OK, I guess," said Debbie, "but I'm tired all the time." (Well, no shit, Deb. With all the screwin' around yer doin', who wouldn't be? At least I take a nap every once in a while.)

"Well, that's to be expected," said Doc. "Let me give a listen."

Doc gave a listen and said, "I don't know how to tell you this, Debbie, but I'm certain that I hear three different hearts in there." (Were there three different daddies, or was one of the guys the father of twins?)

"Three! Oh no! What will I do, Doctor Fix?" she cried.

With that, Doc consoled Debbie, as he had no other patients scheduled for the day. One thing led to another, and before you could sing "Rock-a-Bye-Baby"...

I couldn't wait to tune in tomorrow when I might find out if "Debbie and Doc really got it on?" and if "Debbie will have *four* different hearts in there at her next checkup?" I'm glad my appointment with Ben Loller wasn't until 3 o'clock.

Right after the show was over, I headed straight for Sloppy Man's, hopin' to get there ahead of Cousin Nick. I knew Glad would be workin' and I thought that maybe Fred, the manager on duty the night Joe died, might be there as well. If Nick was there that evening, I'm sure at least one of them would be able to recognize him. Workin' the bar business, one of their jobs was to be able to remember a face and put a drink with it.

I got to the bar about ten minutes to two, and Nick hadn't arrived yet. Unfortunately, Glad had the day off, and some new girl I'd never seen before was behind the bar.

"Hi, I'm Bev. What can I get for you, sir?"

"Hi, Bev, I'll have a Chivas on the rocks. I'm Dewey Polpulcionski, but you can call me Dewey P."

"Dewey P?" She took the bait.

"Well, I do, and if you don't on a regular basis, yer gonna be in big trouble real soon." A new customer for my old line. They didn't come along much these days.

We both laughed, but I could tell that hers was more of a professional giggle; and the way she was lookin' at me said *What kind of an asshole have I got here.*

"Say Bev, is Fred workin' today? I need to see him about somethin'."

"He's in the office. Do you want me to get him?"

"If you don't mind, I would appreciate it." After all, I was the only customer in the bar at the time.

A few moments later, Bev came back out with Fred. We shook hands, and schmoozed each other about how great it was to see one another.

"Say Fred, you were workin' the night of the wine dinner, weren't ya?" I asked, although I already knew the answer.

"Yeah, Dew, I was here. Why do you ask?"

"Well, I got a guy I'm meeting here at 2:30, and I want to see if you recognize him. I'll introduce you to him when he gets here. Let me know later whether he was here that night or not, but don't let on to him."

"Sure, Dew, no problem. I'll come back out around 2:30. Got some work to finish up in the office."

"OK, Fred. Thanks."

Fred went back to his office, and I started talkin' to Bev.

"So, tell me, Bev, how long you been workin' here?" I asked, eyin' her up all the time.

"I just started last week," said Bev. "My normal lunch day is going to be Wednesday, but since Gladys is off today, they thought I could use the experience."

"I see. You gonna be workin' some nights, too?" Bev looked real good to me. A little like Julie here, a little like Nora there, a little like Sally somewhere else, and a bit like Stella elsewhere. Hey, maybe she was the girl I was havin' the dream about this morning, even before I met her. Maybe I'm psychic! (Some people have told me that I'm *psychotic*, but I don't think that's the same thing, is it?) But with the other four I already had goin', I was afraid Bev would have to stay on the back burner. At least for now.

"Right now I'm scheduled to work Saturdays and Sundays, but I'll pick up other shifts if they need me."

"I usually don't get in much on Saturdays, but I'll probably see you on Sunday once in a while," I said.

Just then I saw Nick standing in the lobby. It was only a few minutes after two, so I knew Fred wouldn't be out for a while, but I figured we would still be there at 2:30.

"Hey Nick, in here."

"Thanks for coming, Dewey," he said. "I hope I didn't keep you waiting long."

"No, not at all. We said about 2:30 and it's only a little after two. Besides, I just got here myself a few minutes ago. You wanna have lunch at the bar, take a table, or go into the dining room?"

"Your call," said Nick.

"Why don't we take a table in here," I said. "As you can see, I don't think we'll be disturbed in here."

"That's fine by me," Nick said. So we moved to a table in the bar area.

"What ya drinkin'?" I asked.

"Oh, I don't know. What are you having?"

"This is Chivas," I said.

"I think I'll have the same thing," he said. I could tell that Nick looked real upset.

"A Chivas for my friend here," I said to Bev. To Nick I said, "I think I'm gonna have the fish and chips, but you order whatever you want."

"Fish and chips sounds good," he said.

"And two orders of fish and chips, please, Bev."

"OK, Nick," I started, "tell me what's goin' on. You sounded pretty serious over the phone."

"Yeah… well…two days after the reading of the will, three guys approached me as I was getting off the elevator at the Sheraton. Said they wanted to talk with me. I didn't know who they were, or how they knew where I was staying, so I didn't want to take them up to my room, so we found a little area off the lobby in the hotel."

"I see. So what did they want to talk about?"

"Well, somehow they knew about the reading of the will. I'm sure I didn't see them there that day; but now that I think about it, I know I saw them the day before at Uncle Joe's funeral."

"Uh-huh. Go on." I had a feeling I knew just who he was talkin' about.

"They said they just wanted to give me some friendly advice. They said I shouldn't leave town until I heard from them again, if I knew what was good for me."

"So, what did you tell 'em?"

"I told them that I wasn't going anywhere for a few weeks. They told me that was a real good idea, and then they left. Do you think there's a connection with Uncle Joe's murder?"

"Oh, I'm sure there is," I answered. "I think the guys you were talkin' to were Vinny, Angelo, and Oscar."

"Oscar?" Nick said.

"Yeah, must be related on his mother's side," I answered.

Just then Bev came over with our fish and chips.

"Care for another drink?" I asked Nick. He had hardly touched the one he had.

"Not yet, thanks."

"I'll have another Chivas rocks," I told Bev.

At that point, Fred walked part way into the bar area and nodded for me to come over. Nick's back was to him, so Nick didn't see this happen. I told Nick I had to use the men's room.

"Never saw the guy before, Dew. I'm sure he wasn't at the dinner, and he hasn't been here before at all. At least not when I've been working."

"Thanks, Fred. I owe you one."

"You're welcome. And Dewey…"

"Yeah?"

"You owe me at least seven," said Fred, and went back to his office.

Gee. Was everybody keepin' tabs on how many I owed 'em?

I went to the men's room, just in case Nick saw me talkin' to Fred. When I got back to the table, Nick and I finished our lunches in silence.

A few minutes later Nick got up to leave and said, "Well, thanks for coming, and thanks for the lunch. This is a nice place. I'll have to come here more often while I'm in town."

"My pleasure," I said. "Don't go anywhere, and let me know if you hear from our three buddies again."

"Oh, I'll certainly let you know, all right."

Nick left. I was more convinced than ever that Cousin Nick was not the one who bumped off Uncle Joe. The only problem was there was still somethin' strange about him that I just couldn't figure out.

It was time to give Julie a call.

"Why Dewey, it's so wonderful of you to call," Julie said without bothering with hello. I'd heard her pissed before, but I never heard her sound so sarcastic.

"Hi, Julie. What's up?"

"Hi, Julie. What's up? Is that all you can say? *Hi, Julie. What's up?* What the hell's going on, *Mister* Polpulcionski?"

That now made *three* people in less than a week. Now I *knew* I'd have to change my last name.

"Now I hear you're seeing my lawyer's secretary, Stella DeRita."

"Gee, news sure gets around fast, don't it?" I said. "Ya gotta admit, though, that I'm comin' up in the world. Remember me tellin' ya that I would eventually go from a bimbo to a floozy, to a *she*, and then to somebody who actually has a name. Looks like I've arrived, boss."

"Cut the bullshit, would you, Dewey. What about me? Here I am, accused of killing my own husband, out on bail, and do you care? No! Do you ever take *me* to dinner? No! All you care about is getting laid!"

"But Julie, I'm doin' it all for you. I'm doin' this to try to keep your pretty little neck out of the slammer...or maybe worse."

"Bullshit! You're doing it for the grand a day I'm paying you."

I felt like adding *plus expenses*, but I figured it wouldn't be a good idea pushin' it.

"Look," I said, "why don't I come over tonight and take you out to dinner. Anyplace ya wanna go. Besides, I got things I need to discuss with ya. Whatd'ya say?" After all, it was her money that would be payin' for the dinner.

"OK," she said. "Why don't you pick me up about seven? And look, Dewey, I'm sorry I get like this, but I'm just so upset with everything that's been happening."

"That's all right. I understand. Why don't you take it easy, and I'll see you at seven. Everything's gonna be fine." This was the first lie of the day. I knew damn well I wasn't any closer to figurin' out who killed Joe than I was a week ago, and it was only a week until Julie's trial started.

Time to take a nap.

I got to Julie's right at seven. She was upset enough the way it was, so I didn't want her to get more upset by me bein' late.

"Hello, Dewey," she said as she answered the door. "I'm glad you could come over."

"No problemo," I said, trying to keep things as light as possible. "So…d'ya figure out where you'd like to have dinner?"

"Oh, Dewey, I'm so upset about everything right now. Why don't we just stay in and order a pizza? I have some beer in the fridge."

"That sounds fine with me," I said. "But why should you be upset? You've got Mary Payson defendin' ya, so how can ya possibly lose?"

"I know Mary's good," Julie said, "but with the peanut oil they found during the autopsy, it sure points to me, doesn't it?"

"There're other people who knew about Joe's allergy, so it has to be one of them," I lied for the second time that day. Julie still didn't smell like a rat to me, but I still couldn't rule her out as a possibility.

"Do you really believe that, Dewey?"

"Of course I do." Like I said, lies are like potato chips. I can never stop at just one.

"Well, that's a relief, at least. So, what did you find out that you want to discuss?"

"I had lunch with Nick Rudawski this afternoon. You know, Joe's second cousin three times removed or third cousin two times removed or whatever the hell he is. Anyway, last Friday he got a visit from the three guys who were at the viewing. From what I found out from Sally, there names are Vinny, Angelo, and Oscar."

"Oscar?" Julie asked.

"Yeah, Oscar. I guess he's related on his mother's side." (Well, she didn't know this. This should be the last time you'll hear it, so just chill out.) "Seems they were some kinda business associates of Joe's, but Sally claims she was never in on any meetin's with them. They sound familiar to you?"

"Vinny, Angelo, and *Oscar*, huh? No, I don't think so, but I never did get into Joe's business dealings very much. Oh, wait, weren't they the three ducks on a cartoon…Oh, no, that was Huey, Dewey, and Louie. Never mind. So what did they want with Nick?"

"They told him not to leave town for a while if he knew what was good for him. Seems like they've got him pretty shook up."

"Well, I don't think he did it, do you?"

"I'm almost certain of it now. We had lunch at Sloppy Man's, and Fred, the manager who was on duty the night that Joe died said he never saw the guy before. Fred's real good with faces, so if Nick was at the dinner, Fred woulda recognized him. I'm pretty sure that leaves

Cousin Nick out. Only thing is, there's somethin' strange about that guy that I just can't figure out."

"Why don't we work on solving my problem first, OK? We can worry about Cousin Nick later," Julie said.

Just then the pizza delivery came. After havin' the different kinda Charlie's food, I was really lookin' forward to a pizza and a few beers.

"Hey, this pizza's really good," I said. "Where'd you order it from?"

"It's from a little place right down the street. It's called McNamara's Pizzeria."

"McNamara's?" I said.

"Must be related on his mother's side," said Julie.

We finished the pizza and a six pack in silence. Julie looked a lot more relaxed than when I first got there, but I knew with all the stress she was goin' through, she needed a lot of consoling.

I knew just the man for the job.

Chapter 17: I COULDN'T HOLLER AT BEN LOLLER…YET

Even though Julie was under a lot of stress with the trial only a few days away, she was still goin' into the office. It didn't do much good, but at least it gave her somethin' to do. So once again I had to get up early.

"Hey boss," I said, "why don't ya let me have a key to yer place? It's gettin' close to the trial, and I might need to drop somethin' off or somethin'."

"That's a good idea. Here you go," she said, handin' me a key. "So when will I see you again?"

"I have a meetin' with my attorney, Ben Loller, this afternoon. My DUI hearing starts tomorrow, you know."

"Tomorrow?" she asked, somewhat surprised. "Why so soon?"

"Ben tried for a continuance, but for some reason they want to get this over with fast. Ben and I are goin' over the game plan this afternoon at three."

"Stop over tonight and let me know how it went," said Julie.

"OK. And maybe tonight we can go out for dinner," I said.

"Sounds like a deal."

We kissed each other goodbye and she wished me luck. Julie headed for the office and I headed for home.

It was only a little after 8:00 when I got home, so it was time for another nap. I skipped breakfast, figurin' I could catch lunch before the soap opera came on. There weren't any calls on my answerin' machine, and I didn't have anyone to get in touch with, so I figured I had a good four hours to snooze.

This time I didn't have any dreams that I could remember, but I woke up screamin', "No, no, I'm not guilty I tell ya. I'm not! I'm not! I'm not!" The only problem was that I didn't know if this was about my DUI trial startin' tomorrow, or whether I was dreamin' about bein' on trial for killin' Joe. I'm sure Freud would have somethin' interestin' to say about that, too.

I went back to sleep for a few more hours, and woke up just in time to turn on the TV. Lunch would have to wait till later.

As soon as the TV came on, I saw the words "Special Announcement" on the screen. I wondered what the hell was goin' on.

"Today's episode of *Debbie and Brad and John and Bill and Sam and...* will not be seen today so that we may bring you a special announcement from the President of the United States," said the announcer.

"Oh, shit," I said, to no one there. "What the hell's this bozo gonna tell us now?"

"We now take you to the White House in Washington, D.C., and to our White House correspondent, Veronica Roses." Thinking that his mic was off, he then added, "Shit! I wanted to see who Debbie was screwin' today. I bet she's gonna get it on with Dr. Fix."

"Yes…well…thank you, Bill, and the best of luck in your new position," said Veronica. "This is Veronica Roses reporting from the White House." Roni looked really hot. She hosted her own late night show called *Run for the Roses.* I've never seen it, but it's all about the Kentucky Derby. I think. One of these nights when I'm not out gettin' lai…I mean doin' my detective work, I'll have to tune in. "In just a few moments, we are expecting President Lawrence I. Everwurst to appear and make a very special announcement. We have no idea what the President is going to say, but, as usual, he probably doesn't either. I see he's coming now."

"Good afternoon, ladies and gentlemen, boys and girls, and the rest of you out there," he started.

"Who the hell writes this moron's speeches?" I said out loud.

"First," he continued, "I would like to apologize for having to pre-empt *Debbie and Brad and John and Bill and Sam and…*today. Personally, I can't wait to see how many kids this girl winds up havin'. But let's face it, folks, this girl really does need a day off."

"Just get on with it, you frickin' idiot," I said.

"With the great shape the country has been in economically ever since this administration took office, I am proud to tell you that just this morning we snuck two more bills by you when you weren't looking…uh, I mean, we passed two bills that will really be great measures in keeping the economy growing strong."

"Uh-oh," I said. "Sounds like we're gonna get screwed again."

The first one is called AFTA, the Antarctica Fair Trade Agreement. We're going to send what few manufacturing jobs we have left to Antarctica, and in return, they are going to ship us 5,000 penguins a month. Don't you think the kids'll just love them at the zoos?"

"Good lord! Is this guy nuts, or what?" I couldn't believe this was happenin'. Even from President Larry Everwurst.

"The second bill is even better," the President continued.

"Oh, I can't wait to hear this," I said, still to no one else in the room.

"The second bill is called FIVA."

"And FIVA'll get ya ten that we're gonna get screwed again," I said. I had to laugh at that one myself.

"Yes, FIVA stands for the Fairness in Voting Act. We think the penguins coming in from Antarctica are so intelligent, that we're giving them the right to vote as soon as they come into the country. We can worry about them becoming citizens later. Doesn't that sound great?"

I guess a lot of the people there at the White House certainly thought it did. Most of them were now yelling, "LIE! LIE! LIE!"

"Thank you for that rousing ovation," President Lawrence I. Everwurst said, holding up his hands for the people to stop. "Do we have any questions from the press?" he asked.

He pointed to a young female reporter holding up her hand. "Yes?"

"President Liverwurst," she began.

"That's *Ever*wurst," he said.

"Yes, I know," she retorted. "Could these bills possibly have anything to do with the fact that you're running for re-election next year, and that your popularity in the polls has started to slip badly?"

"Absolutely not," said the President. "We believe that these two bills will definitely keep our country going strong, and we think that the penguins deserve every right of all the other people in this country, even though they're not. Uh, people, that is. As far as the polls, I've been holding strong at 18 percent for the last three years."

Apparently many people agreed with him, because most of them were back to shouting, "LIE! LIE! LIE!"

"Well, that's all the time we have for questions," said the President. "Thank you all for coming."

"Well, there you have it," said Veronica Roses. "President Everwurst has just announced that two new bills, AFTA and FIVA, have just been signed into law. The most important thing that he said was that he apologized for having to pre-empt *Debbie and Brad and John and Bill and Sam and...* The rest of what he said can be summed up very simply. Screw you, citizens. But since this was the President, we now have to have five people who don't know shit from shinola about politics tell you what he just said. This is Veronica Roses from the White House sending you back to the studio."

Now thinking that *her* mic was off, Roni continued, "Damn right I can say that. I have the highest rated show in my time slot; and besides, Daddy's in charge of the network."

Since Roni Roses was finished, I didn't feel like watching any more. How many ways could these five clowns come up with to say that we just got screwed again?

It was now a little after 2:00, so I just had enough time to grab some lunch before my meeting with Ben.

I got to Ben's office right at 3 o'clock.

"Have a seat, David," he said. "And remember, it *is* David." When ol' Ben shifted into Benjamin Loller mode, he could really be a pain in the ass.

"We've only got one day," he started, "so let's get to it. You sure you won't change your mind about ARD?"

I just shook my head.

"All right, then. As I told you over the phone, I tried to get a continuance, but Beanie wouldn't go for it."

"Who?" I asked.

"Beanie. Judge Roy B. Osbourne. We've known each other for 20 years. He's a real nice guy personally, but as a judge, he's a real asshole. So when we get to court, make sure you say, 'Yes, Your Honor' and 'No, Your Honor.' Just follow my lead."

"OK."

"We'll be in courtroom 10B. We have to be there at 9:00, so meet me out in the hall about fifteen minutes early. Any problem with that?"

"No."

"Good. Now, most of the morning will be spent selecting a jury. Beanie didn't think you could have a jury trial, but we got one anyway. That'll give us a better chance."

"That's good," I said.

"In the afternoon, we'll make our opening statements. Assistant D.A. Suzy K. Sukumupi is handling the case. You know who she is?"

"Yeah, I've seen her in action."

"Then you should know what to expect. After that, Suzy'll call her first witness. That should be Walter Hanley, the cop who pulled you over. I talked to him on the phone. He gave me the name of the other guy who was with him. He's no longer on the force. His name is…let's see, I have it right here…oh, yes, it's Stacy Rickert. I don't know if they'll have him testify or not. I hope not. All he would do would be to back up Hanley's testimony."

"If they do call Rickert, he'll probably take the stand on day two, assuming that Hanley is finished. I don't think they'll call anyone else, so after that, you'll go on."

"I see."

"Can you get any character witnesses? We can put them on after you."

"Yeah, a couple people from the restaurant and..."

"No good. We don't want anyone from a bar. Wouldn't look good."

"OK. How 'bout the girl I had dinner with that night?"

"That was the first time you saw her, right?"

"Yeah."

"No good."

"Well, how about Julie Crinn? I'm workin' for her."

"You mean the woman accused of murdering her husband. Are you kidding? How would that look?"

"Well, how about Zeke Zembrowski?"

"Who's he?"

"Oh, he's my auto mechanic." Zeke would be thrilled to know what a lofty title I just gave him.

"He'll do. Can you tell him to be there on Thursday?"

"Sure. No problem."

"Probably on the third day we'll give our summations to the jury, and they'll take it from there. Any questions?"

"Yeah, just one. Do you think you can time it so that lunch is between 12:45 and 1:45?"

"Why's that?" asked Ben.

"Well, I don't live too far from the courthouse, and I'd really like to get home to see *Debbie and Brad and John and Bill and Sam and*...It comes on at 1:00."

"Is that the show where this broad has more kids than the old woman who lived in a shoe?"

"Yeah, that's the one. She's up to three on the way, but it looks like there will be more. President Everwurst was on today during that time, and..."

"Yes, I happened to catch Larry's speech." Ben said.

"Larry!? You actually know that ah...I mean, the President personally?" I asked.

"Well...no...but I feel like we're two of a kind. Wasn't it wonderful what he did? Don't you just love penguins? I know I do, and so do the grandkids."

I couldn't agree more about them bein' two of a kind. "So, how 'bout it? Think you can work out the lunch schedule?"

"Are you serious? No, I don't think so."

"Any other questions?" asked Ben.

"No, that's about it. Guess I'll just have to tape the show for the next few days."

"Good, I'll see you tomorrow morning at 8:45. Are you *sure* you won't take ARD?"

"See you tomorrow, ol' Ben," was all I said.

Now it was my turn to wink.

Chapter 18: PRIME RIB WITH LEGS

I called Julie at her office right after I got home from my meetin' with ol' Ben...uh, Ben...I mean *Mister* Loller. I had to keep remindin' myself that it was *Mister* Loller, at least until the trial was over.

"Hello." Julie sounded very tired and depressed, so much so that she didn't even bother to check her caller ID.

"Hey, boss," I said, tryin' to keep it very upbeat. "Wuz happenin'?"

"Oh, Dewey, I'm glad you called. How did your meeting go with Mr. Dollar?" Julie sounded terrible.

"That's *Loller*, with an *L*," I said, while all the time thinkin', *For what this guy's chargin' me, it should be Dollar.*

"Right. So how did it go?"

"Couldn't have gone better," I lied. "With Ben defendin' me, I got nothin' to worry about." I just wished I could believe that myself.

"So, what time we havin' dinner?" I asked.

"Oh, I don't think I'm really up for it tonight. Can't we make it some other time?"

"Come on, Jules," I said. "It'll do ya good. Why don't I pick you up around 6:30?"

"Well...OK. Maybe it'll do me some good after all."

"Great. I'll see you then."

I had a little over two hours to take a nap. Had to keep up my strength, ya know.

I got to Julie's place about quarter after six. I rang the bell, but nobody answered, so I let myself in with my key.

"Julie," I called. "Julie? Hello! Anybody home?"

"I'll be down in a minute, Dewey. Make yourself a drink."

Julie came down in a minute. I don't know how anyone could be that tired and stressed out, and still look that gorgeous. That long blond hair… those fantastic legs… those magnificent boobs. The events of the last few weeks certainly hadn't done anything to hurt her appearance.

"Wow! You look fantastic," I said. We kissed.

"Thanks, but to be honest about it, I feel like shit. You sure you want to go out?"

"Absolutely," I lied for the second time that day. I wanted to stay right there. Who could possibly think of food at a time like that? But instead, I just said, "Where would you like to go?"

"Why don't we drive over to Queensville and go to Sloppy Man's?" she said. "I've lived here most of my life, and, you know, I've only been there once."

"Are you sure you want to go there, I mean, after all that's happened?"

"Sure, why not? I'd really like to go where Joe was taking his girlfriends instead of me."

I still didn't think it was a good idea under the circumstances, but I knew it wouldn't do any good to argue, so off to Sloppy Man's we went.

We got to the restaurant a little after seven. Since it was a Tuesday night, we had no trouble getting a table in the dining room.

A waitress that I didn't recognize came over almost immediately. "Hello, my name is April. I'll be your server for this evening. Can I start you two off with some drinks?"

"I'll have a vodka martini, dry, and stirred, not shaken, please," I said. "Whatcha havin', Julie?"

"I'll have a Glen Livet on the rocks, please. No, on second thought, make that a double."

It looked like Julie was still very tired and upset, and was tryin' to drink her problems away. It was a good thing I was drivin'.

"Have you decided what yer gonna order?" I asked, after we had time to look over the menu. "This place is really known for its seafood."

"I've heard that," Julie said, "but I still think I want the king-size prime rib, a baked potato, and some green beans." It looked like she was tryin' to *eat* her problems away, too.

"Ya know, that sounds good. I think I'll have the same thing."

April came over and took our order. Just then I looked across the room and saw Nora havin' dinner with some guy I didn't recognize. I don't know if she saw us or not, but even if she had, I'm sure she wouldn't have come over. She really couldn't stand Julie that much, and the feeling was probably mutual.

Julie caught me starin' into space and asked, "What are you looking at, Dewey? See someone you know?"

Julie's back was to Nora and her date, so I just said, "No, I'm just lookin' at you. You look really fantastic." Although she did look really great, it was the third lie of the day.

Our waitress came back and asked if we would like refills on our drinks. I was just about to order another vodka martini when Julie said, "Since we're both having the prime rib, why don't we order a good bottle of red wine."

"OK," I said. It looked like I might have to carry Julie out of Sloppy Man's, so I knew I would have to take it easy. Besides, I didn't want to be charged with DUI again even before my trial coming up had started.

"So, tell me all about your meeting with Mr. Doll...uh, that's Loller, isn't it, went."

"Oh, he's great." The lies just kept piling up. "He doesn't think we have any problem getting an acquittal." At that point I quit keeping track.

"That's great," said Julie. "Do you think I should go to the hearing?"

I was hopin' this wouldn't come up, because I really didn't know how to deal with it. I decided to go with the truth – for once. "No, he doesn't think that would be a good idea," and left it at that.

"You mean because of my trial coming up on Monday?"

"Yeah, I asked him if you should be there, but he didn't think it was a good idea. Sorry."

"That's OK," she said. "I understand." But Julie now looked more upset than ever. For her sake, I was hoping the alcohol would work its magic very soon.

Being a slow night, April was back with our dinners very quickly. Our good red wine was a bottle of Chateau de Somebody or other – 1979. Julie tasted the wine and decided that it was excellent. But not being much of a drinker, and having polished off her double Glen Livet in short order, she would have thought that anything above Ripple would have been excellent.

We sat there in silence, enjoyin' our meals. I had about three sips of my wine. Julie was on her third glass. "Hey, you better slow down on that stuff," I said, but I really knew that this was exactly what Julie needed to loosen up.

"Ya know, you're c-cute," slurred Julie.

"So I've been told," I replied.

"N-no, you really are c-cute. Say, wuz your real name? I always call ya D-Dewey. D-Dewey Poppaloppadoppalus."

"My real name is David, but hardly anyone ever calls me David, but you can if you want. An' my last name is Polpulcionski."

"Yeah, thas what I said. Poppaloppadoppalus. David Poppaloppadoppalus. I like that. David and Julie Poppaloppadoppalus. I like that, too."

Wait a minute, I thought. *David and* Julie *Poppaloppa...er... Polpulcionski.* I knew that alcohol was a truth serum, so now I would have to be careful that Julie didn't get her hooks into me too deep.

Julie moved across the table and sat down right next to me. If she were any closer, she would have been on top of me. "Kiss me, David Poppaloppadoppalus,"she said. Even though that wasn't my last name, with all the booze she had in her, I was really surprised she could pronounce that.

Before I could say anything, Julie threw the all-time lip lock on me. Without lookin', I could feel the few other diners starin' at us. I knew it was time to leave.

"April, could I have our check please?" While I was saying that, Julie was finishin' what was left in her wine glass, and was startin' to pour what was left in the bottle. I was gonna stop her, but I figured one more drink wasn't gonna matter at that point. Besides, I was drivin'.

"Would you like to take the rest of the food with you, sir?" April asked.

"Sure, but could ya make it quick," I said, nodding at Julie.

"Certainly, sir. I understand. Is she all right?"

"Coursh I'm all right," said Julie, who was now all over me. "David an' Julie Poppaloopadoppaloppa. Tha' souns nice."

April hurried back with the check and the doggie bags. I thought I was gonna havta carry Julie out of Sloppy Man's, but, to my amazement – and I guess everyone else's who was in the dining room – Julie managed to stand on her feet. I put my arm around her to make sure she kept her balance, but I guess she thought I was comin' on to her, and threw a lip lock on me that was bigger'n the one before.

Women! Sheesh!

We were just about to go out the door when I saw Nick Rudawski in the lobby.

"Hi, Nick," I said. "We were just leavin'. Had a little too much to drink." I nodded at Julie.

"I see. Well, that's certainly understandable with everything she's been through. You are driving her home, I hope?"

"Certain…" I started.

"Hi, Nicky," interrupted Julie. "Isn' he cute?" meanin' me. "David Poppaloppadoppaloopa. David 'n Julie Poppaloppadoppaloppa. I like that. D'you like that, Nicky? *I* like that. Whaddya think?"

Nicky…uh, Nick, didn't know what to say.

"You here for dinner?" I asked, trying to get Julie closer to the door.

"I just got here a few minutes ago. I'm supposed to meet someone here, but I haven't seen her yet."

"Well, have a nice evening," I said, wondering who the person he was supposed to meet was.

"Yeah, goo'nigh, Nicky," said Julie. "Isn' he cute?"

"Good night," said Nick, "and good luck," he mouthed so Julie wouldn't hear him.

I managed to get Julie into the car without any problem. She was asleep before we hit the first intersection. Never knew Julie snored before.

When we got back to Julie's, I knew I would have to carry her in from the car. She was still asleep, but the second we got in the door, she woke up.

"Kiss me, David Poppaloppadoppaloppa," she said. She didn't wait for a reply.

She then whispered somethin' else in my ear. Not wantin' to disappoint the boss, I carried her up to the bedroom.

Chapter 19: DEWEY'S DUI DAY DONE...ER...DAY ONE

I knew Julie was gonna have one helluva hangover when she got up, so I tried to sneak out without wakin' her up. Unfortunately, I didn't make it.

"Oh God!" Julie said when she tried to get up. "How much did I have to drink last night? I really don't remember too much, Dewey."

"Well, I see you're back to calling me Dewey again."

"What else would I call you? I don't even know your first name."

"Well, you certainly did last night. My first name is David, and in case you've forgotten, my last name is Polpulcionski."

"That much I knew."

"Yeah, well last night it was Poppaloppadoppalus and Poppaloopadoppaloppa and who knows what else." I certainly wasn't gonna tell her about Julie and David Poppaloppadoppalus.

"Oh, no," she laughed. "Was I really that bad?"

"Only till we got back here. Then you were *fan*tastic."

"Oh, does my head hurt. I think I'll stay home today."

"That might be a good idea," I said. "I have to leave soon. My trial's supposed to start at 9, and I'm supposed to meet Mr. Loller at quarter of. And I have to stop off at my apartment first. I'll see you later in the day."

"What time do you think it will go to?" asked Julie.

"Well, Mr. Loller told me that they don't like goin' later than 4:30, so if it goes all day, it oughta be done for the day about then."

"Good luck." She kissed me. "Stop by later and let me know how it went."

The reason I had to stop at my apartment first was to tape that day's episode of *Debbie and Brad and John and Bill and Sam and…* I didn't want to miss two days in a row. Someone left a message on my machine that she needed me to find her lost cat, but I called her back and referred her to someone else. I had enough problems with pussies at the moment.

I showed up outside of courtroom 10B right at 8:45, just like Mr. Loller said. I was wearin' my best suit, which was still the only one that fit me. Mr. Loller got there five minutes later.

"Now, you remember everything I've told you, right?" he asked. "It's 'Yes, Your Honor, and No, Your Honor.' Also, if you've got something to say to me, either write it down or tap me on the coat. I'll get the judge to give us a few seconds so we can discuss whatever you've got. Any questions before we go in?"

"No, Mr. Loller."

"That's good. And remember, it *is Mr.* Loller as long as we're in the courtroom."

We walked in and sat down at the table on the left side of the aisle facing the judge. Assistant D.A. Suzy K. Sukumupi was already sitting at the table across the aisle, along with Officer Walter Hanley. It was now five of nine, and we expected the judge to walk in at any minute.

At 9:15 we were still expecting the judge to walk in at any minute. I now understood why the courts were backed up. It wasn't the cases that did it, it was the judges who couldn't be there when they were supposed to be.

At 9:30 I asked Mr. Loller, "So when d'ya think the judge'll get here?"

"Beanie? Who knows? He doesn't give a shit. Like I told you, he thinks he's the law *east* of the Pecos."

Finally, at 9:45, Beanie...I mean Judge Roy B. Osbourne, came into the courtroom. He looked either very sleepy or very hung over. I couldn't tell which.

"Goo' mo'nin', la'ies and gen'lemen," he said. He definitely wasn't sleepy.

"The first thing we're going to do is to select a jury for this trial. I don't think this should be a trial by jury, but what do I know. I only read up to the fifth amendment in law school."

There were 24 people waiting to see which 12 would be selected for the jury and which two would be the alternates. They had also been waiting since 9 o'clock.

"This trial is about a very serious offense – DUI. Driving under the influence. I was stopped myself just las' nigh', but the cop lemme go when I covin…convit…uh, when I tol' him I was a ju'ge. But today, the defendant is Mr. Davi M. Popple…Davi M. Popel…Mr. Davi M. Uh, Mr. Loller, since the defendant has a rather…"

I knew what the judge was gonna say before he even finished. I tapped Mr. Loller on the coat.

"Could I have a moment with my client, Your Honor?"

"Certainly, Mr. Loller."

"He can call me David under two conditions." I said.

"And what are they?" asked Mr. Loller.

"If I can call him Roy or Beanie. If not, he can either learn to pronounce my last name correctly, or he can refer to me as either Sir or Your Highness. And while you're at it, ask him how Cecil's doin'."

"Don't get smart," he said to me. To the judge he said, "Your Honor, since this is a courtroom, I believe that my client should be addressed as Mr. Polpulcionski or Sir. Unless, of course, Your Honor, we may refer to you as Roy."

"A-hem," I cleared my throat.

"Or Beanie, Your Honor," said Mr. Loller.

"No, you certainly may not call me Roy *or* Beanie in this courtroom, Mr. Loller. So, those are the only two options I have? Call him by some name I can't pronounce, or call him *Sir*?"

"A-hem." For some reason, my throat was very dry.

"Well...no...Your Honor. There is one other option."

"That's better," said the judge. "And just what is that option?"

"He said you can call him...*Your Highness*...Your Honor, if you prefer."

"Your Highness," he practically screamed. "And just why would I call him *Your Highness?"*

"I have no idea, Your Honor."

"Well, Mr. Popple...Pipel...ooooh! Would you mind telling the court, *Sir*, why I would even consider calling you *Your Highness?*"

"Certainly, *Your Honor*," I said as sarcastically as I thought I could get away with. "Ya see, Yer Honor, I'm either the eighth cousin twelve times removed, or the twelfth cousin eight times removed – I'm not real sure which, Yer Honor – of the last King of Poland." I doubted that this was really true, but hearin' about Nick at the readin' of the will gave me the idea, so I thought I'd give it a shot. "Anyway, Yer Honor, I had it checked out, and if Poland still had a King, I'd be the guy. The King of Poland, that is. So, if ya want, Yer Honor, ya can call me Your Highness."

"Well, that's very interesting...*Sir*," he practically choked on the word, "but this isn't Poland, so I'll just call you *Sir*, if that's all right with you."

"Certainly, Your Honor." I gave Mr. Loller a quick wink. Loller looked like he was gonna barf.

"Well, as I was saying, la'ies and gen'lemen, the defendant, who shall be referred to as *Sir*, is charged with DUI. In just a few moments, the prosecutor and *Sir's* attorney will be selecting 12 of you to serve on the jury, and two others to be alternates. If you're not selected, don't worry about it, cuz you probably didn't want to be here anyway, an' you'll git to go home early. But before we do that, I need some aspirin, so we'll take a short recess."

It was only 10:15. We'd been there about half an hour. "So, what the hell is this?" I asked Mr. Loller, "a courtroom – or Ding-Dong School?"

"Looks to me like Beanie really tied one on last night. Say, what was all that crap about being the King of Poland?"

"Who knows? I coulda been, ya know. Besides, I ain't under oath yet, am I?"

Mr. Loller just shook his head. He still looked like he was ready to barf.

After 20 minutes, the judge came back, but he still didn't look any better. He musta *really* tied one on last night.

"Now, la'ies and gen'lemen," he didn't sound any better, either, "Assistant D.A. Sukumupi and counsel for the defense, Mr. Loller, will go through the process of selecting 12 jurors and two alternates out of the 24 of you. Will Ms. Sukumupi, Mr. Loller, and the defendant please rise and face the prospective jurors?"

"Now, la'ies and gen'lemen, if any of you happen to know any of these three people, please hold your number up. When I call your number, please rise, tell the court which one you know, and how you know him or her."

I saw four numbers go up – 6, 13, 19, and 24 – but I didn't recognize the first three, and until 24 stood up, I couldn't see who that was either.

"Number 6," said the judge, "could you please stand, tell us which one you know, and where you know that person from?"

"Yeah, Yer Honor," said a lady I thought looked vaguely familiar. "I know him, the defendant," she said, pointin' at me. "I work at Barney's Bar and Grille. It's about two blocks from here. He used to come in all the time. Say, where you been? Weren't you supposed to call me? An' what about you, Yer Honor? I ain't seen you recently either."

Now I remembered her. Betty, from Barney's Bar and Grille. I used to go there when I was still chasin' cats for a livin'.

"Yes...uh...well...thank you, number 6. You're excused," said the judge.

"Thanks, Beanie...uh, I mean *Yer Honor.* An' don't be a stranger."

"Number 13. Would you rise please and tell the court which one you know, and how you know him or her?"

"Yes, Your Honor. I also know the defendant. I work at Pete's Place, a restaurant in Pantstown. He used to stop by once in awhile. I haven't seen him recently, though. And Betty, Beanie comes into our place all the time. That's why you haven't seen him recently. As a matter of fact, he was there last night until…"

"Thank you, Number 13. You're also excused."

Now I recognized her, too. It was Paula from Pete's Place in Pantstown. (Say *that* five times fast.) I woulda hit on Paula, but I heard she was on her third husband and had five kids. Or was she on her fifth husband and had three kids? Either way, no thanks.

This was not lookin' too good. Two people who knew me, and they both worked at bars. I was hopin' 19 would be my lucky number.

"Number 19, would you rise, please?" said the judge.

"Yes, Your Honor. I know the defendant, too."

"And which bar do *you* work at, number 19?" At this point, I was thinkin' that I would be better off havin' Cecil as the judge.

"Oh, no, Your Honor. I'm a nurse at the Red Cross Donor Center. The defendant comes in every month and donates a unit of blood. Very good quality, and a very good yield, too."

It was Fran from the Red Cross. I didn't recognize her at first without her nurse's outfit on. Knowing that my blood was good enough to be taken by the Red Cross every month had to score some points with the people who would be on the jury.

"And finally, Number 24. Would you rise please and tell us who you know and where you know him or her from?"

It was my old buddy, and auto mechanic, Zeke Zembrowski.

"Yeah, Yer Honor. I know Dew...I mean, the defendant, too." Zeke almost blew it for me by callin' me Dewey, but caught himself in time. "I take care of his car, an' such a beautiful car, too, Yer Honor. You really should..."

"Yes. Well, thank you, Number 24," said the judge.

I was real proud of Zeke. Not only was he honest, but he actually had two words in the space of three sentences that had three syllables in 'em. (One had four syllables if you consider the way he pronounced *beautiful*.) Probably a record for Zekey.

"Ms. Sukumupi and Mr. Loller, will you now select the 12 jurors and two alternates, please? But make it quick, cuz it's almost lunch time – and I gotta pee."

Within five minutes, Sukumupi and Loller – a comedy team if I've ever heard one – exchanged names and selected the 12 jurors and two alternates. They gave the list to the judge.

After reading the list, Judge Osbourne thanked the people who were not chosen. "Yer dismissed," he said rather curtly. "We will now recess for lunch. Court will reconvene at 1:15."

He ran out of the courtroom.

Mr. Loller and I went a block away from the courthouse to grab a slice of pizza.

"Well, it looks pretty good so far," said Loller. "And we scored a few points by having the judge call you *Sir*, but I'm still not too crazy about that shit you pulled about being the King of Poland."

"Hey, like I said, I wasn't under oath at the time."

"OK, but just be a little more careful. And since he's not on the jury, do you really want that character…what's the guy's name?…Zeke whatever to be your character witness?"

"I sure do. Zeke may not be the brightest bulb in the lamp, but he's very honest. An' besides, he's the only one I got."

"Well, OK. I guess I'll keep the questions very simple when I put him on the stand."

We ate the rest of our pizza in silence. Loller had to make some phone calls, so he told me to meet him back in the courtroom no later than 1:10.

We met back in courtroom 10B at 1:10, just like Loller said. The judge came back at 1:35.

"Mr. Loller and Ms. Sukumupi will now present their opening statements to the jury. By the rules of the court, Mr. Loller, you get to go first. I'd much rather play eeny-meeny-miny-mo to see who gets to go, but I have to let you go first. Yer on, Mr. Loller."

"Thank you, Your Honor," Loller started. "Ladies and gentlemen of the jury. Although the judge stated that this case is about DUI, this is really a case about honesty and integrity. My client, Mr. David M. Polpulcionski, will admit under oath that he did have a few drinks on the night in question, but that he was nowhere near being under the influence. You will also hear Mr. Polpulcionski state, also under oath, that he was totally cooperative with the police, answered all their questions, and gave them no trouble whatsoever. We will prove, beyond a shadow of a doubt, that Mr. Polpulcionski is not guilty of the crime of which he is being accused."

"The Assistant D.A., Ms. Suckemuppi, on the other hand…"

"I object, Your Honor," said Suzy Sukumupi. "Mr. Loller is perfectly aware that my name is pronounced Soo-koo-moo-pee. And, may I say, Your Honor, how distinguished you look today; and how wonderfully your red eyes blend in perfectly with your black robe."

"Thank you, Ms. Suckem…uh, Soo-koo-moo-pee. Objection sustained. You may continue, Mr. Loller."

"Thank you, Your Honor. My apologies, Ms. Soo-koo-moo-pee. Now, ladies and gentlemen of the jury. As I was about to say, Ms. Soo-koo-moo-pee will try to convince you that my client was totally inebriated on the evening in question, and that he is lying out his ah…I mean, is lying under oath. That would be perjury, ladies and gentlemen; and may I assure you that my client is the most truthful man you will ever want to meet."

I had to cover my mouth to keep from laughin' at that last part myself.

"I urge you to find my client innocent of the crime he is accused of today. Thank you for your time and your attention. I now turn it over to you, Ms. Suckem…I'm sorry, Ms. Soo-koo-moo-pee."

"Thank you, Mr. *Holler*," she snarled. Before Loller could object, she added, "Oh, I'm sorry. That's *Loller*, isn't it." *Touche*.

"Ladies and gentlemen of the jury," she began, "today, we will prove beyond any doubt that the defendant, Mr. David M. Poppel… Pollip…Poopel…the *defendant*, who will be addressed as *Sir*, was indeed guilty of the crime of DUI – Driving Under the Influence. We will hear testimony from the arresting officer, stating that *Sir* was not in control of his vehicle that evening, did not pass any of the roadside tests that were administered, and was *not* –contrary to what Mr. Loller would have you believe – was *not* at all cooperative with the police. Once you have heard the testimony, you will have no choice but to convict the defendant of this heinous crime of which he is being charged. I thank you."

"Thank you, Ms. Soo-koo-moo-pee. And may I say how lovely you look today."

"Why, thank you, Your Honor," said Sukumupi.

The only thing I could figure is that they were related on his mother's side.

"Well," said the judge. "I see it is now almost three o'clock, so we will recess for 15 minutes. Besides, I have to pee again. Court will resume at 3:15."

Everyone was back in the courtroom at 3:15. Well...*almost* everyone. The judge, however, was gettin' better. He made it back at 3:28.

"You may call your first witness, Ms. Soo-koo-moo-pee."

"Thank you, Your Honor. I call to the stand Officer Walter Hanley."

After Hanley took the oath and stated his name, the questions began.

"Do you recognize the defendant, officer?" began Sukumupi.

"Yes, I do," replied Hanley.

"And did you pull him over for DUI the night in question?"

"Yes, I did."

"Could you tell us, in your own words, why you pulled him over?"

"Yes. He was not in control of his car. In fact, he almost ran over two old ladies who were trying to cross the street."

"That's a lie," I whispered to Loller. "What would two little ol' ladies be doin' crossin' the street at that time? It was almost midnight!"

Loller remained silent.

"Did he immediately pull over?" continued Sukumupi.

"No, he did not. We actually followed him for several blocks, and had our siren and our lights going all the time."

"Another lie," I told Loller. "I pulled right over."

"And what did the defendant do when you asked him to step out of his car, officer?"

"He gave us a real hard time. Started swearing at us. We almost had to drag him out."

"All these things are total lies," I said. "Ain't you gonna object or somethin'?"

"I can't," said Loller. "It wouldn't look good to a jury if I objected to a cop's testimony."

At this point, I was wonderin' if I made a mistake gettin' rid of Barbara Rhodenbaum so fast.

"And when he finally got out of his car," continued Sukumupi, "how did he react?"

"Oh, I could tell he was drunker than a skunk," answered the officer.

"Objection," shouted Mr. Loller.

But before the judge could rule on the objection, I shouted, "We withdraw the objection, Yer Honor."

"I object," insisted Loller.

"No he doesn't, Yer Honor," I said. Ben just glared at me.

"Look, *Sir*," said the judge, "I highly suggest that you listen to your attorney."

"Look, *Yer Honor*," I shot back, "I highly suggest that my attorney listens to me. After all, I'm the one who's payin' him."

"Your Honor," said Ben, "this is ridiculous. I insist that we object to the last question."

"And why would you do that now, ol' Ben? You didn't object to anything else." Now it was my turn to holler at Loller. "Ol' Ben," I continued, "yer fired. Get the hell out."

"Are you saying that you're dismissing your lawyer in the middle of the trial?" asked the judge.

"That's right, Yer Honor."

"And on what grounds are you doing this?"

"Insubordination, Yer Honor. I'm payin' him. That makes me his boss, and he ain't followin' my orders."

"Well, I'm afraid I can't allow that," said the judge. Ben just sneered at me.

"In that case, Yer Honor, you'll have to pay him, cuz I ain't."

"Goodbye, Mr. Loller," was all the judge said.

Ol' Ben packed up and left. But before he went he yelled, "You'll be hearing from my lawyer, *Dewey*. What the hell am I saying! I *am* my lawyer!"

"So, *Sir*, who's representing you now?" asked the judge.

I had to think fast. "I am, Yer Honor. I'm representin' myself."

"Now look...*you!*" Apparently it was no more *Sir.* "I've had all the nonsense I'm gonna take from you. Calling you *Sir.* Being the King of Poland. Now this. You cannot represent yourself in a court of law."

"Oh yes I can, Yer Honor." I figured if he didn't know about the sixth amendment, I didn't think he would know much else. "The precedent for defending yourself in a court of law was established in 1839...in...uh, the United States versus Jonson."

"We'll see about that, Mr. Polapinski. I've got a book right here that lists all the cases dealing with precedents. Now, let's see. U.S. versus Jonson, 1839, huh?"

I figured this time I had gone too far – even for me. I'd be spendin' the night in the slammer, and that wasn't for the DUI charges.

Just then I heard a very hoarse voice from the back of the courtroom say, "I am now representing Mr. Polpulcionski, Your Honor."

I turned around and saw Mary Payson approachin' the bench. Julie musta called her and let her know what was goin' on.

"Your Honor," said Mary, barely above a whisper, "since I've just taken over this case, may we have a brief recess so that I may meet with my client in private for a few minutes."

"I object, Your Honor," said the Assistant D.A.

"Too damn bad, Ms. Suckemuppi," said the judge. "This is Mary Payson, so you know yer gonna lose anyway. Objection overruled. We will take a brief recess until 4 o'clock."

Mary and I found an empty room down the hall from courtroom 10B and ducked inside.

"Julie called me to tell me what was going on," Mary said in a very clear voice.

"Thanks for comin'," I said. "I guess I didn't see you walk in. Say, what was with yer voice in there?"

"I came in during the cop's testimony. As far as the voice, I don't know anything about your case, so I'm going to tell the judge that I have laryngitis, and convince him to let you question the witness. I'll take over tomorrow if necessary. Unless I'm mistaken, it looks like you've got something up your sleeve."

"Oh, I got somethin' up my sleeve, all right. Somethin' more than my arm. And, thanks again for comin'."

"You're quite welcome…and Dewey…"

"Yeah?"

"I'm very surprised at you. United States versus Jonson wasn't in 1839…"

"I know, I just made that…"

"…it was in 1842. And it wasn't about representing yourself in court, either. It was about Jonson's right to let his cows shit on federal property. Jonson won the case, by the way. He was defended by a lawyer by the name of Abe somebody or other. I wonder what ever happened to Abe after that?"

"Gee. And I thought I just made the whole thing up. And, thanks again, Mary. I owe ya one."

Mary just looked at me and laughed. "It looks like we'd better be getting back," she said. "And Dewey…"

"Yeah?"

"That's three you owe me now."

Great. Another one keepin' track.

When we got back to 10B, Judge Osbourne was already there waiting for us – for a change. I guess he really wanted to get out of there that day. Over the objection of Ms. Sukumupi, Mary convinced the judge that she had laryngitis, and he allowed me to question the witness.

"You may continue with your questioning, Ms. Soo-koo-moo-pee," said the judge. "Will Officer Hanley please take the stand."

"That won't be necessary, Your Honor," said Sukumupi. "I was finished with the witness. But may I say that it was very kind of you, Your Honor, to consider the fact that I wasn't finished. Thank you so very much."

"Oh, why don't you put a sock in it, sister," was all Beanie said. For a second, I actually was beginnin' to like the guy.

The feeling didn't last long, however.

"So, Mr. Polipinski," – I could tell *Sir* was out the window, but I wasn' gonna push it – "do *you* have any questions for the witness, *Mr. Big Shot wannabe lawyer*?"

"Just a few, Yer Honor. Thank you, Yer Honor."

"Will Officer Hanley please take the stand? And remember, officer, you're still under oath."

"Now, Officer Hanley," I started, "before the recess you were asked how I reacted when I finally got out of my car. Do you remember that, Officer?"

"Certainly."

"And could you please tell the court what yer answer was?"

"Yes. I said I could tell that you were drunker than a skunk."

"I see. And could you please tell the court, Officer Hanley, exactly how a skunk acts when he is drunk."

"Objection," yelled Sukumupi.

"Overruled," yelled Osbourne.

I looked over at Mary. She gave me a very quick smile.

"Well...Officer?"

"I...I don't know."

"I see. Well then, Officer Hanley, could you please tell the court how many years you've been on the police force."

"Certainly. It's been 18 years."

"Eighteen years, you say. And in 18 years, Officer, exactly how many drunk skunks have you run into?"

With that, the whole courtroom was in stitches.

"Order! Order in the court," yelled Osbourne. "We will have no more outbursts, or I will have the courtroom cleared!"

Then he turned his head away from the court. I'm pretty sure he was laughin' himself.

"Well...*none*, I guess."

"None, you say. Well, in that case, you were either lyin' before or yer lyin' now. In either case, that's perjury. I want this man charged with perjury immediately, Yer Honor."

"Oh, for the love of..." said Osbourne. "We will deal with this issue tomorrow, *Sir*. Court is adjourned. We will reconvene tomorrow morning at nine a.m."

I walked over to Mary and gave her a big hug.

Sir was back in action.

After Mary and I left the courtroom and were out of earshot of everyone, I said, "Thanks again for bein' here, Mary. I told Julie I'd stop by and let her know how things went."

"Why don't you give her a call, Dewey? We've got a lot of things to go over for tomorrow."

I gave Julie a call on my cell phone. She sounded real happy about the way things turned out on day one, but wasn't too excited that I wouldn't be right over. After I told her that I still had a lot of things to go over with Mary, and that I would try to get there later, she said she understood and wished me luck.

"Why don't we go grab a pizza and a few beers," said Mary. "I hear it's the perfect thing for laryngitis." We both laughed.

"Today went pretty well, but you're not out of the woods yet," Mary said during dinner. "Got anything else up your sleeve for tomorrow?"

" 'Deed I do." I told Mary what I thought we should do, and continued by saying, "An' feel free to take over the questioning. If your *laryngitis* is better, that is."

I was reaching for my wallet to pay for the pizza when Mary said, "Dinner's on me."

"Well, thanks, Mary, and thanks once again for bein' there today." I was ready to head over to Julie's.

"Uh...Dewey?"

"Yeah?"

"That's four you owe me now, Dewey."

"Yeah, I guess it is. Well, thank you, Mary."

"Uh...Dewey?"

"Yeah?"

"My place?" (Admit it. You *knew* I'd get to her sooner or later. Didn'cha?)

I spent the night at Mary's. She was still doin' a lot of heavy breathin'.

Funny thing is, though. She never asked for her inhaler. Not once.

Chapter 20: DEWEY'S DUI...DAY DU

I wanted to get up early on Thursday, but Mary beat me to it. There was a "sticky" attached to my pants that said, "You were wonderful last night. I had to go to the office early. Meet me outside of 10B at 8:45."

I went home to take a shower and change clothes, but, more importantly, to tape that day's episode of *Debbie and Brad and John and Bill and Sam and...* There were no calls on my answering machine, so I decided to give Julie a call while I had the chance.

"Well, hello, Dewey," she said. I was glad to see she was back to using caller ID, but I couldn't tell what kinda mood she was in. "So...did you get things straightened out with Mary last night?"

"Yeah, I think we got things pretty straight between us," I said. "Looks like we got a good chance of winnin'."

"Oh, that's great! Why don't you give me a call when it's over." It seemed like Julie was in a good mood and genuinely happy that things were going well for me.

"I got a better idea," I said. "Why don't you take another day off and come to the trial. We're in courtroom 10B. Ben Loller doesn't represent me any more, and I don't think Mary would mind."

"That's a great idea. What time does it start?"

"Well, it's supposed to start at 9, but it all depends on when the judge decides to show up. It's anybody's guess what time he'll get there."

"OK. I'll be there no later than 9:30. Good luck, Dewey."

"Thanks, Julie. I'll see you later."

I met Mary outside of courtroom 10B at 8:40. Stella, wearing her usual professional-looking pants suit and her secretary-style glasses, was with her. We exchanged "good mornings" and walked in.

Assistant D.A. Sukumupi was already seated at her usual table, along with Officer Walter Hanley. The only other people in the courtroom were workers. Julie hadn't arrived yet.

"Do you think this will work, Mary?" I asked. "Does Stella know what's goin' on?"

"Yes, I informed Stella on the way over. Saul really had to perform some magic to do it, but I think it will work out just fine. We'll know soon enough. And Dewey…"

"Yeah?"

"That makes five you owe me now."

"Hey, what about last night?" Stella just looked at me and shook her head. "Don't that count?"

"Right. I almost forgot about that. That makes *six* you owe me." Mary just laughed.

It was now 9:00 on the dot, and as usual, Judge Roy B. Osbourne had yet to make his appearance.

"Does this guy stay out every night, or what?" I asked.

"From what I've heard," said Stella, "not every night. Only on days that end in *y*."

"Good," I said, sarcastically. "It oughta be another fun day."

Mary went over to talk to Suzy Sukumupi. Stella and I couldn't hear what was bein' said, but from the looks of things, Suzy wasn't too happy that Mary was now handlin' the case. This gave Stella and me a chance to talk.

"You two got things pretty well figured out last night, I see," she said.

"Yeah, looks like. Thanks mostly to Saul, from what I hear."

"Well, I just hope everything goes as planned."

"So what else did you to do last night?" Stella continued. She got off the subject of the trial in a real hurry.

"Oh, a little of this, a little of that. You know."

"Yes, I'm sure I do. Look, Dewey, it's really none of my business, but don't expect much personally out of Mary. She's a really nice lady and everything, but ever since her split with Nathan Bricks, I hear she just doesn't seem interested in much except her cases."

"Nathan Bricks? Why do I know that name?"

"Nathan's a multi-billionaire real estate developer. They split up a little over five years ago. Mary and Nathan used to be married."

The look on my face must have told Stella everything she needed to know.

"You mean she didn't tell you?"

"This is the first I've heard about it. She didn't mention anything to me."

"Oh, she will. Believe me. She will."

Julie walked into the courtroom at 9:30 and took a seat in the back. Zeke Zembrowski, my main – and only – character witness was already there. Mary was now back at our table, and Julie waved at the three of us. Judge Roy B. Osbourne still hadn't shown up.

"Does this guy ever show up on time?" I asked. "Are the rest of the judges like him?"

"Beanie. Oh, Beanie comes in whenever he's good and ready. Once, we were kept waiting for..."

It was now 9:40. Judge Osbourne had arrived – five minutes earlier than yesterday, but still 40 minutes later than *he* told the rest of *us* to be there.

"Your Honor," said Mary, "may we approach the bench?"

"Certainly, Ms. Payson."

"Your Honor, as you are well aware, I have taken over the defense of Mr. Polpulcionski. As you can tell, Your Honor, I am now over my bout with laryngitis; so, if it please the court, I will take over the questioning of the witnesses." Assistant D.A. Sukumupi didn't look real happy, but she didn't object, either.

"Any objections, Ms. Sukumupi?" asked the judge.

"No, Your Honor." Sukumupi wasn't kissin' up to Judge Osbourne like she usually did. I wondered whether she was savin' it, or concedin' defeat.

"Very well. You may call your next witness, Ms. Sukumupi."

"Your Honor, the prosecution has no further witnesses to call at this time. However, Your Honor, we do reserve the right to call other witnesses at a later time."

"Any objections, Ms. Payson?" Beanie actually sounded like he took a night off from the bottle.

"No objections, Your Honor."

"Very well. You may call your first witness, Ms. Payson."

Expectin' Mary to call me as her first witness, both Sukumupi and Officer Hanley stared in amazement as Mary said, "I call Mr. Stacy Rickert to the stand."

"Objection!" yelled the Assistant D.A.

"On what grounds?' responded the judge.

"On the grounds, Your Honor, that…uh…that we didn't want him here, and that we didn't think the defense would want him here, either. And may I say, Your Honor, how…"

"Save it, Ms. Sukumupi. I don't have a hangover today. Objection overruled. Will Mr. Stacy Rickert take the stand, please?"

The rear door of the courtroom opened, and in walked Stacy Rickert, the other cop that was there the night I was arrested. Naturally I remembered him from that night, but he looked familiar from somewhere else, too. I just couldn't figure out where.

After Rickert took the oath and stated his name, Mary began her questioning.

"Tell the court, if you will, Mr. Rickert, what your occupation is?"

"Objection, Your Honor. Mr Rickert's occupation is irrelevant to this case."

"On the contrary, Your Honor," said Mary. "As I will show very shortly, Your Honor, Mr. Rickert's occupation is *very* relevant to this case."

"In that case, I will overrule the objection for now, Ms. Payson. But please, make it *very shortly*. I may not be hung over today, but I still have to pee. Please answer the question, Mr. Rickert."

"I run a family flower shop in East Arthur."

"I see. And on the night the defendant was arrested, did you run the flower shop?"

"No, I did not."

"I see," continued Mary. "At that time, what was your occupation, sir?"

"Objection," yelled Sukumupi. "Your Honor, everyone here knows what Mr. Rickert did for a living at that time."

"Oh, but that's just it, Your Honor," replied Mary. "Do we really know what Mr. Rickert's job was on the night in question?"

"Objection overruled." It was now 10:10. "This is all very interesting," added the judge, "but I've got to pee, so court will recess until 10:30."

This *was* very interesting. What was Mary gettin' at? If the judge wasn't hung over, why did he have to pee already? Most importantly, who was screwin' Debbie on *Debbie and Brad and John and Bill and Sam and...*

Even though I didn't know where Mary was goin' with Rickert, I trusted her enough to know that she did. And I certainly had no idea why Beanie was peein' so much. Probably cuz he was gettin' older, and the plummin' was breakin' down. But I sure wanted to find out what was happenin' with Deb. I missed Tuesday cuz o'President Everwurst, and yesterday's episode was on tape. The way it looked, I'd miss today's, too, although my TV was set up to tape today's show as well.

We were all back by 10:28, and this time Judge Osbourne was there waitin' for us. The way he was runnin' things, I figured we would break for lunch no later than 11:30, so he should be able to hold out on his next pee until then.

Rickert went back up on the stand.

"Now, Mr. Rickert," began Mary, "could you please answer the question I asked you before the judge had to p…I mean, before the recess. What was your occupation on the night in question?"

"I was unemployed at the time," answered Rickert.

Normally there would have been a gasp from the spectators in the courtroom; but since the only two who were there were Julie and my buddy Zeke Zembrowski, there was total silence. I'm pretty sure Zeke new what *unemployed* meant, even though it was another three-syllable word.

"Let me get this straight, Mr. Rickert. You say that you did not have a job on the night in question?"

"That is correct."

"And yet, you were riding in a police car, wearing a police uniform, and from what I understand, you performed some of the field tests on the defendant. Is that correct, Mr. Rickert?" asked Mary.

"Yes, that is correct."

"Could you please tell the court how this was possible, since you didn't have a job, and, therefore, weren't a police officer that night?"

"Certainly. I was in training to be an officer."

"I see. Well, did Officer Hanley say anything to you before the two of you stopped the defendant?"

"Objection, Your Honor," said the Assistant D.A.

"Overruled," said the judge. "I'd like to hear this myself."

"He said that since it was a slow night, we would pull the next car over and I could get some practice on a DUI arrest."

"You mean to tell me that the defendant was pulled over so you could get some practice?"

"Yes. That's what Officer Hanley said."

"And what kind of *practice* did you get, sir? Did you do any of the field tests?"

"Only the portable breathalyzer."

"I see. And were you, at that time, certified to perform such a test?"

"No, I was not."

"And what type of reading did you get, sir?"

"The first time I did it, I didn't get any reading at all. I probably didn't know what I was doing."

"I see," said Mary. "So then what did you do?"

"Well, I looked over at Officer Hanley. I didn't say anything, I just kind of shrugged."

"And did Officer Hanley say anything?"

"Yes, he said, 'Have him do it again.'"

"And did you have the defendant do it again?"

"Yes, I did."

"And did the defendant say anything or object to this in any way?"

"No, he did not."

"So, would you say that the defendant was being cooperative, Mr. Rickert?"

"Objection, Your Honor," yelled Ms. Sukumupi.

"I withdraw the question, Your Honor," countered Mary.

"And did you get a reading a second time, sir?"

"Yes."

"And what was that reading, Mr. Rickert?"

"Objection, Your Honor," said Sukumupi. "Inadmissible in court."

"Under the circumstances with what this witness has said so far, I'm going to overrule the objection. I think this is vital to the case, and I'd like to hear this, Ms. Sukumupi."

"Thank you, Your Honor," said Mary.

"Well, Mr. Rickert? Please tell the court what your second reading was."

"It was .028," answered Rickert.

Mary turned to me and smiled. "Just a few more questions, Mr. Rickert. First, did the defendant appear to be driving under the influence in your estimation?"

"No, he did not."

"Last question, Mr. Rickert. Why aren't you on the police force, if that's what you were training for?"

"I saw that night how they operated and I knew I couldn't be a part of it. And, if I may, I would like to apologize to Mr. Plowpa... Mr. Pelpi....the *defendant*. I'm really sorry I had anything to do with this."

Sukumupi and Officer Hanley looked like they were having a very serious discussion. Now it looked like Sukumupi was ready to barf.

"No further questions of this witness," Your Honor. "Your witness, Ms. Sukumupi."

"I have no questions of this witness," Your Honor.

"Very well, you may call your next witness, Ms. Payson," said the judge.

"Your Honor, the defense would like to recall Officer Walter..."

"That won't be necessary, Your Honor," said the Assistant D.A. "The prosecution wishes to make a motion to dismiss the case, Your Honor."

"No objection, Your Honor," Mary said as fast as she could.

It was over. We won. Time to celebrate.

Chapter 21: PARTY TIME...OR...DEWEY DOES A FOURSOME

Only kidding! At least about the foursome. We did go out to celebrate after the trial, but after all, my good buddy – and only character witness – Zeke Zembrowski was there with us. What was he supposed to do? Sit there and watch!?

This was the first time that I had ever seen Zeke in a suit, and, quite frankly, he looked very handsome. (Hey, don't get the wrong idea. I mean that in a compliment kinda way. This ain't that kinda book. I swing pretty good, but only from one sida the plate, if ya follow my drift.) In fact, Zeke looked so good that I hardly recognized him.

We went to Sloppy Man's to celebrate the victory, and got a table for five in the dining room. (We sure as hell weren't gonna go to Charlie's.) After we got our first round of drinks, I was gonna introduce Zeke to the ladies, but I was in for a surprise.

"Oh, I know all these people, Dew. Julie drives a Mercedes, Mary got a BMW, and Stella got a Lexus. But nobody got a car like yours, Dew. Such a classic! A more beautiful car I ain't never seen in..."

"Yeah, I know, Zeke." I had to interrupt him. He looked like he was gonna cry.

"So Mary, what gave you the idea to put Rickert on the stand?" asked Julie.

"Actually, that was Dewey's idea. He said there had to be something strange about him. The way he didn't talk much and the way he handled the test at the car, Dewey figured it was worth a shot. When he remembered his name from Ben Loller, I had Saul track him down. It took most of the night to find him, but it certainly was worth it."

"I'll say," I said. The waiter came and took our food order, and we ordered another round of drinks.

"If it hadn't worked out," said Mary, "I would have put Dewey on the stand, and then called Zeke as our character witness. I don't think we would have had anything to worry about either way."

"Yeah, my old pal Zeke woulda come through, wouldn' ya, Zeke?" But Zeke wasn't payin' any attention. It looked like Zeke and Stella were havin' their own private conversation; and it didn't look like he was tellin' her about my beautiful bucket o'bolts.

Just then our food came, and we ordered our third round of drinks. I knew I'd have to take it easy, cuz I'd have to keep an eye on both Mary and Julie. Zeke looked OK, and looked like he was more than willin' to keep an eye on Stella.

"So, chalk up another victory for Mary Payson," I said. "How many does that make now, Mary?"

"I quit counting around 864," said Mary, "but you know, it wasn't always that easy."

Julie gave me a kinda look that said *Here we go. I was wondering when this story would come out.* I could also tell that Mary was starting to feel the drinks.

"Years ago," continued Mary, "I fell in love with a man by the name of Nathan Bricks. I'm sure you've heard of him. Nathan Bricks, the multi-billionaire real estate developer?"

"Sure, I know the name," I said. I wasn't about to mention that before old Nate made it big, we used to call him Brick the Pr…uh…well…you get the idea, I'm sure.

"Well, in no time, Nathan and I got married. I was just out of law school and Nathan was just starting to make it big. Things went very well for the first few years, but then Nathan decided that he wanted a nice little stay-at-home wife. I tried that for awhile, I really did, but I just knew it wouldn't work out. We couldn't have any children, so when I found that out, I knew I couldn't be the wife he wanted. Nathan and I are still good friends, but we called it quits five years ago."

"So, what did you do after that?" I asked. Julie sat there like she already knew the answer.

"After the divorce, I set up my own law office," Mary went on. "At first, it was really hard getting clients, but then I came up with a brilliant idea, if I must say so myself."

"Really? And what was that?" I asked. This was gettin' rather interestin', although I could tell Julie was bored out of her mind.

"What I did was, I decided to Anglicize my name. You see, my real name isn't Mary Payson, it's Maria Paisana. I thought that with a name like that, and being a lawyer, everyone would just assume that I won every case that I ever handled. Once I did that, the clients just started rolling in, and they haven't stopped ever since."

"Wow! Maria Paisana, huh? Who'd a thunk it?"

The food hadn't arrived yet, so Mary excused herself to go to the ladies' room.

"You don't know how lucky you are, Dewey," Julie said.

"Whaddya mean?"

"Mary gave you the condensed version of that story. It used to be that she was the one that made Nathan what he is today, and how hard she had to work to set him up in business. According to the way the story used to go, Nate the Great was out cheating on her almost every night, while she was slaving away."

"Well, I can certainly believe that one. Once upon a time I knew old Nate. And let me tell ya, we had a nickname for him, too, but it wasn't exactly Nate the Great."

"Looks like Mary's mellowed some," said Julie, "if they're the good friends she says they are."

Mary got back to the table just as the dinners were bein' delivered. We ordered two bottles of excellent wine – one red, one white – and after some crazy toasts to everyone at the table, we ate our dinners in relative silence. I looked over at Zeke, and he seemed to be fine. I knew he would take good care of Stella. Ya never know where true love will show up – or maybe he just had the hots for her Lexus.

Mary and Julie were another matter. I knew Mary wasn't in any shape to be drivin' anywhere, right after she started her story. Julie wasn't nearly as bad as she was the last time we were here, but dinner wasn't over yet. After a glass or two of wine, Julie's car would be stayin' overnight in the parkin' lot, too. I knew I had to get her to slow down some.

"Hey Jules, how ya holdin' up?" I whispered in her ear.

I got the answer I was hopin' I *wouldn't* get. She was in worse shape than I thought.

Julie musta thought I was comin' on to her, cuz before I could turn my head away, she kissed me like I just got off the boat comin' back from the war.

When she said, "You know, *David*, yer awful c-cute," I knew it was time to leave. I was just hopin' we could make it before she started talkin' about David and Julie Poppaloppadoppalus.

Everyone was finished with their dinners, and what wine was left wasn't enough to worry about. I got the waiter over to our table as fast as I could, and took care of the check. It was goin' on my expense account anyway, and Julie would never know the difference.

"Hey Zeke, we're gonna take off. Thanks for bein' here, old buddy. You OK to drive?"

"Yeah, Dew, I'm OK. Stella and I are goin' into the bar for a nightcap. Sounds like they got a real good group in there playin' tonight."

"Yeah, well, I wish I could join ya," I said. But with Mary fast asleep and Julie hangin' all over me tellin' me how *c-cute* I looked, there was no way. "Stella, could you do me a favor and get Mary's keys for me? We're gonna take her home."

"Sure, Dewey. Here you go," she said, handin' me the keys. I thought maybe she would volunteer to take Mary home, but it looked like she was really into Zekey. Go figure!

"One more thing, guys," I said. "Could ya keep an eye on Julie until I get back? I gotta carry Mary out to the car. Looks like she's dead to the world."

I picked Mary up and deposited her into the back seat of her BMW. I decided to take her car and leave mine in the parkin' lot. I'd rather see somebody steal my junk pile than Mary's BMW; and if they did, I could use the insurance money. Even if I knew that Zeke would be brokenhearted.

When I got back inside, Julie was just tellin' Zeke and Stella about David and Julie Poopaloopadoopaloppadoopaloppus. I guess she was worse off than I thought.

"Good luck, Dewey," Stella said.

"OK, let's go, Julie Poopaloopa..." But before I could get even half of the name out, Julie laid one on me again.

Musta been one helluva war.

Mary was sound asleep on the back seat, and, fortunately for me, Julie was able to make it to the car on her own power. Once inside, however, she was out like a light. Good thing I got Mary's address from Stella before we left.

I found Mary's place without any problem. The *problem* now was to get Mary from the back seat into her house.

"Hey Mary!" I said as loud as I could, hoping I wouldn't wake up Julie. "Mary! You awake back there! Mary!"

"Huh? I'm awake. Where are we, and how'd we get here?"

"We're at your place, Mary. I drove you home from Sloppy Man's. I'll bring your car back in the morning. Think you can walk if I help you get inside?"

"Oh, sh…" Mary was sound asleep again.

I got out and picked Mary off the seat and carried her to the door. Just as I was gettin' the key in the lock, Mary woke up. "So, you coming in?" she said, kissin' me all over.

"Sorry, Mary, but I gotta take Julie home."

"Oh, just for a little while," she said, starting to unbutton her blouse.

"Not tonight, Mary. Maybe some other time." I deposited Mary on her sofa, and she promptly fell fast asleep.

I just hoped that Mrs. Poopaloopa…uh…I mean, *Julie*, didn't see any of that.

When I got back to the car, Julie was still fast asleep. I drove the few miles from Mary's to Julie's in complete silence. Well, *almost* complete silence. Julie was snorin' away.

Once we got to Julie's, I carried her into the house without any problems. Just as I was about to put her down on the sofa, she woke up and said, "So, David, - yer cute, ya know tha' – why're we stoppin' here?"

Never disappoint the boss is a rule I always try to live by.

Chapter 22: DEBBIE AND BRAD AND JOHN AND BILL AND SAM AND…

Julie didn't have to get up the next day, but I did. Julie decided to take a long weekend off before her trial began, and she wouldna been in any shape to go to work anyway. I snuck out the door without wakin' her up, remindin' myself to call her later.

I really wasn't any closer to figurin' out who bumped old Joe off than I was right after I heard he got it. Only two things I knew for certain. (Pay attention to this. There'll be a quiz on it later.) First, I knew *I* didn't do it. (Or did I? How many times have I lied already? If you said 43…it really doesn't matter since I wasn't countin'. If you were, stop it! It ain't gonna help!) Second, I knew Joe didn't take the pipe. (That's PI talk for committin' suicide. Who the hell knows where that came from? If you do, please e-mail me at dewpol@zyx.com., an' you'll get a message sayin' that your message is undeliverable. Sheesh!) But what can you expect from the 358th best private investigator east of the might Manatawny. I only hoped that Mary Payson – *nee* (fancy, ain't it) Maria Paisana - and her PI, Saul Swann, were figurin' out more than I was. After all, he was the *number one* private eye east of the mighty Manatawny, so he should know more.

But, first things first. And, no, for once I did not have to take a nap when I got home. Julie was her wonderful self on Thursday night. Problem was, she was already snorin' before I got my second wind.

The first thing I had to do was watch the two episodes of *Debbie and Brad and John and Bill and Sam and...* Any phone messages I had could wait.

In Wednesday's episode, I saw that they had yet another actress playin' Debbie. This made the fourth – or was it the fifth – one in the last three months. I told ya they were wearin' the poor girl out.

Anyway, on Wednesday's show, the new Debbie is now with John. (I wondered when he was gonna show up. I still haven't seen Bill, and Sam hasn't been in it for a long time.)

"I'm really sorry, John," said Debbie, "but I can't see you any more." Geez, John's name's in the title and everything, and all he gets is a cameo appearance? And could it be that Deb is actually saying no to a guy?

"But...why...Debbie?" John cries – literally. "You know how much I love you." Hey, calm down, Johnny. How could you *possibly* love her? This is the first time you've even *seen* her. And if you love this one, boy...you shoulda seen the last Debbie. This one ain't bad, but the last one...OH!

"Oh, John, I hate to see you cry like that."

"I'm sorry, Debbie, but it's the only way I know how to cry." (Hey, you've been good now for how many chapters? Don't start with the booin' again. OK?)

"But John, I'm havin' triplets, and I don't think any of them are yours." Hold on there, Deb. What about the Doc? After all, the Fix was in. (Come on! I like that one!)

"But, Debbie," John was still cryin', "when I asked you if I was the first, you said yes, didn't you?" (Hang in there, reader. It'll be outta my system in a minute.)

"No I didn't, John. I distinctly remember saying, *I'm not sure, but you sure look familiar.*" (There! That did it!)

"Oh, Debbie!"

"Oh, John!"

Oh my! It looks like Debbie couldn't say no to a guy after all.

Just then the announcer cut in and said, "Tune in tomorrow when we might find out if Debbie is gonna have kid number four – or is it five – with John. We also might find out which last name they're going to give which kid. And, on tomorrow's show, we might find out where they're gonna put everybody when the family gets together for Christmas."

Then he added, "*Debbie and Brad and John and Bill and Sam and...*has been brought to you today by SafOne Condoms – the brand you can trust." That really cracked me up. But that's show business, I guess.

I couldn't wait to see what was gonna happen the next day to Debbie, so I didn't. Wait, that is. I pulled Wednesday out and put Thursday in.

Thursday's show was a lot more disappointin' than Wednesday's. Debbie had another appointment with Dr. Fix.

"So, how is my little mother doing today?" asked Dr. Fix.

"How should I know?" questioned Debbie. "Why don't you call her and find...Oh, you mean me."

"Of course I mean you, Debbie. Now let me give a listen. Yes, there's one. There's two. And there's three. I definitely hear three."

"Oh, Dr. Fix," cried Debbie, "that's terrible."

"I know, Debbie. You're going to have three babies, you're not sure who the fathers are, and you're not even married. I know how you must feel."

"No, Dr. Fix, you don't understand. That's not what I'm upset about."

"Well then, Debbie, tell me what the problem is."

"The problem is that I'm sleeping with a few guys who are shooting blanks. I've got to find out who they are and get rid of them. Think what that would do to my reputation if this ever got out."

"Indeed, Debbie. We certainly can't have that."

After a few commercials, Debbie spent the rest of the show talking the situation over with her mother. Unfortunately for Debbie, Mom couldn't stay long. She was due to baby sit 14 of her 19 grandchildren that afternoon, and told Debbie she would think of something and get back to her.

The show was over, and not a minute too soon. The announcer then said, "Tune in tomorrow when we might find out who's playing with cap pistols, what advice Mommy will give to Debbie, and if the writers can come up with a better script. Frankly, I think today's show really sucked." Fortunately for him, he was *Ron* Roses, brother of *Roni* Roses, and Dad still ran the network.

I knew the show had been on for over 10 years, so they all couldn't be winners. And lucky for Debbie, she was still holdin' at three kids.

Usually when I set the timer to tape a show, I add an extra five minutes to the time, just in case my clock ain't in synch with theirs. I decided to let the tape run and see what I had extra on it. It turned out to be the *Sister Margaret Mary Story*, and you'll never guess who was playin' the lead role. (Well! Go ahead and guess! I'll wait...No, but yer close.) It was the girl who played Debbie before the one playin' Debbie now. I'm really sorry I didn't tape the whole thing. It looked real interestin', especially the first part. It showed Sister Margaret Mary goin' to confession, and her first line was, "Help me Father, for I have sinned." That really cracked me up.

When I got done watchin' the tapes, it was only 11 o'clock, so I went out for a pizza and a few beers. Had to keep up my strength for the afternoon's show.

It was five minutes to one when I got back from lunch. The light on my answerin' machine was blinkin', but the calls could wait until after the show was over.

As the show opens, we see Debbie talkin' to five guys. I've heard of a *ménage a trois,* but five? Well, if anybody could pull it off, Debbie sure could.

"Let's see," said Debbie. "There's Bill. Hi, Bill. There's Sam and John. Over there's Brad. And there's Dr. Fix."

It looked like they had a new guy playin' the part of Sam, and Bill looked too old to be on the show, but somehow he looked familiar. Oh, yeah…now I remember him. He was one of the stars on one of those detective shows back in the late '70s. Things must be tough all over, but I guess it's a livin'.

"OK, guys," Deb said, "I see you're all here. First, I'd like to thank you all for comin', but we got a little problem. Seems like at least two of you are shootin' blanks, and we can't have that on *my* show." Gee, the new Debbie seemed like a real b-i-t-double hockey sticks. No…wait… That don't make no sense. That would be *bitll*, an' whoever hearda bitll. Anyway, you get the idea. I bet *this* Debbie'll never get to play a nun on TV!

"So, over on the table, I've got five jars. One for each of you. Your names are on the jars, so please make sure you take the right one. Please go into a room by yourself, and give me a good sample in the jar. If you need any help, there are magazines and videos in each

219

room." (Man, this was one tough broad!) The guys just looked at each other, but nobody said a word.

After a few commercials, we come back to find Debbie talkin' on the phone with her Mom, Sara Jones Smith Brown Lewis Orkwist. I wasn't sure whether she sounded more like a law firm or an accounting firm. No wonder she had 19 grandkids.

"So, Mom, what should I do about this situation?"

"Well, Deb, I think you should…Oh, but before I forget, you can congratulate me."

"Congratulate you, Mom? What for?"

"I'm gettin' married again, that's what for. Barry Davis asked me last night, and…well…you know me. I just *can't* say no." And I thought the old sayin' was *like father, like son.* Shows you what I know.

"Wow, Mom. That'll make six now, won't it?"

"Nah! Actually it'll be seven. Remember, I was married to Stan Brown twice, but the post office said I could only put the name on the envelopes once, or they'd have to charge me extra postage?"

"Well, congratulations, Mom. Now tell me, what should I do about *my* situation?"

"Oh, yeah. Let me see. You still know Fred and Art?"

"Yeah, why?"

"Well, have 'em come over and tell 'em to be ready. Only this time, check 'em out *first*. Ya don't want the same thing happening again."

"Right, Mom. And thanks. I knew I could count on you."

After a few more commercials, the guys came out holdin' their...jars. (Hey, get your mind outta the gutter.) And the show was over for the day.

"Tune in Monday," began the announcer, "when we might find out if Fred and Art were now in the title; how Mom handled 14 grandkids; and, if the five guys all filled up their jars. Today's episode of *Debbie and Brad and John and Bill and Sam*...was brought to you by Wipems." Boy, they sure had some appropriate sponsors.

I knew I wouldn't be tuning in Monday because of Julie's trial, so I set up the VCR to tape the show.

I checked my answerin' machine and had two calls. The first one was from a lady who wanted me to find her lost cat. I told her I was gonna be tied up till at least Thursday, and referred her to the *359th* best private investigator east of the Manatawny. I hoped that didn't jeopardize my spot on the list. I couldn't afford to drop any lower.

The second call was from Nick Rudawski. He said he received another visit from our three amigos, so I agreed to meet him at Sloppy Man's for dinner at 6:00.

When I arrived at Sloppy Man's at 5:45, Nick was already there, workin' on his second Glen Livet. I decided to join him in one at the bar.

"So Nick," I said, "you got another visit from our friends, huh? Whad they want this time?"

"Oh, it was Vinny, Angelo, and Oscar all right. They were just checking up on me to make sure that I wasn't going any place. They said I was being a good boy, and that they would see me again after the trial was over. What do you think I should do?"

"Just lay low and don't panic. Sounds to me like they may know more about the murder than they're lettin' on, so we'll just have to wait and see how it plays out."

We ordered dinner at the bar and Nick ordered his third Scotch.

"Better slow down on those things, Nick. Too many cops around here. Wouldn't want to see you get into any trouble."

Nick just smiled. "Speaking of cops, do you think we ought to let them know about my visitors?"

"Nah. We got plenty o'time to do that. If they're gonna do anything, it won't be till after the trial anyway. Let's just wait and see what happens."

I excused myself and went outside to call Julie on my cell phone. I wanted her to join us, but she said she wasn't feeling all that well, and was gonna go to bed early. I told her I would be in touch with her tomorrow.

By the time I got back, our dinners had arrived. It was now too crowded and noisy to talk any more, so we ate in silence.

"Hang in there, Nick," I said, and wished him good night. There was still somethin' about that man I just couldn't figure out.

I got home about 8:30. Since there were only a few days left until the beginning of the trial, I thought it might be a good idea to see Nora Klause and Sally Roberts one more time before Monday. I tried Nora first, but got her machine. Sally picked up on the third ring.

"Hi, Sally, it's Dewey. Been a few days. How ya doin'?"

"Fine, Dewey. I've been busy in D.C. How are you?"

"OK, I guess. Just waitin' for the trial to start on Monday. Say, what'cha doin' tomorrow night? Wanna have dinner?"

"That sounds good. There's a new seafood place that just opened in East Arthur. Would you like to go there?"

"Sure. Why don't I pick you up around seven. Would that be OK?"

"Seven it is. I'll see you then."

For the first time in a long time I was alone on a Friday night. There wasn't anything more I could do about the case – at least until I saw Sally and Nora again – so I decided to grab a beer outta the fridge and do a little light readin'. I just bought a copy of the number one best seller *Saloken has Spoken* by Dag Williams. Boy, can that guy tell a story. If ya don't already have the book, do yerself a favor and pick up a copy.

The book was such a quick read and so enjoyable that I was still wide awake at 11:30. I decided to see what was on TV, so I started flippin' around the dial. I came to a show on one of the cable channels that was just about to start, and realized that it was *Run for the Roses* with Roni Roses. I thought I'd watch it. Always wanted to learn more about the Kentucky Derby.

Well, was I in for a surprise. It didn't take long to realize that it wasn't about the Kentucky Derby, or races, or even horses; unless you considered that the six guys sloshin' around in the mud with Roni were all hung like them. There was Roni, in all her…uh…*glory*, and these six guys who were actin' like they just got rescued from a deserted island after 20 years. I can't describe everything that went on without turnin' this into an x-rated book; but I could see why it was on at 11:30, and why Roni had the number one rated show in her time slot. With her…uh…*actin' ability*, she probably didn't even need Daddy.

It was a little after 1:00 a.m. when the show ended.

This was the first time that I would be sleepin' in my own bed in quite some time.

Chapter 23: SALLY AND THE SEAFOOD

It was Saturday. I didn't have nothin' to do, so I got up when I got up. (OK, if ya wanna get technical, it was 11:28 a.m. Eastern Standard Time. Let's not get picky here, OK?) *Debbie and the Daddies* (hey, maybe that would make a good name for a spin-off) wouldn't be on until Monday and I had the VCR ready to go. I told Julie I would get in touch with her, but I could do that later. There was nothin' else I could really do about the case until I saw Sally and Nora, so I did somethin' that I really enjoyed. (No, *not* that!)

I had my favorite breakfast. If you were payin' attention from before – and shame on you if you weren't – my favorite breakfast is two bowls of Frosted Flakes; four Twinkies (if you said the regular ones, not the strawberry, go to the head of the class. If you see Dr. Mousskowsky when ya get there, tell her I said hello.); and one can of Jolt. After that I really didn't have anything to do until around quarter to seven when I would leave to pick up Sally, so I did somethin' else I really enjoyed. (*Wrong again, Bucko.*) I took a nap.

I really wish I could tell ya all about the dream I had about the girl with the long blond hair, the great pair of legs, and the terrific set of boobs, but I can't. If I had any dreams at all, I sure didn't remember 'em.

I got up around 5:30, took a shower, and shaved. No AquaKarate, no HaiVelva, and certainly no Midnite Madness for Men. I put on a nice pair of dress pants, with a dress shirt and a pullover sweater. I really needed to go out and get some new clothes. All the women I was seein' saw me in – and out of – all the clothes I had. But that could wait till after the trial. I decided to give Julie a call while I was still thinkin' about it.

"Hi, Dewey," she said. "How's it going? Why don't you come over and we'll have dinner."

"I'd love to, Boss, but I'll be busy workin' on your case for most of the evening. Maybe I can stop over later."

"So, *Mr. Polpulcionski*" – I could tell she wasn't drinkin', since she didn't call me Poppaloppadoppalus – who will you be *working on* tonight? Sally, Nora, or Stella?"

"Gee, Jules, there's no need to get sore. We've only got two days till your trial starts. If you must know, I'll be with Sally tonight, tryin' to pump...I mean *get*...information out of her. She's still on my suspect list, ya know. As you know, I saw Nick last night, and tomorrow I'll try to get in touch with Nora one last time. I won't see Stella until we get to court on Monday. I really don't think *she* did it, do you?"

"No, certainly not. Well, just be careful, Dewey."

"You can count on that. If it's not too late when I get done with Sally…uh…I mean…when I've gotten all I can out of her…uh…you know what I mean, I'll try and stop over. OK?"

"Sure, Dewey, and good luck *getting* whatever it is you're *getting*."

Before I could thank her, Julie hung up.

I left to pick Sally up at quarter to seven, and all the way over I could tell somethin' just wasn't right. I got to Sally's without any problems, but I felt real uncomfortable. Sally met me at the door before I even had a chance to ring the bell.

"So, stranger, how've you been?" she asked. Sally looked as gorgeous as ever, but for some reason she looked very tired.

"Real busy, with Julie's trial comin' up in a coupla days. How was your trip? They got you relocated yet?"

"Not yet, but it should be next week right after the trial. I know you don't want to hear this, Dewey, but Julie *had* to murder Joe. I don't think she stands a chance of getting off. Do you?"

"Oh, I don't know about that. Remember, she's got Mary Payson defendin' her, and Mary hasn't lost a case in over her last 800 cases, so I think Julie has a pretty good shot."

"Well, I think her streak is about to be broken. That bitch should be in jail where she belongs, for a long, long time."

I didn't want to get into an argument with Sally – at least until after I had a chance to pump her – so I just said, "We'll see. Don't you think we should get going to dinner? I hear this place is real good, and it gets pretty crowded on Saturday."

"OK, but why don't we take my car. I'll drive."

Regardless of what my buddy, Zeke Zembrowski, thought, it was great to be goin' in style for once.

I was right. When we got to Salty's Seafood Restaurant in East Arthur, the place was packed. Salty's had just opened, and taken over the building formerly occupied by Charlie's Chop House. (I *knew* that place wouldn't last long!) We walked over to the *maitre'd* to put our name in for a table, and guess who it was. (Go ahead, guess. No…No… No…Geez, you must have no imagination at all!) It was our old buddy, Reginald, from Charlie's Chop Suey House.

"Ahoy, mates!" said Reggie. But he dropped the act real quick once he recognized us. "Oh, hello, suh," Reginald said in his best British accent, although very quietly. I still didn't buy the British act, either.

"So, Reginald," I said, "still havin' trouble gettin' actin' jobs, I see."

"Yes, suh," he said, again very quietly. "But my name's Captain Bob, and welcome aboard to Salty's Seafood Restaurant," he continued, sounding very New Englandy. (Had to hand it to…whatever his *real* name was. He could sure do accents. Maybe he should forget acting and try to get voiceover work?)

"So, Cap'n Cru...uh, Bob, what happened to Charlie's Chop House?"

"Well, matey," he said, staying in character, "Salty bought him out. If ya evuh in the mood for lunch, try Salty's Sub Shop. It's right down the street."

"We'll keep that in mind, Cap'n. So how long's the wait?"

"About an hour and a half, but for you, I'll see what I can do."

"Thanks, Cap'n. We'll just go into the bar."

The bar was packed, but two people were just getting up as we walked in, so we took their seats. Once we were seated, I looked at the couple next to us, and who do you think they were? (OK, I won't make you guess this time.) It was Stella DeRita, looking very stunning in her *very* unprofessional-looking clothes; and someone who looked a lot like Zeke Zembrowski.

"Hi, Stella," I said. "Who's yer friend here?"

"Oh, hello, David," said Stella. "Hi, Sally."

"David?" I began to ask. "Why so form..."

"David and Sally, I'd like you to meet Sanford."

"Hello, David. Hello, Sally," Sanford said very stiffly, but in a voice that sounded vaguely familiar.

Sally and Sanford and I shook hands all around. Then Stella said, "I have to go to the little girls' room. Why don't you come with me, Sally?"

The second they left, I started talkin' to Sanford. "So Sanford, don't I know you from someplace?"

"Yeah, Dew, it's me, Zeke."

"Zeke! For a minute I thought that was you when we walked in. What the hell's goin' on?"

"Ah, Stella's tryin' to turn me into a sophisticated gentleman, or somethin'. I don' like this any better'n you do, but just play along, OK? I can put up wit this shit, cuz the rest o' the package is really wurt it, let me tell ya."

"OK, Zeke…uh…I mean *Sanford.* I'll play along." And Zeke didn't have to tell me about the rest of the package, cuz I already knew. She musta already been workin', cuz this was the first time I could ever remember hearin' Zeke say a five-syllable word and a three-syllable word back-to-back. "Sanford, huh? Where the hell did that come from?"

"Ah, it was my great-granfather's name on my mother's side. Dad gave me the nickname Zeke when I was jus' a little kid. But I sees 'em comin', so jus' play along, OK?"

"No problem, *Sanford.*"

"So David – I hope you don't mind that I call you David. I think it's so much nicer than Dewey. What do you think of Sanford?" Stella asked, after they sat down.

"You can call me anything you want, Stella. And Sanford, he's quite the guy," I said, givin' my old buddy a quick wink. "Where'd you find him?"

"See, Sally. I told you he wouldn't recognize him."

"What're ya talkin' about? Recognize who?" I said, playin' along just like Zeke wanted me to.

"Sanford is your old friend Zeke. Dress him up and teach him to talk English, and even his friends won't recognize him. He's still a work in progress, but he's coming along just fine. Don't you think so, David?"

"Oh, sure Stella," I answered. What I really wanted to say was *oh boy*, and from the look Zeke was givin' me, it looked like he felt the same way.

Just then, Cap'n Bob...or Reginald...or whatever his name was, came over and told us he had a table for four ready in the dining room. For Sanford's sake, it didn't come a moment too soon.

With Stella bein' Mary's secretary an' all, we really didn't get a chance to talk over the trial. Fortunately for Zeke, very little was said at the table at all. I was wonderin' how much of this nonsense the guy was gonna put up with, package or no package. We all did agree, though, that the food at Salty's Seafood Restaurant was a major improvement over anything that Charlie had served. After a little over an hour at the table, Stella and Zeke got up to leave.

"Well, this certainly was a lovely evening, Sally and David," he said, although not quite as stiffly as earlier. I guess the three glasses of wine he had with dinner helped with that. "I hope you two have a lovely evening."

"Why, yes, Sanford, it was lovely, quite lovely," I said. "Just take it easy drivin'. You know the cops around here."

A few minutes after they left, Sally and I decided to leave too. Time for a little pumpin'.

When we got back to Sally's, I noticed that my car was right where I left it and that both back tires were perfectly inflated. Unfortunately, the front two were flatter'n a proverbial pancake. I also noticed a note stuck on my windshield. It said, *This is your next-to-last warning, so why don't you just be a good boy and mind your own business.*

"That's weird," I said to Sally. "Whaddya think it means by *next-to-last* warning?"

"I don't know, but I'd be very careful if I were you," answered Sally.

Since I knew that it wouldn't do any good to call Sanford... uh...I mean Zeke at that point, I figured it was a good time for a little pumpin' with Sally.

"So, Sally, I got two days left to go till the trial, and I'm stumped. You think Julie did it. But what about Vinny? How about Angelo? What about Oscar? Maybe it was Nurse Nora? How about Cousin Nick?"

"Oh, face the facts, Dewey! Any one of them could have done it, but who had the most to gain with Joe out of the way? Julie would get a bundle, and she would be free of a husband that was over twice her age. I'm sorry, but she had to do it."

"Maybe so, but she's sure got me fooled."

"Let's face it, Dewey. If Ma Barker had looked like Julie, she would have had you fooled too."

"I still don't know. What about his three business associates? The ones where you were never in on the meetin's with?" I didn't tell her about *their* meetings with Nick.

"Now that Joe's gone, I don't think we'll see them again. Do you?"

I just shook my head. "I'll be back in a minute," I said. "I have to go outside and check my car again, and give Zeke a call. Maybe I can catch him and he can bring over a coupla tires."

I walked out to my car, still thinkin' about the message. My *next-to-last* warning, it said. Before I could figure it out, someone clubbed me over the head. I woke up in the street the next morning with my cell phone ringin' and one helluva headache.

It was Julie. "Where the hell have you been, Dewey? I've been trying to reach you all night."

"Well, believe it or not, Boss, I've been out all night, and I do mean out – literally. Look, here's Zeke's number. Have him bring two tires over to this address." I gave her the number and the address. "I'll be over as soon as I can. I'll explain everything when I get there."

Chapter 24: FINDIN' CATS IS EASIER, BUT IT DON'T PAY THE BILLS

Right after I hung up with Julie, Sally came runnin' out the door.

"Oh my God," she yelled. "Are you all right? I fell asleep as soon as you went outside and I just woke up."

It appeared she was telling the truth. Sally was still in the same clothes she had on Saturday night and it was obvious that she hadn't taken a shower.

"Yeah, I guess I'm OK. I came out to look at the tires, and somebody clubbed me over the head. I sure hope this was my *last* warning. Zeke should be over soon with some tires. As soon as he gets here, I'm gonna get goin'. I've got a lot of things to do today." I didn't tell her that I already talked to Julie.

"Well, you just be careful," Sally said. She sounded sincere, but she only gave me a small peck on the cheek.

"So, you comin' to the trial tomorrow?" I asked.

"I wouldn't miss it. I hope that bitch gets everything she deserves."

Before I could say anything, Sally turned and walked back into the house.

A few minutes later Zeke showed up with a new set of retreads for my car.

"What happened this time, Dew?"

"When we got back here last night, the front two tires were just like you see 'em. I also got a note on the car sayin' that this was my *next-to-last* warnin'. When I came out later to look around, somebody clubbed me. I was out cold in the street all last night."

"Gee, Dew, that's too bad. Who would want to do a thing like that?"

"I don't know for sure, but I got a fairly good idea. Problem is, how do I go about provin' it, especially with the trial startin' tomorrow?" I didn't mention it to Zeke, but I think Stella was already workin' her magic on him without him even knowin' it. It was the first time I heard him say *want to* instead of *wanna* since our zip English course.

"So, tell me, *Sanford*, how did the rest of the night go?"

"Aw, Dew, it was great. Stella and me, we spent the night together. I jus' don' know how long I can put up wid this stuff o'tryin' to turn me inta somethin' that I ain't."

I was real glad to hear that from my buddy Zeke. Apparently Stella still had a long way to go.

After Zeke changed the tires, I slipped him a ten. I was feelin' extra generous that day, and besides, it was goin' on my expense account with Julie any way. I thanked Zeke and told him I would look for him at the trial on Monday. He said he'd be there and wished Julie and me good luck.

When I got over to Julie's, she was just about finished making breakfast. It wasn't my usual high-sugar, high-caffeine breakfast, but I was hopin' that I would have plenty of time to work her into that once this business was over. The three-cheese omelet with sausage and pancakes would just have to do for now.

"So, tell me what happened," she said, after we kissed. "And don't leave anything out."

"Well, like I told ya, I wanted to see Sally last night to see if I could get any more info out of her. We were gonna have dinner at Salty's Seafood Restaurant in East Arthur. You know, it used to be Charlie's Chop House, only Salty's is much better. Well, anyway, when I got to Sally's place, she wasn't quite dressed yet, so I helped her..."

"Maybe I should rephrase what I just said, Dewey. Don't leave anything out *that involves the case.*"

I wasn't sure whether she was pissed or jealous, or maybe a little of both. I know nothin' happened Saturday night with Sally, and you know nothin' happened on Saturday night between me and Sally, but Julie didn't know that. And I sure didn't want her to start feelin' too secure.

"So anyway, we drove over to Salty's in her car, and guess who we ran into? Go ahead, guess."

"Oh for God sakes, Dewey. I'm not in any mood to play games. Who the hell did you run into?"

"Well, if that's the way yer gonna be, I ain't gonna tell ya," I said. But I was only kiddin' around.

"Well, in that case, you're fired." She wasn't.

"Well, in that case, I guess I'll tell ya. It was Stella and Zeke. I think they make a great couple, only Stella's really tryin' to change Zeke into…"

"Look, I'm really not interested in Stella and Zeke's social life at the moment. So what happened?"

"Well, the four of us had dinner, so I really couldn't get any info out of Sally with Stella and Zeke there. They left a little before we did, and we went back to Sally's. When we got there, my two front tires were flat, and I had a note on the car sayin' this was my *next-to-last* warnin', and that I should *be a good boy and mind my own business.* I went inside with Sally and…"

"Dewey!"

"Hey, it was only for a minute or two, and then I went out to look around. The next thing I know, you're callin' me on my cell, only I'm in the middle of the street."

"Wow! Do you think somebody thinks we're getting close to finding out anything?"

"Sure looks that way to me. Only I wish I knew what I thought they think I know, cuz I sure don't know nothin' that I think I know."

"Huh?"

"Yeah, whatever you said."

"Oh. OK."

"Any way, Sally still insists that you killed Joe, even though you got Mary Payson defendin' you. I brought up Vinny, Angelo, and Oscar, but Sally doesn't think we'll see them again, but I ain't so sure about that. But I'm still stumped."

"Do you think someone followed you last night when you went to pick Sally up?"

"It's possible, but somebody coulda been waitin' for me when we got back, too."

"It seems like the only time anything happens to you or your car is when you're at Sally's. Do you think there's a connection?"

"I don't think so," I answered, "and for two very good reasons. First, Sally couldn't have done it, or I woulda heard her come after me. And second, and I guess I can tell ya, Sally is really with the F.B.I."

"What?"

"Yeah, I know it's hard to believe, but Sally was a plant by the F.B.I. They thought that your late husband had some dealings with the Mafia and wanted to keep an eye on him, so they got Sally in there to do it. Matter of fact, her name's not even Sally."

"I can't believe it. Joe and the Mafia? Sally with the F.B.I?"

"Yeah…well…you never know," was all that I could say.

"So who else could have hit you? You said Stella and Zeke left the restaurant before you did. Do you think Zeke could have done it?"

"Come on! My old buddy Zeke! No way! We've known each other since we were kids. Why would he do it?"

"I don't know. But who else knew where you would be?"

"Well…there are two other possibilities."

"OK, and who might they be?" Julie asked.

"Well…maybe the unknown person who killed Joe for whatever unknown reason followed me."

"Maybe. But we both know that most of us don't like that kind of story. What's the other possibility?"

I hated to say it, but since she asked, "Maybe somebody else had ties to the Mafia, too, and that person bumped Joe off or had them do it?"

"Really? And who might that be?"

"Well," I said, "that might be…you."

"Me!?" she yelled. "You can't be serious! Why would I do it?"

"Oh, I don't know. Maybe everybody is right. Maybe you wanted to get rid of a cheating husband who was more than twice your age, get his money, and enjoy life. I don't really want to believe it, but you *were* the only other person who knew where I would be."

"I think you should go, Dewey."

"Yeah, maybe I should." I tried to kiss her, but she just turned away. "See you at the trial tomorrow."

"That won't be necessary. And figure out what I owe you and I'll mail you your final check."

I started to walk out, but I had to turn around one more time. "Good luck, Julie," is all I said.

I still knew I would be attending the trial.

When I got home, I tried givin' Nora a call. It wasn't that I was in the mood for any action; but, even though I was no longer gettin' paid, I wanted to take her to dinner to see if I could find out anything more from her. Unfortunately, I never did get in touch with her.

I made a few other calls before I went to bed.

It was gonna be one helluva long evening.

Chapter 25: JULIE'S TRIAL DAY ONE… or… IS DEWEY DONE?

It made no sense to go to bed Sunday night. I was all alone, plus I didn't get any sleep at all. I got up early Monday morning to have breakfast and set the VCR to tape *Debbie and Brad and John and Bill and Sam and…*I really wasn't hungry, but I did force myself to have my usual breakfast, only this time I had *two* cans of Jolt. (Chasin' lost cats can really take a lot of energy, and I figured that's what I would be doin' from now on.) I hated to admit it, but I did miss the omelet with the sausage and the pancakes.

After breakfast, I put on my new suit that I just bought specifically for the trial. I did look rather handsome if I must say so myself. The only problem was that I probably wouldn't get to wear it too often after Julie's trial. Lost cats really don't care what you look like.

The trial was supposed to start at 9:00 in Courtroom 6A. One of the calls I made on Sunday night was to Zeke. I told him what happened and we agreed to meet in the hall outside the courtroom at 8:45. I knew Julie couldn't have me thrown out of the courtroom, but I didn't want to walk in or sit by myself, either.

All the way over I kept asking myself if I did the right thing. I was 99 percent sure Julie wasn't the one who bumped Joe off, but I had to be absolutely certain, so I took a gamble…and *won.* From Julie's reaction I positively knew she was innocent, but I felt terrible. How can you take a gamble and *win* and still feel like you've lost...*everything?* I guess Julie really did have her hooks into me a lot deeper than I realized.

I got outside the courtroom right at 8:45. Fortunately, Zeke was the only person there. I guess Julie and Mary and Stella were already inside.

"How are you holding up, Dew?" asked Zeke, even though it sounded more like Sanford.

"Well, Zekey, I guess I'm doin' OK, but I didn't get any sleep at all last night."

"Aw, that's too bad, Dew. I was hopin' you'd be over wid that by now, jus' like the ol' Dew." (Maybe he was turnin' into Dr. Sanford and Mr. Zeke, but he was still my best friend and I was very glad he was there.) "Is that a new suit? It looks real sharp."

"Yeah, thanks. I got it a few days ago. Probably won't have much use for it after the trial. You look real good too."

"Thanks. Stella's still tryin' to turn me inta a real gentleman, but it'll be a long process. An' don' worry, Dew, I'm sure things'll work out for ya."

It was five of nine when we walked into the courtroom. As I suspected, Julie and Mary and Stella were already up front sittin' at their table. Nobody bothered to turn around when we walked in. Nora Klause was already there with Nick Rudawski. (Were these two now a couple, or were they just there together?) Zeke and I took the two seats next to them. There was no sign of Sally Roberts or anyone else.

The prospective jurors were already there, too. Since it was only a few minutes to nine and there was no sign of a judge, I was wonderin' if it would be my ol' pal Beanie. The D.A. handlin' the case didn' look familiar to me either, although he made both me and Zeke look like two guys who just played a football game that went overtime…in the mud.

At 9:05 the judge's door opened and out walked a female judge I'd never seen before. If I wasn't so upset, I mighta thought about checking her out later, but that was definitely on hold.

The judge, according to her nameplate, was the Honorable Saundra Helene Pants, great-granddaughter of the founder of Pantstown, Jeremiah S. Pants. After seein' the name, I remembered bein' told about her. Judge Pants was very *friendly*, if ya get my meanin', thus the nickname Sandy to her friends – and *Hot* to everyone else.

"Good morning, ladies and gentlemen," she started. "Today, we will begin the first-degree murder trial of Mr. Joseph J. Crinn…" She kept on goin', but I quickly tuned her out. I was wonderin' how Julie was holdin' up, and kept starin' at her, even though she was still facing the judge.

"…and so we will now begin the jury selection. The defendant is Mrs. Julie Crinn, the widow of the deceased, who is accused of the first-degree murder of her husband, Mr. Joseph J. Crinn. Mrs. Crinn's attorney is Mary Payson." I thought I saw a very quick smirk on the lips of the judge, but if I did, it disappeared just as quickly.

"The prosecuting attorney is the D.A. for this county, Mr. Phillippe Auguste Mignon." There was no mistaking the smile on the judge's face, and it didn't disappear all that quickly. Even though Mary had won over 800 cases in a row, it seriously looked like her streak might be in jeopardy.

Phillippe Auguste Mignon was about 35 and strikingly handsome. I guessed that Judge Pants was about the same age, and wasn't all that bad herself, so it wasn't any wonder that she would find him attractive. Phillippe, from what I'd been told, had been born in Paris, France, but was brought over to the US when he was about five. He considered himself to be totally American, and insisted that everyone call him Phil, so… (If you don't get it right away, it'll hit ya later, I promise.)

The judge informed the prospective jurors as to what was about to happen, and said the words that I was waiting to hear. "Will Mrs. Crinn, Ms. Payson (I definitely saw the smirk that time), and Mr. Mignon (same smile) rise and face the jurors please?"

I knew that with only the four of us in the visitors' section, Julie couldn't help but notice that I was there. When she turned around, I thought I saw just a tiny smile on her face, but it was gone quicker than the judge's smirk. Maybe there was hope yet, or maybe Mary told her to smile at the jurors. Either way, I had my work cut out for me if I ever wanted to see Julie again.

"If anyone from the prospective jurors knows any of these people, could you please hold up your number and rise when I call it, please?" said Judge Pants. Only three people held up their numbers.

"Number 12, could you rise please, and tell us who you know?"

"Yes, Your Honor," said Number 12. "I know the defendant, Mrs. Crinn. I used to work at Petunia's Peanut Pieces."

"Thank you, Number 12. You're excused, but thank you for coming. Number 18, could you rise please, and tell us who you know?"

"Yes, Your Honor. I know Mary Payson. She defended me in court a few years ago."

"Thank you. You are also excused." The smirk on her face didn't exactly say *And thank you for coming, too.*

"Number 21?"

"Yes, Your Honor. I know the D.A., Mr. Mignon."

"I see," snarled the judge. "And just how do you know him?"

"Oh, we've been dating for the last three months, Your Honor."

"You're definitely excused," Hot Pants continued to snarl.

"Now, since this is a first-degree murder trial," continued the judge after she regained her composure, "if there is anyone who is against capital punishment, could you please hold up your number?"

Hot waited for a few seconds, but not a number went up. I really hoped Mary's winning streak would continue.

After about 15 minutes, the 12 jurors and two alternates were selected, and the rest were dismissed.

It was time for the first recess of the day.

After the recess ended, it was time for the real show to begin.

"You may call your first witness, Mr. Mignon," said the judge.

"I call Dr. Urnot Lyve to the stand, please."

Dr. Lyve was the medical examiner for the county. He placed his hand on the Bible and swore "to tell the truth, the whole truth, and nothing but the truth." I find it amazing that the only people involved in cases who don't have to do this are the ones who actually should – namely the attorneys and the judge.

"Would you state you name please, sir?" began D.A. Mignon.

"My name is Urnot Agostine Lyve," Dr. Lyve stated in an accent that I couldn't place.

"And what is your profession, doctor?"

"I am the Medical Examiner for the county."

"I see. And as the Medical Examiner, did you perform the autopsy on Mr. Joseph J. Crinn?"

"Yes, I did."

"Could you tell the court, Dr. Lyve, what was the cause of death of Mr. Crinn?"

"Mr. Crinn was poisoned."

"Could you be more specific, doctor?"

"Yes. Actually, Mr. Crinn died from peanut oil in the body."

"Peanut oil? But doctor, peanut oil isn't a poison. Could you explain, please?"

"Yes, peanut oil is usually not poisonous, but to someone like Mr. Crinn, who is highly allergic to peanuts, peanut oil can be very deadly."

"And you're sure it wasn't something else, perhaps a heart attack?"

"Well, it was made to look like a heart attack, but it certainly wasn't."

"Thank you, doctor. No further questions. Your witness, Ms. Payson."

It certainly looked like Mignon had scored a number of major points. Mary and Phil had been arch-rivals for years, and Mignon was doing everything he could to stop his losing streak.

"Thank you, Mr. Mignon. "Would you be so kind as to tell the court, Dr. Lyve, if there was anything else you found in the body?"

"Yes. There were the usual things. Some food, some alcohol, some other medication that he was on."

"Medication, you say? What types of medication, Dr. Lyve?"

"Oh, some of the usual medication. Things for high blood pressure and cholesterol, mainly."

"I see," said Mary. "You said *mainly*, Dr. Lyve. What else was there?"

"Well, there were definitely traces of Norpramine."

Norpramine, I thought. Even though I didn't even know what the hell Norpramine was, or what it was used for, my first thought was *No, No, No, No, No. Could No have killed Joe with Norpramine?* (Wow, six negatives together. That oughta get me the silver in the Olympic English-butcherin' competition. I figured that Zeke had the gold wrapped up, but with Stella trying to change Zeke into Sanford, I was closin' in fast.)

"And could you tell the court, doctor, what Norpramine is used for?"

"It's an antidepressant."

"I see. And could the wrong amount of Norpramine prove fatal to someone, doctor?"

"Well, yes, it could."

"And what symptoms, if any, would occur before death, doctor?"

"Well, in most cases, an overdose would cause a heart attack."

Since there were only four of us in the courtroom, no one gasped, but the jury sure looked very confused.

"A heart attack, you say? So, Dr. Lyve, how do we know it was the peanut oil that killed Mr. Crinn and not the Norpramine?"

"Well," stuttered Dr. Lyve, "we really don't. But with Mr. Crinn's reaction to peanuts, we just assumed…"

"You just *assumed?* Dr. Lyve. Just a few more questions, Dr. Lyve. How is Norpramine administered?"

"It's usually in tablet form, but sometimes it can be taken in a syrup."

"I see. So it would be fairly easy to slip some into someone's drink, Dr. Lyve, especially someone who had a few drinks already?"

"Objection," yelled the D.A.

"I withdraw the question," Mary shot back. "No further questions of this witness, Your Honor."

"Any rebuttal, Mr. Mignon," Judge Pants purred.

"Not at this time, Your Honor," replied Mignon.

"In that case," said the judge, "I see that it is the noon hour. Court will recess until one o'clock."

I went up to the railing to see if I could talk to Julie, but Mary just shook her head, and Julie wouldn't even turn around to look at me.

It was gonna be an uphill battle.

Even though Judge Pants was very biased towards D.A. Mignon, I will give her one thing. (No, *not* that!) She was on time. When she said one o'clock, she meant one o'clock.

"Please call your next witness, Mr. Mignon," said Hot Pants, like she was on one of those sexy shave cream commercials from the '70s.

Mignon called Sally Roberts. I didn't see Sally enter the courtroom after lunch, but when her name was called, she got out of her seat which was a few rows behind us. She walked to the witness stand without looking at any of us.

"This oughta be real good," I whispered to Zeke.

After the swearing in part, Mignon began his questions.

"Could you please tell the court, Ms. Roberts, how you knew the deceased, Mr. Joseph Crinn?"

"Certainly. I was Mr. Crinn's personal secretary."

"I see. And about how long did you work for Mr. Crinn in that capacity?"

"Well, I started right out of high school, and worked for him up until he died."

"And as his personal secretary, what were your duties?"

"I attended most of his meetings and took the notes, I took dictation, and generally ran the office for him. Things like that."

"Did you ever see Mr. Crinn outside of the office?" asked Mr. Mignon.

"Yes, on several occasions after a long day, we would have dinner together."

"Then, would you say that being at the wine dinner with Mr. Crinn on the night he was murdered was nothing out of the ordinary?"

"Objection!" yelled Mary Payson. "Leading the witness, Your Honor."

"Sustained," growled Judge Pants.

"But you were with him for dinner at Sloppy Man's the night before he died, is that correct?"

"Yes, I was."

"About what time did you leave Sloppy Man's that evening, Ms. Roberts?"

"We left right after it was over. I'd say it was about 10:45."

"And where did you go from there?"

"Well, Mr. Crinn drove me right home. I have no idea where he went after that."

"I see. Tell me, Ms. Roberts, did you know about Mr. Crinn's allergy to peanuts?"

"Yes, I did. After working for him for almost 18 years, I did know about that."

"How did Mr. Crinn look to you when he drove you home?"

"Other than looking a little tired, he appeared fine to me."

"You say he looked a little tired?"

"Well, yes. But it was late, it had been a long day, and Mr. Crinn was 83 years old."

"Yes, that certainly would explain it. Other than being a little tired, were there any other signs that Mr. Crinn was in any way not feeling well?"

"No. Other than being a little tired, he looked fine to me."

"Thank you, Ms. Roberts. Oh, just one other question," said D.A. Mignon. "Did you know that you were in Mr. Crinn's will?"

"I certainly did not. I didn't know anything about that until I got a call to be at the reading of his will."

"Thank you, Ms. Roberts. No further questions. Your witness, Ms. Payson."

"If there is no objection, Ms. Payson," said Judge Pants as civilly as possible, "I think it would be a good time for a 15 minute recess."

"No objection, Your Honor."

"Court will recess for 15 minutes. Please be back at 2:30. And ladies and gentlemen of the jury, please do not discuss the case with anyone while you are outside the courtroom."

I went up and had a few words with Mary.

Julie never even turned around.

When court reconvened at 2:30, it was Mary's turn to question Sally Roberts.

"So, Ms. Roberts, you say you were with Mr. Crinn at the wine dinner the night before he was found dead?"

"Objection, Your Honor. That has already been established."

"Sustained!" sang out Judge Pants. It looked like she wanted to stick her tongue out at Mary.

"Yes, it has, hasn't it? Well, in that case, were you with Mr. Crinn at all times at the dinner?"

"The only time we weren't was when one of us had to use the bathroom. I don't think they would let us go there together."

"Just answer the questions, please, Ms. Roberts," said the judge.

"Certainly, Your Honor. Sorry, Your Honor."

"Now, Ms. Roberts, did you see anyone else you knew at the dinner that evening?"

"Yes. I saw Nora Klause. She was there with Dewey Popple... Pollup...Dewey. The guy sitting back there," she said, pointing at me.

"Let the record show that the witness is pointing to Mr. David Polpulcionski," said Mary.

"Did you and Mr. Crinn talk to Mr. Polpulcionski or Ms. Klause at any time during the evening?"

"Yes, we talked to them after the first course."

"And did anyone leave your group while you were talking?"

"Nora...I mean Ms. Klause did. She said she thought she saw someone she recognized and was going over to talk to them."

"And could you see where Ms. Klause went?"

"No, we were talking, so I didn't watch her."

"And Mr. Polpulcionski? Was he there all the while, or did he go somewhere else too?"

"No, he was with us all the time."

"Did you see them later on during the dinner?" asked Mary.

"No," replied Sally. "We were sitting on the other side of the room, and we left right when it was over, so we never saw them again."

"I see," said Mary. "Now, getting back to your position with Mr. Crinn. You said you were his personal secretary, is that correct?"

"Yes, that is correct."

"And as his personal secretary, did you attend all his meetings?"

"Well, I attended most of them?"

"So, you didn't attend them all then, is that correct?"

"Yes, there were a few I did not attend."

"Could you tell the court why you were not at those meetings, Ms. Roberts?"

"Well, the only meetings I didn't go to were the ones Mr. Crinn had with three guys named Vinny, Angelo, and Oscar."

"I see. And why didn't you go to those?"

"I really don't know. Joe…uh…Mr. Crinn said I didn't have to be there. I guess they were personal."

"And you don't know anything else about these three men?"

"No. Nothing at all."

"Thank you very much, Ms. Roberts. I have no further questions of this witness at this time, but I would like to recall the witness, if necessary, at a later time, Your Honor."

"Very well, Ms. Payson," Hot snarled. "Any rebuttal, Mr. Mignon?" she purred.

"Nothing further for the witness, Your Honor."

"Very well, then," said the judge. "Since it is just after four o'clock, if there are no objections, court will recess till tomorrow morning at nine o'clock."

"No objections, Your Honor," said D. A. Mignon.

"No objections, Your Honor," said Mary Payson.

"Court is adjourned," said Judge Pants.

Mary turned around and gave me a brief smile. I knew somehow that things would be all right.

Julie never looked my way.

Chapter 26: DEBBIE AND BRAD AND JOHN AND BILL AND SAM AND…REVISITED

I knew there was nothing more that I could do, so on the way home I grabbed a six pack and a pizza. When I got in, it was time to turn the VCR on and watch that day's episode of *Debbie and Brad and John and Bill and Sam and…*

"In our last episode," began the announcer, "Debbie had just given Brad, John, Bill, Sam, and Dr. Fix their tests to see which ones weren't exactly playing with a loaded gun. Today's episode is brought to you by the state lottery, where Edgar, the 43rd most popular anteater in the state reminds you to "Just rub 'em, baby."

That really cracked me up. Since nobody on the show was usin' any protection, it's a wonder some of them weren't rubbin', and I don't mean lottery tickets.

Once again, the scene opens with Debbie talkin' to the five men.

"Hello, guys," said Debbie. "Gather round, please. I have the results of your tests, and I'm afraid that we're gonna hafta say goodbye to some of you."

The five men, plus two new ones I hadn't seen before, were paying strict attention.

"As you know," continued Debbie, "I've been sleeping with all of you, and some of you have not been performing up to expectations. I'll do this as mercifully as I can, but three of you will have to go."

"But first, the winners. I'm happy to announce that Brad and Dr. Fix will remain with the show. As you all know, I'm expecting three new arrivals, so one of you guys must be on hi-test. I'm not sure which one yet, but we can worry about that later."

"And now, for the rest of you. Bill, I know you gave it your best shot, but at your age you could barely get it up. Sorry, Bill."

"Sam, you just started with the show, and I was hoping for *big things* from you, but it just didn't work out. Good luck with your career."

"And John, what can I say?"

"But Debbie," John started to cry, "I really…"

"Oh, knock it the hell off, would you John. Save it for your next show."

"Brad and Steve, on our next show you will be joined by Fred and Art. I've already had both of them tested, and I'm happy to report that they're *more* than ready to go. Starting tomorrow, the show will be called *Debbie and Brad and Steve and Fred and Art and…* Are there any question?"

"But why, Debbie?" cried John.

"Stuff a sock in it, will ya, John," replied Debbie.

"Gentlemen, I'll see you tomorrow. Right now I have to go and help my mother prepare for her latest wedding."

"Tune in tomorrow for the first episode of *Debbie and Brad and Steve and Fred and Art*. And remember, as our sponsors would say, "If you don't want to *just rub 'em,* remember to use SafOne Condoms, and after you're finished remember to reach for the Wipems."

Today's show wasn't all that great, but the sponsors really outdid themselves.

I had nothin' to do and nowhere to go, so after a long nap I got up in time to see *Run for the Roses*, starring Roni Roses. There was Roni, still sloshin' around in the mud with nothin' on but a smile, and six horny studs just waitin' for action. I was wonderin' if Roni was gonna give Bill and Sam and John a shot now that they were out of work. I definitely had to tune in again tomorrow.

It was now a little after 1:00 in the morning. I set the VCR for the shows for the next day and went to bed.

Alone.

Again.

That's all. (I really hope you weren't expectin' me to add *Naturally.*)

Chapter 27: JULIE'S TRIAL DAY TWO… or… DEWEY'S STILL IN THE DOG HOUSE

I got up the next morning and had my regular breakfast. I shouldn't hafta tell ya what that is by now, so I won't. I'd set the VCR the night before, so I didn't hafta do that either. I was really beginnin' to wonder why the hell I got up so early, but I guess it was because I didn't get a lot of sleep again the night before. No point in goin' back to bed.

I decided to wear my new suit again for the trial. I knew everybody had seen me in it the day before, but I figured I might as well get as much use out of it as I could. Apparently it wouldn't be all that much longer.

Since court was to resume at 9:00, I got there around 8:45 and caught Zeke just as he was about to walk in. He had a big smile on his face, so I guess things were still goin' OK with Stella, but he did look a bit tired. We both grunted "Mornin'" and walked in together. Nora Klause and Nick Rudawski were already sitting there together. It now appeared that they were definitely a couple.

Mary and Stella and Julie were already in their seats on their side of the aisle, and D.A. Phillippe Auguste Mignon (see, the guy's name is…Oh, never mind! If ya didn't get it by now, it ain't worth explainin'.) was on his. Judge Pants had yet to make her appearance. I gave Mary a quick look and she nodded back, but Julie never turned around.

At 9:02, Judge Saundra H. Pants walked into the courtroom and we all stood. Judge Pants wasn't exactly on time, but she was a lot closer than Beanie. She sat, we sat, and the second half was about to begin.

I hoped Mary got her second-half strategy all worked out in the locker room, cuz it sure looked to me like the score was still tied.

"Good morning, ladies and gentlemen," said Judge Pants. "It is now the defense attorney's turn to present her side of the case," snarled Hot. "Are you ready with your presentation, Ms. Payson?" Then she added, "Hey, I'm a poet and don't know it."

"Yes, Your Honor, the defense is ready to present its case."

"Very well then, Ms. Payson, you may call your first witness."

"Thank you, Your Honor. Defense calls as its first witness Mr. David Polpulcionski."

I took the oath to tell the truth, although it woulda been a lot more fun to lie. I hadn't told any good ones in some time, and I was afraid I might be outta practice, but since I swore...

"For the record," Mary began, "could you state your name please?"

"Certainly. It's David Polpulcionski." I felt like addin' *but you can just call me Dewey P,* but I didn't think it was the place for it. But don't think I wasn't tempted.

"Could you please spell that for the court stenographer, Mr. Popple…Mr. Poppy…Mr. Popeye (Hey, that was one even I hadn't heard before.) uh…Sir?" said the Judge.

"Sure," I said, not bein' able to resist the chance at a little humor. "T-h-a-t," I said.

Everyone in the courtroom broke up, and I even thought I saw Julie give a little chuckle. Maybe things weren't as hopeless as I thought.

Everyone in the courtroom broke up, except, of course, for the judge.

"Order! Order in the court!" yelled Judge Pants. I was thinkin' of sayin' *I'll have a ham and cheese on rye, with a diet rootbeer,* but even I didn't have the guts to push it.

After the courtroom settled down, Mary continued with her questioning.

"Could you please tell the court, Mr. Polpulcionski, what your occupation is, sir?"

"Certainly. I'm a private investigator."

"And as a private investigator, did you ever do any work for Mr. Joseph Crinn?"

"Yes, I did."

"And could you tell us what Mr. Crinn hired you to do?"

"Yes. He hired me to keep tabs on his wife."

"And by 'keep tabs' I assume you mean you were paid to watch her?"

"Yes. That is correct."

"Why did Mr. Crinn pay you to watch his wife?"

"Because he said he thought she was cheatin' on him."

"And according to what you found out, was she cheating on him?"

"Objection, Your Honor," shouted D.A. Mignon. "I've let this line of questioning go on long enough, but this is totally irrelevant to the case."

"It does seem that Mr. Mignon has a good point, Ms. Payson."

"Your Honor," replied Mary, "if you will allow me to ask just a few more questions, I assure you that it will become very relevant to the court."

"In that case, Ms. Payson, I will overrule the objection for now," snarled Judge Pants. "But please show the relevancy very quickly or I will have to sustain the next objection."

"Certainly, Your Honor," said Mary. "Thank you, Your Honor."

"Now, Mr. Polpulcionski, according to what you discovered, was Mrs. Crinn cheating on Mr. Crinn?"

"From what I could see, no, she wasn't. As a matter of fact, it appeared to be just the opposite."

"Objection," yelled Mignon. "The witness is drawing his own conclusion, Your Honor."

"Sustained!" replied Judge Pants. "Please just answer the questions, Mr...Mr...OH...Sir."

"Yes Your Honor," I said, barely keeping myself from laughing.

"Well, tell me, Mr. Polpulcionski, did you see Mr. Crinn on the night he was murdered?" asked Mary.

"Yes I did."

"And could you please tell the court exactly where you saw Mr. Crinn that evening?"

"Yes. I saw him at a wine dinner at Sloppy Man's in Queensville."

"And was he alone?"

"No, he was not."

"And who was he with at this wine dinner?"

"He was there with his secretary, Sally Roberts." The spectators at the trial normally would have at least stirred at this revelation; but since Sally, Nora, Nick, and Zeke were the only ones there, they were doing all they could just to stay awake.

"Are you quite sure that it was Mr. Crinn and his secretary, Ms. Sally Roberts, that you saw together at the restaurant?"

"Oh, quite sure. We were talking to..."

"The prosecution will concede that Mr. Crinn and Ms. Roberts were at the wine dinner together on the evening in question, Your Honor. Could we just get on with this, please?"

"Thank you, Mr. Mignon," purred Judge Pants. "If you intend to make a point with this line of questioning, Ms. Payson, I hope you can get to it soon," she snarled.

"Certainly, Your Honor. If you will allow me just a few more questions, I will soon get to the point."

The judge just nodded.

"Mr. Polpulcionski," Mary continued, "were you alone at the dinner, or did you have a date?"

"I was with Nora Klause."

"And were the two of you together the whole time at the dinner?"

"Most of the time. The only times we weren't was when one of us had to…uh…use the…you know."

"You mean the restrooms, Mr. Polpulcionski?"

"Yeah, the restrooms."

"Any other times you weren't together?"

"Just once. That was when Nora said she thought she saw somebody she knew and went over to the other side of the room."

"I see. And did you see Mr. Crinn and Ms. Roberts the whole evening?"

"No. We only saw them for a few minutes. They were sittin' on the other side of the room, and they musta left as soon as it was over, cuz we didn't see them after that."

"Thank you, Mr. Polpulcionski. No further questions. Your witness, Mr. Mignon."

"Thank you, Ms. Payson. Now, Mr. Polpulcionski," Mignon started, "you stated that you were working for Mr. Crinn, is that correct?" (Somebody else who could pronounce my name correctly. I wonder how many that made at this point? If you were countin', STOP! It don't matter!)

"Yes sir, that is correct?"

"And did you like Mr. Crinn, sir?"

"Objection!" yelled Mary.

"Overruled," yelled back Judge Pants. "Please answer the question, Mr. Popple...Mr. Poople...SIR," she snapped. (At least there was one person I didn't have to worry about getting it right.)

"I really didn't care one way or the other. He paid me on time. That's all I cared about."

"And how did you feel about Mrs. Crinn, sir?"

"Objection, Your Honor," Mary said, rising to her feet.

"Overruled!" yelled Judge Pants, once again. It looked like Mary really had her work cut out for her. "Please answer the question, Mr. Polpulcionski." (Oh no! Now even the judge was gettin' in on the act.)

"I really didn't know Mrs. Crinn at that time," I answered.

"I see. Well, isn't it true that you and Mrs. Crinn planned to murder Mr. Crinn that evening by having you slip something in his drink so that you and Mrs. Crinn could be together and have Mr. Crinn's money?"

"Objection! Objection! Objection!" yelled Mary.

"I withdraw the question, Your Honor. I have no further questions for the witness at this time."

"Very well," said the judge. "Any rebuttal, Ms. Payson?"

"No, Your Honor."

"Before you call your next witness, Ms. Payson, I think this would be a good time for a brief recess, if there are no objections." Not hearing any, the judge continued, "Court will recess until 10:30."

Mary and I looked at each other.

Julie still didn't turn around.

When court resumed at 10:30, Mary called her next witness, Nora Klause.

"Now, Ms. Klause," Mary began, "you heard Mr. Polpulcionski state that you were his date for the wine dinner the night that Mr. Crinn was murdered. Is that true?"

"Oh yes," Nora answered. "We were at the wine dinner together."

"And were you together the whole time?"

"Yes, except for the times that one of us used the restroom, and the one time that I walked to the other side of the room."

"Could you tell us, Ms. Klause, why you went to the other side of the room?"

"Because I didn't want to be around Joe…I mean Mr. Crinn."

"And why was that, Ms. Klause?"

"Because I couldn't stand to see him with Sally Roberts."

"And why would that be, Ms. Klause?" continued Mary.

"When Joe and I broke up, he told me that Julie, Mrs. Crinn, was the one love of his life. Now I knew it wasn't true."

"I see. So you and Mr. Crinn had an affair?"

"No, not really. Mr. Crinn and I were going together before he met Mrs. Crinn."

"I see. Tell me, how did you meet Mr. Crinn?"

"I was the nurse at the doctor's office Mr. Crinn went to."

"And being his nurse, did you know about his allergy to peanuts?"

"Yes."

"And being a nurse, would you know what effects the drug Norpramine would have if administered in the wrong dosage?"

"Yes, I suppose so. But I didn't…"

"Thank you, Ms. Klause," said Mary. "No further questions. Your witness, Mr. Mignon."

"Just one question, Ms. Klause," said Mr. Mignon. "Did you know that Mr. Crinn would be at the wine dinner that evening?"

"No, I certainly did not," answered No.

"You may step down, Ms. Klause," said Judge Pants. "You may call your next witness, Ms. Payson."

"I call to the stand Mr. Oscar Smallings."

Oscar had been sitting behind us in the courtroom, and I hadn't noticed when he came in. Even though I'd seen him briefly at old man Crinn's funeral, somethin' looked awful familiar about him other than that. I just couldn't quite figure out what it was.

"Mr. Smallings," began Mary, "did you know the deceased, Joseph Crinn?"

"Yes, I knew him." Oscar's voice sounded a bit familiar, too. But again I couldn't quite place it. Only I knew I'd heard it somewhere before.

"And exactly how did you know him, sir?"

"Mr. Crinn and I had some business dealings together."

"I see. And what kinds of business dealings would they be?"

"Well, my associates and I invested in many of Mr. Crinn's businesses. You might say we were kind of like a syndicate."

"And were your business dealings on good terms, sir?"

"Oh, yes. Very good terms. Mr. Crinn was making us a lot of money."

"And did you ever see Mr. Crinn other than through your business dealings?"

"No. We made it a rule to never mix business with pleasure."

"I see. So then you were not at the wine dinner the evening Mr. Crinn was murdered, I take it?"

"That would be correct."

"I have no more questions of this witness, Your Honor. Your witness, Mr. Mignon."

"No questions, Your Honor."

Mary looked at me and I looked at her. I knew her winning streak was in jeopardy.

"You may call your next witness, Ms. Payson," said Judge Pants.

"If it please the court, Your Honor, since it is approaching the noon hour, I would suggest that we take our noon recess before I call my next witness."

"Any objections, Mr. Mignon?" asked the judge.

"No objections, Your Honor," replied D.A. Mignon.

"Court will recess until 12:45," said the judge.

I knew that Mary was now stallin' for time. I knew that the solution to the entire case was starin' me smack in the kisser, but I just couldn't seem to see it.

I also knew that unless I figured out what it was, Julie was in big trouble.

Chapter 28: CAN YOU OUTDO DEWEY?

Well, like I said, I knew the answer to the case was starin' me smack in the kisser, but I just couldn't see it yet. But if it's starin' me smack in the kisser that means that it must be starin' you smack in the kisser, too. You have all the clues you need, so before I reveal the thrillin' climax to the murder trial of Joseph Crinn, can you figure out who done it?

You have many suspects to choose from, so let's take one last look at the lineup.

Was Nora jealous enough to slip some Norpramine into Joe's drink when she went to the other side of the room? And did she know, by any chance, that she was in Joe's will? Nora usin' Norpramine to get Joe does have a nice ring to it, but I gotta admit, it's also more than a bit corny.

What about Sally? She was with Joe most of the evening and had the best advantage to do it? Did she know she was in his will? But it sure seemed like Joe was takin' care of Sally pretty good, so would she bite the hand that was literally feedin' her...among other things?

What about Oscar? Did he lie about bein' at the restaurant the night of the wine dinner, and could I have missed seein' him? Joe was supposedly makin' money for him and his pals, so why would he do it?

Speakin' of his pals, where were they? Could one of them have done it?

How about my old pal Zeke? Nah, I'll tell ya right now, ya can forget about him.

What about Cousin Nick? Did he know he was in the will? What was it about him that I couldn't figure out? And why wasn't he called to testify at the trial?

Could it be the person we don't know for some reason we don't know, either? If you expect somebody not in the book yet to come into the courtroom screamin', "I did it! I did it!" then you need to go back and read the book again.

Even though I didn't think so, could it really be Julie? She had enough motives. Could she actually be foolin' everybody?

And last, but certainly not least, did I bump off the old man cuz I wanted Julie all to myself? Am I really writin' this from some maximum security prison, just hopin' that Mary can get me a pardon from the governor – after the temporary insanity plea didn't work? (I guess there's a good shot since I did vote for the guy.) I don't think so, but then you should know by now how much I...shall we say...like to stretch the truth.

Oh, but there is one other possible solution. Maybe Joe really isn't dead. Maybe I got real bored with just sittin' outside Julie's office, so I let my imagination run wild and made the whole thing up. Maybe I'll be back to tailin' Legs again tomorrow.

I'll give ya a few minutes for you to figure it out before you turn the page to find out what really happened.

Chapter 29: THE ANSWER REVEALED

Well, the lunch recess was over, and we were back in the courtroom, so you can forget about me makin' the whole thing up. Julie, Mary, and Stella were back at their table, and D.A. Mignon was back at his, lookin' rather smug. I sure hoped that Mary figured somethin' out during lunch, cuz even though it was starin' me smack in the kisser, I still couldn't come up with the answer.

"Are you ready to call your next witness, Ms. Payson?" asked Judge Pants.

"Well, Your Honor…"

Just then it hit me. I went runnin' up to Mary.

"May I have a moment, Your Honor?" Mary said.

"A very brief moment," snapped the judge.

"Your Honor," started Mary, "I would like to recall a witness."

"And which witness would that be, Ms. Payson?"

"Your Honor, I would like to recall Sally Roberts."

"Any objection, Mr. Mignon?" Hot Pants purred.

"No objection, Your Honor," replied Mignon, almost returning the purr.

After Sally was reminded that she was still under oath, Mary started with the questions.

"Could you tell us, please, Ms. Roberts, the name of the director of the F.B.I?"

"Objection, Your Honor. How can that possibly be relevant to the case?"

"May I assure you, Your Honor, that if you permit me to ask Ms. Roberts just a few more questions, I will show the court that it is *very* relevant to this case."

"Very well, Ms. Payson. But only a few questions. I really can't see the relevancy myself. Objection overruled."

"Thank you, Your Honor. Now, Ms. Roberts, could you please tell the court who the director of the F.B.I. is?"

"Well, I think it's J. Edward Hooper." Everyone in the courtroom busted out laughin'. Even Judge Pants couldn't believe her answer.

"Don't you mean J. Edgar Hoover, Ms. Roberts?"

"Yes, I suppose that's who I mean."

"Would it surprise you to know, Ms. Roberts, that J. Edgar Hoover is dead?"

"Oh, I'm so sorry," said Sally. "I really didn't know."

"Ms. Roberts," continued Mary, "Mr. Hoover died in 1972."

"I must object to this line of questioning," Your Honor. "I don't see how this can possibly be relevant to this case."

"I can't see the relevancy either, Mr. Mignon, but this is too precious not to continue. Objection overruled."

"Thank you, Your Honor. Now, Ms. Roberts, you said you thought that J. Edgar Hoover was the director of the F.B.I. and you didn't know he had been dead since 1972?"

"That's right," said Sally. "Why should I know who the director is? What difference does it make to me?"

"Because didn't you tell Mr. Polpulcionski that you really worked for the F.B.I. and were planted to keep track of Mr. Crinn because the F.B.I. thought he had mob connections?"

"I did no such thing!" shouted Sally.

"And didn't you tell Mr. Polpulcionski that you made several trips to Washington, D.C., in the last few weeks because you had to report your findings now that Mr. Crinn was dead?"

"No!"

"And didn't you also tell Mr. Polpulcionski that your real name was not Sally Roberts, but was, indeed, Teri Smallings?" With that, Oscar Smallings, who was sitting in the back of the courtroom, tried to make a break for the door, but Nick Rudawski tripped him and the bailiff handcuffed him immediately. I was still tryin' to figure Nick out.

"No!" shouted Sally. "That's another lie. They're all lies!"

"All lies, you say, Ms. Roberts. Or should I call you Mrs. Smallings? Would you like Mr. Polpulcionski to return to the stand and see what he has to say about that?"

"No, that won't be necessary," said Sally, finally calming down. "I poisoned Joe at the wine dinner all right, but it was all his idea," she finished, pointing at Oscar.

"She's lying," yelled Oscar. "It was all her idea. I had nothin' to do with it."

"Yes he did, the rotten bastard. Oscar, Vinny, and Angelo were trying to get Joe to sell them his businesses, but he wouldn't do it. Oscar told me that if I didn't kill Joe, he would blow the whistle on me, and leave me for good this time."

"Under the circumstances, Your Honor, I make a motion that all charges against Mrs. Julie Crinn be dropped."

"No objections, Your Honor," said Mignon, although he sounded very disappointed having lost again to the great Mary Payson.

"Very well," said Judge Pants. "All charges against you are dismissed, Mrs. Crinn. Bailiff, please hold Mr. and Mrs. Smallings."

It was finally over. Julie was free. I went up to congratulate everyone, but Julie still wouldn't even look my way.

"Julie," Mary said, "I think you're being unfair to Dewey. After all, he was the one who remembered that Sally was really Teri Smallings. He's the one who saved you."

Julie finally looked at me with tears in her eyes and said, "I'm sorry, Dewey. I really…"

"Yeah, I know," I answered. "Me too."

"Your Honor," I said. "May I have a word with Ms. Roberts… uh… I mean Mrs. Smallings?"

"I suppose so," said Hot Pants.

"Why the hell did you have to get involved? Why couldn't you just go on finding cats, you…you?" Teri said, before I could get a word in.

"Just one thing I don't get, *Teri*," I said. "What did you mean by *he would leave you for good this time?*"

"Oh, this is the second time we've been married. See, we were married once, right out of high school, but we were too young and thought we'd made a mistake. So I got a divorce and married somebody else. But then Oscar and I realized we were meant for each other, so we got married again."

"Oh, so you divorced your second husband to marry Oscar again?"

"Well, not exactly."

"Well, what happened then?"

"Well, actually, my second husband, he…uh…he had a little accident. Tragic. Very tragic."

"I can imagine," I said.

They were ready to take Teri and Oscar into custody. But before they did, I had to know one thing. "Excuse me, but could I have a word with Oscar?"

"Oscar," I said, "I know you look vaguely familiar and I know I've heard your voice somewhere before, too, but I just can't seem to place you."

"Oh really, suh," was all he said.

Well I'll be damned. I knew the British accent was a phony, but it looked like he was a much better actor than I gave him credit for.

So it looked like everyone was gonna live happily ever after. Julie and I were back together, Nick was with Nora, and Zeke was with Stella. It even looked like Sandy Pants was gonna get together with Phil A. Mignon (come on, you had to figure it out by now), and even Teri and Oscar would be together for as long as they had left. Mary was still alone, but I'm sure that wouldn't last long. Yes, it looked like one big happy ending.

Well, if I were writin' a novella, that would be the case. But since novellas don't pay, and this is supposed to be a novel, the happy endin' is just gonna hafta wait.

Chapter 30: SOMEBODY GETS PERSONAL WITH THE IMPERSONATOR

It was time for a party. We all headed over to Sloppy Man's to celebrate the capture of Joe's real killers and the release of Julie Crinn. Everyone was there. I was with Julie, Zeke was with Stella, Nick was with Nora, and even Phil was there with Sandy. Mary wasn't there yet, but she said she would catch up to us later. Of course, Oscar and Teri weren't there. It appeared they wouldn't be goin' anywhere for quite some time.

Since it was a Tuesday night, and my friend Tommy wasn't playing, we decided to sit in the dining room instead of the bar area.

Samantha came over to take our order. Samantha had only been at Sloppy Man's for a few weeks, but already was the favorite waitress in the place. It looked like all the other waitresses were jealous, and for good reason. Once Samantha – you would never refer to a girl like this as *Sam* – entered the room, all eyes were on her. Gorgeous, long blond hair, even longer legs, and a great pair of…well…you should know my taste in women by now. It's a good thing Julie didn't bump Joe off. I never would have been able to afford Samantha on the money I was makin' chasin' lost cats. Not that I was interested, you understand.

"Hello, folks," said Samantha. "My name is Samantha, and I'll be your server tonight. Can I start you off with a round of drinks?"

Before anyone could say anything, Phil said, "We'll have the best bottle of champagne that you have. It's on me."

"Why, thank you, Phil," said Sandy Pants. If she would have been purrin' any louder, I woulda sworn that Phil was strokin' her. Now that I think about it, since I could only see one of his hands, I'm pretty sure that he was.

No one quite knew what to say until Julie said, "I sure hope Mary gets here soon. I'd really like to thank her."

"She'll be here in a few minutes," said Stella. "She just went to pick someone up."

Just as she said that, Mary walked in with someone I hadn't seen in quite some time, but whose picture I had seen many times in the papers. Nathan Bricks, Mary's ex. Now the party was complete. Boy-girl, boy-girl, boy-girl, boy-girl, boy-girl. It's a good thing they had big tables at Sloppy Man's.

Phil called Samantha over. "It looks like you'd better make that two bottles of your best champagne."

Sandy continued to purr. I couldn't wait to see what she was gonna do with a few drinks in her.

When the champagne arrived and the glasses had all been filled, Phil proposed a toast. "To the best defense attorney I've ever had the pleasure of losing to."

Everyone went "Here, here."

"But I'll beat you yet one of these days," he continued.

Little did I know at the time how prophetic that would come to sound.

Samantha brought over the menus, and since Sloppy Man's specialty was seafood, that was what most of us had. Actually, all of us, except, of course, for Phil A. Mignon. He had exactly what you would expect him to have.

Chicken.

Everyone was enjoying the meal so much that very little was said during dinner, until Nick came back from the men's room.

"Hey, Dewey," he said. "What was the guy's name at your trial who was the police impersonator?"

"I'm pretty sure it was Stacy Rickert. What brought that up?"

"I stopped in the bar a few seconds to watch the news on TV. Apparently Mr. Rickert's body was found this afternoon. Seems he was murdered late last night or early this morning."

"That's a shame," I said. "He seemed like an all right guy." Then I added, "Hey, Mary, maybe you'll have a new client one of these days."

Now it was my turn to sound prophetic.

Everyone was really enjoying dinner, and, for once, no one was having too much to drink. But it had been a long, mentally-exhausting day, so our group started to break up.

First Mary and Nathan left.

Then Stella said, "Well, Sanford, I think it's time we got going, too."

"That's a good idea, honey," Zeke replied. "Goodnight everybody."

I knew I'd lost my old buddy Zeke, but at least I would always have Sanford.

Nick and Nora left soon after, with Nick telling everyone that even though he was now a multi-billionaire, he needed to get back to Tucson in the next few days. He promised to get in touch with me before he left.

That now left me and Julie, and Phil and Sandy; and the two of them were so into each other that they didn't even notice when we quietly slipped out. It was a good thing Phil was pickin' up the tab.

When we got back to Julie's place, she insisted on having a few drinks before turning in. We both had double scotches, and I started to make my move, but Julie wasn't ready.

"So...who did you think killed Rickert?" Julie asked.

"How should I know?" I replied, still trying to get her into the mood.

"Well maybe you should try and figure it out," she said. "It might be a good career move."

"Really? And how do you figure that?"

"Well, if Mary happens to defend the person charged with his murder, and with Saul going to Saskatchewan, maybe Mary would hire you full time when Saul leaves."

"OK, let's see. Well, I know you didn't do it. You were still in jail. I don't see any reason why Teri and Oscar would have done it, unless they were just tryin' to rack up some numbers."

"Would you get serious?" Julie said.

"OK. Then how about Officer Hanley? Rickert blew the whistle on him on the stand?"

"I don't think so. Hanley might have been pissed, but not enough to kill him."

"Then that leaves just three other possibilities as far as I can see."

"Yeah, and who might they be?" asked Julie.

"Well, there's Beanie the judge. Maybe he was pissed cuz I won, he figured Rickert was the reason, he ran into him when he was drunk, and voila."

"Nah."

"Or it could be the unknown person who isn't in the book yet who killed him for some reason we don't know yet."

"Nah. You don't like those kinds of endings, and the book's almost over."

"OK. Then the only person left is yours truly."

"And just why would you do it?" she asked.

"Oh, I don't know. Maybe I had my fill of cops, and since he wasn't one to begin with, maybe I figured he shoulda said somethin' even before we went to trial."

"Sounds possible. Only then, this would be a stand-alone, not a series, and you'd never get this thing published."

"Ya know, I never thought of that."

"Oh well, I'll just have to sleep on it," I said, as I finished unbuttoning her blouse.

Chapter 31: IT'S JUST ANOTHER DAY...ALMOST

I didn't have much time to sleep on it. As a matter of fact, I didn't get much sleep at all, but that was all right by me. Julie and I hadn't been together in quite a while, and we more than made up for it.

However, it was another day, and back to business as usual.

Julie, of course, didn't have to do anything, now being a billionaire and all. I, on the other hand, now had to find some cases to keep me in pizzas and six-packs. You really didn't think I would let Julie support me, did ya? What kinduva cad do you take me for?

Oh! That's a kind I've never heard of before. You'll have to explain it to me one of these days.

Like I said, Julie didn't have to do anything, but she was real anxious to get back into the routine, so she went into her office at Petunia's Peanut Pieces. Since Saul was still around and workin' for Mary – and Mary didn't have any new cases that I was aware of – I went to my apartment to check my e-mails and phone messages. Hopefully the cats in East Arthur were gettin' lost again.

Julie and I promised to get together for lunch. Maybe I could sweet-talk her inta buyin'.

I had no e-mails waitin' for me, but four phone messages.

The first message was from my landlord, lettin' me know that the rent was over do. Again. Funny how that little thing kept slippin' my mind. But I still had the money to take care of it – at least for now – so I would do that later.

The second message was from Nick Rudawski. He didn't say what he wanted, but I figured he called to say goodbye. I would get back to him later in the day.

The other two were from little ol' ladies in East Arthur whose cats were missin'. I really didn't wanna take the jobs, but my dough was startin' to run low, so I called 'em back. Once I gave 'em my "I'll find your pussy in three days or your money back" guarantee, they both hired me on the spot. Sometimes I found 'em sooner. Dependin' on the client.

It was definitely back to business as usual.

Since I still had some time before I was to meet Julie for lunch, I decided to watch the latest episode of *Debbie and Brad and Steve and Fred and Art and…* that was waitin' for me in the VCR.

It was the same announcer with the same Debbie and Brad and Steve, but now Fred and Art were new to the show. I didn't recognize either of the actors, but by the way they both looked, I figured they were ex-jocks just breakin' into show business.

"Today's episode of *Debbie and Brad and Steve and Fred and Art and…* is brought to you by Jocks and Socks, the perfect combination to put next to your man," began the announcer. "All that's missing is you." With this kind of show, I really didn't expect it to be sponsored by Gay Blades.

Debbie was still her bitchy self. "So Fred and Art," she said, "I had you guys tested before I agreed to put you in the show. I hope you don't let me down. You *do* know what happened to Bill and Sam, don't you?"

"You got nothin' to worry about with me, babe," said Fred, as he gave Debbie's ass a little pinch.

"Ooh, Fredsie," cooed Debbie, "you certainly know how to sweet-talk a girl. I'll get back to you in a minute, Fredsie. And what about you, Art?"

"Gee, I don't know, Debbie. It's all right if I call you Debbie, isn't it? Or should I call you something else? I don't even know your last name. Should I call you Miss something, or Mrs., maybe? Or do you prefer Ms? And do you expect me to grab your rear end too?"

"I think we need to have a little talk, *Arthur*," said Debbie.

Either that, or maybe *tomorrow's* episode would be sponsored by Gay Blades. But I wouldn't count on it.

"Well, Fredsie, looks like it's back to you. You know I have three or four kids on the way by a few different guys. I can never keep count, you know. That's why I have Dr. Fix around. He keeps track of the kids I'm havin'. That and the fact that he's one of the daddies. At least I think he is. I'm sure we'll find out in a later episode. But there's always room for one more, so whadyah say, Fredsie?"

"What're we waitin' for, babe?" was Fredsie's reply.

"Oh, *Arthur*, wait for me in my dressing room, and if I don't show up in an hour, start the conversation without me. One other thing, *Arthur*. Shape up! You still could be playing in Japan, you know."

"Today's episode of *Debbie and Brad and Steve and Fred and Art and...* was brought to you by Jocks and Socks, the perfect combination to put next to your man. All that's missing is you," said the announcer. "Tune in tomorrow, same time, same channel for *Debbie and Brad and Steve and Fred and Art and...* or will it be *Debbie and Brad and Steve and Fred and Arthur and...* or maybe just *Debbie and Brad and Steve and Fred and...* Oh, I don't know. Just tune in tomorrow."

Debbie was up to her eyeballs in babies and daddies, and the show was startin' to show its age, but I just had to tape today's show to see what would happen with Art...or was it *Arthur*?

It was time to meet Julie for lunch.

When I picked Julie up at her office, she insisted that I meet her at the rear entrance. After all, I was still drivin' my clunker.

"Hi, Julie," I said. "So, how'd your first day back go so far?"

"So far, so good, although we didn't get too much work done talking about the case. But I'm sure I'll change that tomorrow. We can't have people missing their Petunia's Peanut Pieces, now can we? Where would you like to go for lunch, Dew?"

"Oh, I don't know. How 'bout a pizza and a few beers," I said, just in case I had to pay.

"I have a better idea," said Julie. "There's a new place that just opened up a few days ago called Sammy's Steak House. Why don't we give that a try? And don't worry, Dew, it's on me."

"Sammy's Steak House it is."

Sammy's was in a new shopping center just outside of East Arthur, only about ten minutes away from Petunia's Peanut Pieces if you took the Route 58 bypass. The place looked like a lot of other new restaurants, with outdoor seating when the weather was nice. Today wasn't one of those days.

The host greeted us as soon as we walked in the door, even though it was the lunch hour. I didn't know if the place actually had some class or if this was just because it was new and they were tryin' to put on the dog.

"May I help you?" he asked.

Julie and I really weren't payin' much attention when we walked in, so when we looked up, we couldn't believe our eyes. Neither one of us said anything. We just stared at each other.

"Oscar!" I finally said. "How could you possibly be…"

"I'm sorry, sir," replied the host, "but my name is Vincent. Vincent Billings. You must have me confused with someone who looks like me. Will there be two for lunch, sir?"

"Yes, Vincent. Two for lunch, please. I'm sorry, Vincent, but you look just like someone who is being held on the charge of murdering Mrs. Crinn's husband. Perhaps you heard about it on the news?"

"Actually, sir, I did. My sincere condolences, Mrs. Crinn. You see, my real name is Vincent Smallings. Oscar and I are identical twins, but we haven't had anything to do with each other in some time. I changed my last name over ten years ago."

Julie and I didn't know what to say for a few seconds. Then Julie said, "I'm sorry that things turned out that way for you. And thank you for the condolences."

Vincent then took us into a very elegant dining room and gave us a table that would allow us a lot of privacy. Since it was lunchtime, almost any table would have done that.

Within seconds of being seated, our waiter came over to take our drink orders. Even though it was lunch, he was dressed in a very nice tux, first-class all the way. This definitely was not Sloppy Man's. I looked around, but didn't see one long-legged, big-boobed waitress in the entire place.

Damn!

Since Julie had to go back to work after lunch, she ordered decaf coffee. And since I had to start findin' a few lost pussies, I ordered a non-alcoholic iced tea.

Our waiter, Claude, was back with our drinks within a matter of seconds, and was ready to take our order. If the food here was anywhere as good as the service, I would definitely have to check it out for dinner.

Maybe that's when the waitresses worked.

Julie and I both ordered the New York Strip with a baked potato and green beans. We both like our steaks medium rare, and thought they were the best we had in quite some time.

While we were eating, the topic of conversation shifted back to the murder of the police impersonator, Stacy Rickert. We were going through our usual list of suspects, which included the unknown person not yet in the book, as well as myself, when Vincent came by our table.

"How is your lunch today, folks?" he asked. "I assume this is your first time here."

We both agreed that the lunch was fabulous. "It's our first time here, but it definitely won't be our last."

"Very good, sir. And, by the way, your lunch is compliments of the management. We certainly would like to see you two again."

"Why, thank you very much, Vincent," said Julie.

"Our pleasure, ma'am."

"Say, Vincent," I said. "Did you happen to see where a man by the name of Stacy Rickert was murdered a few days ago? I hate to bring this up, but do you think that Oscar might have had something to do with it?"

"I really don't know, sir. As I said before, Oscar and I have had no communications with each other in quite some time. Why do you ask?"

"Well, Vincent, first of all, could you please stop calling me *sir?* Since we'll be coming in here on a regular basis, my name is Dewey and her name is Julie, OK?"

"Yes sir, I mean…Dewey. I don't think I've ever met anyone named Dewey before."

"Well, Vincent, my real name is David Polpulcionski, but everybody just calls me Dewey P."

"Dewey P?"

"Well, I certainly do, and if you don't on a regular basis, you'll be in trouble real soon." (Come on! You knew I had to get it in at least one more time.)

Vincent laughed kind of a professional-type laugh, and looked at me like he thought I was half nuts. He probably wasn't very far off.

"The reason I'm asking, Vincent, is that Rickert was a police impersonator traveling with the East Arthur Police for a short time. I was wondering if Oscar had any dealings with them, or just had a thing for bumpin' off cops, even though Rickert really wasn't one."

"I really don't think so, Dewey. Oscar, at least the last time I saw him, seemed to *associate* only with people who had lots of money, if you get the idea. I don't think a police officer, whether an impersonator or not, would fit into that category."

"No, I guess not," I said. That seemed to eliminate Oscar from our suspect list for the murder of Stacy Rickert.

We told Vincent goodbye, thanked him for the lunch, and left a generous tip for Claude, our waiter. Julie wound up gettin' off pretty cheap. All she had to do was leave the tip.

All the way back to Petunia's Peanut Pieces I tried talkin' Julie into takin' the rest of the day off, but she wasn't bitin'."No, Dew, I have too much work to catch up on, but you'll come over for dinner tonight, won't you?"

"Sure. Actually, I've gotta start trackin' down some lost cats this afternoon, so maybe it's a good idea that I get started. How about six for dinner? Is that OK?"

"Six sounds fine. And make sure to find those cats. You don't want to have to pay off on your guarantee."

We both laughed.

When I got back to my apartment, I saw a police car in the parking lot, and it looked like my old friend Sergeant Hanley. And he was walking my way.

"Well, if it ain't my old pal *Private* Hanley," I said, before he had a chance to say anything.

Just then my cell phone started to ring.

"I see…Uh-huh…What?…Yeah, I'll be in touch…Well, thanks for callin'."

"That's *Sergeant* Hanley, Mr. Popple...Mr. Poople...Mr...Oh, you know who you are!" he shouted. "Could you step out of the car please, sir?"

"Sure, pal," I said, real cocky-like. "What's up?"

"I'm placing you under arrest for the murder of Stacy Rickert. Could you get in the car, please? I won't use the handcuffs unless I have to."

"Gee, what a surprise," I said. "The call I just got was from Nick Rudawski. You remember him from my DUI trial, don't you, Sarge? I don't know how he found out, but he told me this was about to happen. You're makin' another mistake, Sarge!"

"Yeah, well, just get in the car, OK?"

"Sure, Sarge. Just one question."

"Yeah, what's that?"

"Don't you *ever* read anybody their rights?"

It was time to call Mary Payson.

Chapter 32: MARY'S NEXT CASE

I was given a free ride to the East Arthur Police Station, compliments of Sergeant Walter Hanley. He said nothin' all the way to the station, but once we got there he started right in.

"OK, Mr. P. (I guess he'd given up on tryin' to pronounce my last name), why'd you do it? Why did you murder Stacy Rickert?"

"Hey, I ain't sayin' nothin' till I get a chance to talk to my lawyer. I'm allowed one phone call, ain't I? You ain't gettin' nothin' outta me." I felt like addin' *Copper,* like they did in all the old movies, but I thought that would be just a bit too corny.

"Yeah, you'll get your one call all right, but why don't ya start singin' and make it easy on yourself."

"Ya know," I said, "maybe yer right."

That certainly got Hanley's attention. "Now you're talkin' some sense. OK! Sing!"

So sing is what I did. At least that's what I started to do.

"Come to me my melancholy ba-a-a-a-a-by. Cuddle up and don't be bl…"

"Hey, just what the hell d'ya think you're doin'"? asked Hanley. Good thing he stopped me there, too. I really didn't know too many other words to the song.

"Look, Sarge, you asked me to sing, so I'm singin'. But if ya don't like that one, here's one that my dearly-departed Dad really enjoyed. Roll out the barrel, we'll have a barrel of fun…"

Once again Hanley cut me off. "All right, we'll go make your phone call. Just knock it off, would ya?"

I really gotta hand one thing to Hanley. His timin' couldn't be more perfect. I didn't know too many other words to the *Beer Barrel Polka*, either.

We walked down a long hallway to make my call. When we got to the phone, Hanley was leanin' all over me like we were…well… never mind. Just leave it at he was leanin' all over me.

"Hey, can't a guy get any privacy around here?" I said. "Do I lean all over you when you're tryin' to call one a your girlfriends. *You do have girlfriends, don't you, Hanley?"*

Hanley just walked away. He musta figured I wasn't goin' anywhere.

I had Mary's business card in my wallet, but I really didn't need it to dial her number. After all, how hard is 1-800-CALL-MARY to remember? (What did you expect her number to be? Pennsylvania 6-5000? This story don't go anywhere near back *that* far.)

After a few rings, Stella answered the phone.

"Mary Payson's office. This is Stella DeRita. How may I help you?"

"Hi , Stella, it's Dewey. How ya doin'?"

"Oh, hello, Dewey. OK, I guess. You aren't by any chance looking for that no-good boyfriend of mine, Sanford, are you?"

"Who?"

"You know. Sanford!"

"Who?"

"Come on, Dewey. You know. SANFORD!" Now she was really shouting. "Sanford, the auto-mechanic formerly known as Zeke."

"Oh! Him? No. Sounds like trouble in paradise, Stella."

"No, not really. We just had a little misunderstanding last night. I'm sure we'll work it out in a day or two."

Just then Hanley came back. "Hey, would ya hurry it up. This ain't the Polish-American Social Club, ya know."

"No, Stella," I continued. "I was really lookin' for Mary. Can I talk to her a minute, please?"

"I'm sorry, Dewey. Mary just stepped out for a few minutes. Can I take a message?"

"Yeah! Ask her to come down to the East Arthur Police Station as soon as she can. I just got arrested for the murder of Stacy Rickert."

"You got ten more seconds," said Hanley.

"OK, Dewey. I'll tell her. I'm sure she'll be there as soon as she can."

Right after I got off the phone with Stella, Hanley started in on me again.

"Come on, Mr. P., tell me why you killed Rickert." With the Mr. P moniker, I was startin' to feel like a celebrity. First Mr. B, then Mr. C, and now me, Mr. P.

"Tell you what, Sarge. Insteada me tellin' you why *I* killed him, why don't *you* tell me why *you* killed him."

But Hanley jumped over that like he never even heard it.

"The way I got it figured," he said, "is that you knew he really wasn't a cop, so you figured he shoulda said somethin' before the trial even got started. Ain't that right, Mr. P?"

"And the way *I* got it figured, Sarge, is that Rickert made you look like the idiot you really are on the stand. Ain't *that* right, Sarge?"

Sarge and I just sat there and glared at each other for a while, but we both knew that neither one of us was makin' any sense. I knew that he was just doin' his job, and he knew that I was just blowin' smoke. I was half-beginnin' to like the old Sarge.

But only half!

Mary got there about fifteen minutes later. By that time Sarge and I were almost bosom buddies. Enough so that Walt let us go into a room by ourselves and close the door for a little talk.

"Stella told me what happened, Dewey, so I got here as fast as I could. So tell me what happened."

"Well, I just got home after droppin' Julie back at the office after lunch, and Walt was in my parkin' lot to arrest me for the murder of Stacy Rickert. You remember him, right? The police impersonator at my trial."

"Walt? Who's Walt?"

"Oh, I'm sorry. Sergeant Hanley. We've become good buddies waitin' for you to get here."

"You're kidding me, right, Dewey? I mean about the good buddies part."

"Damn right I am. But how do ya think I got us the private room?"

"Oh, don't let that fool you, Dewey. They've probably got the room bugged."

"Really?" I whispered.

"Very likely," Mary whispered back.

"Screw you, Walt," I yelled at the top of my lungs.

"OK, Dewey! OK! So I assume you didn't kill Rickert."

"Of course not. Why would I kill him? He's the one who got me off at my trial."

"Well, do they have any evidence against you?"

"Not that I know of."

"Well then, why did they bring you in?"

"I don't know. I guess Hanley's still ticked off about the DUI trial, and this is his way of gettin' even. Isn't it, Hanley, you son of a..."

"Dewey! Calm down! That won't do any good. So who do you think might have done it?"

"Well, let's see. Julie was still in jail, so that leaves her out. I know I didn't do it, and I really don't think Hanley did, either. Oscar could have done it, but his brother said that bumpin' off cops, whether they were really cops or not, wasn't his style. I'm afraid at this point..."

"Wait a minute," said Mary. "You know Oscar's brother?"

"Yeah. Julie and I just met him over at a new restaurant called Sammy's Steak House. He's the host over there and he goes by the name of Vincent Billings. Said he changed his last name over ten years ago. Hasn't spoken to Oscar since then, but he says Oscar wouldn't do this."

"So who does that leave us with?" asked Mary.

"Right now it looks like it leaves us with somebody who isn't even in the book yet."

"Oh, goody," said Mary, "I just love those kinds of endings." (I knew someone did, but I couldn't remember who it was. Now I knew.)

"Well, I don't, and I'm writin' this thing, so you'd better get Saul workin' on this real quick. I'd really hate to pull somebody new outta the woodwork on my readers."

"All right, Dewey. But just for that you have to promise me that I'll be in the next book."

"OK, Mary. But then Saul has to do somethin' else for me, too."

"What's that?"

"Well, I know I'm only the 358th best private eye east of the mighty Manatawny, and he's number one, but I still havta eat, ya know. I'm not workin' for Julie any more, so I'm back to lookin' for lost pussies, so I was wonderin'…"

"Dewey, Saul's very happy in a new relationship ever since he broke up with Stella. I don't see how you can expect him…"

"No, no, no. I'm talkin' about *real* cats. *Lost* cats. I got two new cases today, and I gotta find 'em soon or…"

"Oh, yeah. How does your guarantee go? Let me see. I'll find your pussy in three days or you don't pay. Isn't that it?"

"All right. Give me the information and I'll pass it on to Saul. He won't be happy about it, but I'm paying him, and things have been pretty slow lately. But this is going to cost you more pages in the next book."

"OK! OK! Thanks, Mary."

"Say, Dewey, I thought you and Julie were living together now."

"Well, let's just say I spend a lot of time over at her place, but she ain't supportin' me if that's what you mean. Just what kinda cad do you take me for?"

Mary answered by telling me *another kind* that I never heard before. I guess I'm gonna havta start takin' notes on these things.

"One other thing, Mary. I'm kinda inta the TV show *Debbie and Brad and Steve and Fred and Art and...* Do you think you could tape it for me till I get outta here?"

"Sure, Dewey. But I guess you haven't heard. The show is now called *Debbie and Brad and Steve and Fred and...*Art just signed a contract to go back to play baseball in Japan."

Just then Hanley stuck his head in the door. "Hey, let's wrap it up, OK? Whaddya think this is, the No-tell Motel?"

After he closed the door, Mary said, "So hang in there. I'll try to get your bail hearing set as soon as I can, but don't expect to go anywhere until at least Monday. It'll give Saul some time to start digging around. Oh yeah, that reminds me. About those pussies?"

Mary was right. She was back the next day, but the bail hearing wasn't set until Monday, four days away. She told Saul about the cats, and he wasn't real thrilled, but he was goin' to Saskatchewan soon, so he didn't complain too bad.

Mary also brought Julie with her.

After Julie and I kissed, she said, "I missed you, Dewey. And don't worry about bail. I've got that covered regardless of what it is." Fortunately Hanley was givin' us some privacy, but maybe the room was bugged.

Mary then informed us that I had the Honorable Abraham J. Moses for the judge at my bail hearing.

"Hey, wasn't that the old guy that Julie had at her bail hearing?" I asked.

"The one and the same," said Mary. "Bail hearings are about all he does any more, but they're more than enough to keep the old boy busy."

"Make sure you bring along some Petunia's Peanut Pieces," I said to Julie. "I could use all the help I can get."

I was about to fill Julie in on some things that Mary didn't tell her, but just then Hanley came along.

"OK," he said. "You two lovebirds have had long enough. Your time's up, so kiss him goodbye."

Good old Walt. What a guy!

Mary gave me some instructions for the trial, and said it would start at 9:00 a.m. That meant that *we* had to be there at 9:00, and the judge would waltz into the courtroom about 9:45. Well, maybe at Judge Moses's age it would be more like shuffle in.

Until then, I had room and board compliments of the East Arthur Police Department.

I sure hope Saul found those pussies.

Chapter 33: DEWEY'S MEETING WITH MOSES

I spent a rather uneventful weekend in the East Arthur jail. A little time was spent shootin' the shit with Hanley, but he was off most of the weekend. Julie came to visit me every day, but there really wasn't anything new to discuss, and East Arthur certainly wasn't gonna allow us conjugal visits.

Mary contacted me on Sunday night and told me that she would be there at 8:30 on Monday morning to take me to the courthouse. She didn't say anything about Saul, so I suspected that I wouldn't be making any money from my two clients with the lost cats. I also suspected that he hadn't turned up anything interesting about the murder.

Mary, along with Julie, turned up at exactly 8:30 on Monday morning, just as she had promised. Stella would meet us in the courtroom at 9:00.

"They're having a new Assistant D.A. handle this," said Mary, "so I really don't know what to expect. His name is W. H. Everett, Jr. I'll certainly try to get you out on bail on your own recognizance, but I really wouldn't count on that happening if I were you."

The three of us walked into the courtroom a few minutes before nine. Stella was already there, but there was no sign of Zeke. I didn't know if that meant that they hadn't patched things up yet, or if he was just at work. I would try to talk to Stella later.

I was surprised to see Nick Rudawski sitting in the back of the courtroom. I really thought he would be in Tucson by now, but it was good to see him again. Since Nora wasn't with him, I thought that she must be working, too. There was still something about Nick that I couldn't figure out. When this was all over, I would have to ask him what it was.

It was now nine o'clock. I figured we were in for a least a half-hour wait before the judge arrived, but the Honorable Abraham J. Moses surprised me and was there five minutes later. He didn't exactly waltz into the room, but for someone his age, he didn't exactly shuffle in, either.

"Ladies and gentleman," the judge started, "this is the bail hearing for Mr. David M. Polpulcionski."

I really had to hand it to the old fella. He must have done his homework, because he had no problem pronouncing my last name. I just hoped he would go easy on the bail, even though Julie was payin' it.

"As you may or may not know," he continued, "Mr. Polpulcionski is accused of murdering Mr. Stacy Rickert. I see Mr. Polpulcionski's attorney is Ms. Mary Payson, and the Assistant D.A. handling the case is Mr. W. H. Everett, Jr. Are you ready to present, Ms. Payson?"

"Yes, Your Honor."

"Well, that's good. But since there is such a small crowd here today, and since I like to keep this as informal as possible, I see we have a celebrity with us here today. Right here in this very courtroom we have the lady who, just a short time ago, was acquitted of murdering her husband, Mr. Joseph Crinn, Mrs. Julie Crinn. Stand up and take a bow, Mrs. Crinn."

Everyone in the courtroom was completely stunned. Nobody could believe that Judge Moses was doing the best Ed Sullivan any one of us had heard in years.

"Come on, Mrs. Crinn. Stand up and take a bow," the judge insisted. Finally we all started clapping, so Julie stood up. She didn't say anything, but the look on her face said *What the hell's goin' on here*, and she quickly sat down.

"Oh, by the way, Mrs. Crinn," said Judge Moses, "you wouldn't just happen to have any Petunia's Peanut Pieces with you, by any chance? I just love those things."

I was very surprised that Assistant D.A. Everett didn't say anything, but I guess he figured it was in his best interest not to.

"I just happen to have two whole boxes here just for you, Your Honor," said Julie. I could see bail being lowered with every piece.

"Thank you, Mrs. Crinn. How thoughtful of you."

"It was my pleasure, Your Honor."

"Are you now ready to proceed, Ms. Payson?"

"Yes, Your Honor, I am. We contend, Your Honor, that my client, Mr. David Polpulcionski, is, and always has been, a law-abiding citizen. While it is true, Your Honor, that Mr. Polpulcionski has been arrested for driving under the influence on three separate occasions, he was acquitted in each case. Furthermore, Your Honor, Mr. Polpulcionski resides in this community and has done so for many years; plus, he operates his own profitable business, and contributes to the community through the taxes that he pays."

I wasn't quite sure what Mary was spittin' out, but I guess she meant I made enough to keep myself in pizzas and six-packs, and paid my taxes on time.

"Therefore, Your Honor, we feel that Mr. Polpulcionski should be released on his own recognizance without forfeiting any bail. Thank you, Your Honor."

Judge Moses just sat there and didn't say anything. Apparently he had dozed off during Mary's little speech.

The bailiff walked over and gently nudged the judge.

"Uh...yes. Thank you, Ms. Payson. Mr. Everett, let's hear your side of this."

"Thank you, Your Honor. Your Honor, Mr. Polpulcionski is being charged with first-degree murder. His bail should be set at one million dollars. Thank you, Your Honor." Everett, apparently not one to waste words or time, sat down.

"I see," said the judge. "Well, this is a very serious crime, but then again Mr. Polpulcionski has never really been in serious trouble before; and it seems that he has access to a large supply of Petunia's Peanut Pieces – I just love those yummy things – so I am going to release Mr. Polpulcionski on his own recognizance. Any objections, Mr. Everett?"

"Yeah, whatever," said Everett. "I mean, uh, no objections Your Honor."

Even though the judge just saved Julie a bundle, I couldn't imagine that Everett would be in his current position all that long.

"Your trial will start one week from today, Mr. Polpulcionski. Please do not leave the state without notifying the court. Court is adjourned. Oh, Mrs. Crinn, could I speak to you for a moment, please?"

While Julie was talking to the judge, I went over to catch Everett before he left the courtroom.

"Excuse me," I said, "but I want to thank you for not fighting the judge's decision."

"Yeah, whatever."

"Frankly, you didn't seem too interested in what happened."

"Yeah, whatever."

"Well, if you don't mind my askin', how did you get to be the assistant D.A?"

"You may have heard of my father, W.H. Everett, Sr? He's on the State Supreme Court."

My only response was "Yeah, whatever."

Julie walked over after talking to Judge Moses.

"What was that all about?" I asked.

"You won't believe this," she said, "but the judge wanted to know if I could send him a case of Petunia's Peanut Pieces every month. He even offered to pay for them. I told him that I would be delighted to send him a case every month, and that they were on me."

Mary and Stella then came over. As it turned out, Stella and Zeke did patch things up, but he had a lot to do at his shop. She was sure that he would be in the courtroom once my trial started.

Mary then said, "Well, that certainly went a lot easier than I ever imagined. I'll be in touch with you before the trial, so just stay out of trouble."

She handed me Friday's tape of *Debbie and Brad and Steve and Fred and*...I was sure I could make it home in time to watch it before today's episode came on, but first I had a little catchin' up to do with Julie.

"By the way, Dewey," Mary said, "Saul found those two cats and gave me the money after he took his fee. I'm keeping it as your fee for my services for today."

That was fine with me. It looked like I wasn't the only one would could find lost pussies within three days.

Chapter 34: A WEEK OFF

Once my bail hearing was over, I was real hungry. But it wasn't for food. Julie and I went back to her house as fast as we could without gettin' a speedin' ticket.

As soon as we were inside, all Julie said was, "Do me, Dewey!"

I was only too happy to oblige.

Since I was still in my new suit, and since it was the only one that really fit me, Julie very tenderly helped me out of it, kissing and caressing as she went along. Once she was finished undressing me, it was my turn. I very quickly ripped her dress off – literally – and returned the kissing and caressing. I was quite sure that Julie didn't care – about the dress, I mean. After all, she had closets full of clothes, and since she was now a billionaire, and not just a measly millionaire, she could certainly afford a new dress.

We were going at it for quite some time, but I'm afraid I can't give you the blow-by-blow details. If I did that, I would probably turn this into an X-rated story, and I'm afraid I've already pushed it from a PG to an R. Sorry, but you'll just have to use your imagination.

After we finally got out of bed, we decided to take a shower – together, of course. Once in the shower, the passion continued. Only this time it was a lot wetter – if that was possible.

When we finally got out and dried each other off, Julie said, "Honey, why don't we go away for a few days? We could both use the time to unwind before your trial starts."

"I'd really love to, Babe," I replied, "but I really should start checkin' around to see what I can find out about the murder; and besides, I still need to make a livin', ya know."

"Oh, come on, Dewey. You're the one writing this story, so you *know* who did it! Why don't you give the readers some time to try and figure it out? Besides, Mary has Saul working on the case, so I'm sure he can handle it. And if you're worried about the money, I'll gladly pay for the trip. What do you say?"

"That's really very kind of you, Julie, but I couldn't let you do that. What kind of a cad do you take me for?"

She told me yet *another* kind that I never heard of before. It was gettin' to the point that I really needed to go out on the Internet and look up *cad*. Maybe the next time somebody told me another kind, at least I would be able to say that I heard of that one. Maybe I could even argue with them.

"Dewey," Julie said very seductively, as she started to rub me the *right* way in all the *right* places.

"Yes, Hon?" I asked, really startin' to get into it again.

"You don't want to sleep on the couch for the next week before your trial begins, do you?"

"No, of course not!"

"Well then, where would you like to go?" she asked, grabbin' me in the right place, only way too hard.

"Anywhere you say, sweetheart," I said.

"That's more like it, darling," she said.

"But I'll need to go back to my apartment and pack some things for the trip. Why don't you start packing, and I'll be back in about two hours. Think about where you'd like to take me."

I knew it would only take me about fifteen minutes to pack. I just wanted to watch the episode of *Debbie and Brad and Steve and Fred and...* that Mary taped for me, and thought I would still have time to see the current episode as well.

When I got back to my apartment, I checked my e-mails and my phone messages. No e-mails, so at least I wouldn't have to worry about any other pussies for awhile. Julie would like that.

I did get one phone message. It was from Nick Rudawski. He said he was in no big hurry to get back to Tucson, and would stick around until after my trial, and he wished me luck. That was real nice of him, but I still knew that there was somethin' goin' on there.

It was time for the taped episode of *Debbie and Brad and Steve and Fred and...* I knew that if I fast –forwarded through the commercials, I would be able to see that day's episode, too.

When I put the tape in, Debbie was once again in Dr. Steve Fix's office.

"Oh, Doctor Fix, Doctor Fix," cried Debbie. "What am I going to do?"

"What's the matter *now*, Debbie?" asked Doctor Fix.

"Oh, Doctor Fix, Doctor Fix (it really sounded like the writers doing the scripts were the ones who needed the help), Arthur went back to play ball in Japan, and now I'm down to only you and Brad and Fred. What am I going to do, Doctor Fix?"

"Well, for starters, Debbie, this will give you a chance to slow down just a bit. I mean, after all, you've got four babies on the way, and you're only 22. You've got a long way to go, so why not take it easy for a little while?"

"Gee, Doctor Fix, do I really look 22?" Debbie said, making it sound like she was a lot older.

"That's what it has here in your records," said Fix.

"Well, I really don't know where you got that information. You see, Doctor Fix, I'm really only 17."

After Doctor Fix took his time consoling Debbie – could baby number five be on the way? – the commercials came on and the show was over, so I fast-forwarded and tuned in just in time as that day's episode was just about ready to start.

That day's story was really something else. Either Doctor Fix really was concerned for Debbie's well-being, or the writers were gettin' very desperate. Fix and Debbie spent the whole show arguing because Fix had her committed to the hospital. It was a new ward that was just created, probably just for the show.

The nymphomaniac ward for unwed mothers was one I never heard of before, but what did I know. I was still tryin' to figure out how many different kinds of *cads* there were.

Right after the show, I called Mary Payson's office. I told her that Julie and I would be going on a trip until my trial started, but I didn't know where we were going, so I told her I would have to call her back if we were goin' out of state. Couldn't do that without notifyin' the authorities. Mary also agreed to tape that week's episodes of *Debbie and Brad and Steve and Fred and...* I knew the shows were gettin' to be pretty lame, but a habit like that is pretty hard to break.

Since Mary didn't say anything about Saul, I assumed that he hadn't found out anything about the murder. But Saul was *numero uno*, and still had a week to go, so I had faith in him.

And you, my faithful reader, still have a week – at least in the book – to go, too. I know you won't let me down.

After talkin' to Mary, it took me 15 minutes to pack, and I was back on the road to Julie's.

When I got back to the house, Julie was ready to go. She was dressed in a halter top and a pair of very short shorts. It only took me a few seconds to heat up again.

I reached for Julie, but she avoided my grasp and said, "Un-uh. We've got plenty of time for that, but we've got to get going."

I noticed that she only had one bag packed, so I figured that we couldn't be goin' too far. "So where you takin' me?" I asked.

"It's a surprise," she answered. "We're taking my car and I'll drive."

"But if we're goin' out of state, I have to call Mary and let her know so she can notify the court. I don't want to have my bail revoked."

"Oh, you don't have to worry about that. We aren't going that far."

When we got out to the car Julie said, "Here. Put this blindfold on. I want this to be a total surprise."

With the blindfold on, I dozed off for awhile. But before I knew it, Julie said, "Well, you can take the blindfold off now. Here we are."

When I took the blindfold off, I was in for a *real* surprise.

"Where the..? This looks like the parking lot of a Stay Over Inn."

"It is, silly," she answered. The Stay Over Inn in Walterville.

Walterville is about 30 miles west of East Arthur, a little more than half way between Manatawny and Riten. There really isn't anything to do or see there, and its claim to fame – if you can call it that – *is* that it's located a little more than half way between Manatawny and Riten. Not that they're exactly known for being the fun capitals of the world, either.

"So," I said. "This is the big surprise? You brought me to a Stay Over Inn in Walterville?"

"I told you we both needed the rest before your trial got started, and that's exactly what we're going to do until then. Well, at least we'll be in bed till then."

For the next five days, we did very little other than stay in bed. Occasionally we would order room service, but that was the extent of our *other* activities. That and taking showers every day. Together, of course.

An old friend of mine once told me that her idea of roughing it was spending a night in a Stay Over Inn.

When we were ready to leave, I couldn't have agreed *less*.

Chapter 35: BEANIE AND DEWEY – PART TWO

When we got back to Julie's, there was a call waitin' for me from Mary.

"Hi, Dewey, it's Mary. Hope you enjoyed your trip. As you know, your trial starts tomorrow morning at nine o'clock. We'll be in courtroom 6B, so I'll meet you in the hall about quarter of. We got Judge Osbourne, so it ought to be interesting. By the way, I also left this message on your machine at your apartment, just in case you go there first. Unless I hear from you tonight, I'll see you tomorrow morning."

"Mary called," I told Julie. "We're in 6B tomorrow at nine a.m. And we got Beanie again."

"Oh, that's just great. He should be in rare form. Did she say whether Saul found out anything yet?"

"No, she didn't mention it. I don't know if that's good news or bad news."

After Julie and I had something to eat, I went back to my apartment to pack some things and check my emails and my phone messages.

I got neither. That was good *and* bad.

Good because I wouldn't have been able to do anything for the next few days anyway. Bad because I really had to start thinkin' about findin' some clients.

And the rent would be due soon again.

After gettin' my things together, I went back to Julie's, and we replayed our vacation at the Stay Over Inn.

We got up very early for the first day of the trial. I, of course, had on my one suit that fit me. Julie wore a very professional-looking business suit. I couldn't imagine that showing any skin – Julie's, not mine – would have impressed Beanie in the least. Assuming, of course, that he would be able to see that far with his hangover to begin with.

Since it was still very early, we stopped and had breakfast at a restaurant in downtown East Arthur, within walking distance of the courthouse. Even though I knew I didn't do it, the tension was still very thick, so we said almost nothing during breakfast.

We arrived outside courtroom 6B at exactly 8:45. Mary and Stella were already there waiting for us.

"So, how was your mini-vacation?" Mary asked.

That must have brought a big smile to my face, because she followed that up quickly with, "Don't bother. With that look on your face, I can just imagine what went on. I just hope you got at least *some* sleep."

I didn't bother to answer.

"Saul's still digging around, but so far he hasn't been able to come up with anything. I hope he has some good news for us today."

"That would be nice," was all I could say.

"Sanford said he would be over around nine," Stella said. I assumed that meant that everything was back to normal between the two of them.

"Well, shall we do it?" said Mary.

We walked into the courtroom at ten of. Nick Rudawski and Nora Klause were already there, sitting in the back. Since they were both billionaires now, they could do anything they wanted, but it was still good to see both of them there. We all waved on the way in.

D.A. Phil A. Mignon was already sitting at his table, so there was nothing to do now but wait for Judge Roy B. Osbourne to show up.

And wait is what we did! Nine fifteen came and went, as did nine thirty. Finally at 9:45 the door to the judges' chambers opened, and out walked – actually, *staggered* would be the correct word – the Honorable Roy Bean Osbourne.

"Goo' mornin', la'ies 'n gen'lemen," Beanie slurred. "Lemme see. Oh, yes. Today we have the trial involving the murder of…"

"Well, well, well, so we meet again, *sir*," Beanie said sarcastically. "I knew you wouldn' be able to stay outta trouble long. But this time I'm ready for ya."

"La'ies 'n gen'lemen, as I was sayin', today we start the murder trial involvin' the murder of Mister Stacy Richards…er, Ricketts…uh,

Rickert. Thas it. Rickert. The accused is Mister David Plopopinski...
no, David Poplodinski...Ooh! And I practiced so hard, too."

I actually thought old Beanie was gonna cry.

"Well, until I get his name right – and I will, too – the defendant
will be known as Sir."

Mary and I just grinned at each other.

"Sir," he continued, "is being defended by Ms. Mary Payson,
and the District Attorney handling the case is Mr. Phil A. Mignon."

I didn't notice her before, but apparently the D.A. had his own
one-woman rooting section sitting right behind the rail in the person of
Judge Saundra H. Pants.

"The first thing we will do is select a jury. But before we do
that, I'm going to call a brief recess. I gotta pee."

Good old Beanie. Obviously nothing had changed.

We were back in court fifteen minutes later.

"We will now select a jury. Twelve of you will be chosen to be
on the jury and two of you will be selected as alternates in case one or
two of the people get thrown off the jury or somethin'. If more than
two get the boot, I'll be damned if I know what to do. Wha' do I look
like? A judge or somethin'? The rest of you'll get to go home. I sure
wish I could."

"I will now ask the defendant, counsel for the defendant, and
the District Attorney to rise and face the persep...the prospect... Ooh!

The people who might be on the jury. If any of you know any of these three people, please hold up your number and rise when I call your number."

This time only three numbers went up.

"Number six, could you rise please and tell the court which one you know?"

"Yes, Your Honor. I know the defendant."

She looked vaguely familiar to me, but for the life of me I couldn't place her. And from the looks of her, she was *way* too old for me to be chasin' her. I was never *that* desperate. Close, but not quite.

"And how do you know the defendant, ma'am?" asked Beanie.

"Oh, Your Honor, he found my little Snuggy Poo about two years ago. And he found her within two days, too. You know his guarantee, don't you, Your Honor? Let me see. How does it go? Oh, yes. *I'll find your pussy in three days or you don't pay.*" Everyone in the court, with the exception of Beanie, got a big laugh out of that. "Such a nice young man, too, Your Honor."

"Yes. Thank you, ma'am. You're excused. And may I remind ev'ryone that we're in a court a law. Any more outbursts and I will be forced to clear the courtroom." Then he added, under his breath, "I just wish I could clear my head."

"Number fourteen, could you please stand an' tell the court who you know?"

Number fourteen rose. Now, she was more my style. I probably woulda found her pussy for nothin'.

"Certainly, Your Honor. I know the District Attorney, Phil A. Mignon. Hiya, Philsey," she squeaked.

On second thought, I probably woulda charged her double. I looked over, and Judge "Hot" Pants was startin' to simmer.

"Philsey, I mean the D.A., Your Honor, we been seein' each other the last few weeks, ain't we Philsey?"

And I thought my English was bad.

The judge – Hot, not Beanie – was about to blow. She managed to keep her cool, but I woulda given eight-to-five that we wouldn't see her back after the noon recess.

"Yes. Well, thank you, number fourteen. You're excused."

"Ah, gee, Your Honor. Are you sure?"

"*Quite* sure," number fourteen. "Thank you."

"Number twenty-three, could you rise please and tell us who you know?"

"Sure, Your Honor. I don't know any of them, but I do know you, Beanie…uh, I mean, Your Honor. So where ya been hangin' out? I ain't seen you in weeks. You hangin' out at the high-class bars now? Huh, Beanie?"

The look on the judge's face – Beanie's, not Hot's – said more than words could ever say.

"Thank you, number twenty-three. You're excused."

"Whazamatter, Beanie? Ain't I good enough for you no more? I thought…"

But Beanie cut her off. "We will now take our noon recess. Please be back in the courtroom by one o'clock."

Everyone was back in the courtroom by 1:00. Well, *almost* everyone. I'm sure I don't have to give ya three guesses to figure out who was backin' up the court.

When Beanie walked in at 1:18, he was in worse shape than I had ever seen him.

"Sorry fer the delay, folks, but it was unadoid…unaboin…It couldn't be helped."

I was wonderin' exactly *what* couldn't be helped. A blond, a brunette, or a redhead. On second thought, it was probably a martini – his third, by the looks of it.

"We will now have the jury selection. Oh, no wait. We already did that. What comes next?"

Beanie seemed really *confused*?

"Oh, yeah. We will now have opening statements from the persecution and the defense attorney."

The bailiff then went up and whispered something to the judge.

"Oh, I'm sorry. I meant to say that we would now have opening statements from the *prosecution* and the defense attorney."

Frankly, I thought he was right the first time.

If you ever get so lucky to be in a court of law, watch how our *justice* system operates. It all seems very fair and on the up-and-up, but is it, really?

The persecu…I mean *prosecution* gets to go first with its opening statement, so the defense gets to go first with its closing argument. Seems fair enough. Right!?

Wrong!!!

It's all stacked in the prosecution's favor.

They get to go first with the opening statement, but by the end of the trial, who the hell remembers opening statements.

Nobody, that's who!

Near the end of the trial, when it's time for the closing arguments, the defense gets to go first.

So, what's the big deal, you ask?

The *big deal* is that the prosecution gets to go last. And with those windbags, what are you gonna remember? Somethin' somebody said fifteen minutes ago, or fifteen *seconds* ago?

Exactly!

The amazing thing is that these asswipes who figure out these things think that we're too stupid to figure out what the hell's goin' on.

Amazing!

Anyway, D.A. Phil A. Mignon got to present his opening statement first.

"Ladies and gentlemen of the jury," he started, "today we begin the trial of the murder of Mister Stacy Rickert. The most serious, the most heinous crime of the murder of Mister Stacy Rickert, who was cut down in the prime of his life. The murder of Mister Stacy Rickert, a stellar resident of this community who left behind his lovely wife, three young children, two dogs, one cat, and one hamster. Oh, and four goldfish."

I thought it was rather odd that none of these people and animals were present in the courtroom. Where the hell were they? On a field trip to the zoo – or was it the local pet shop?

"If you're wondering why Mrs. Rickert isn't here today, it's quite simple. She has been undergoing psychological therapy since the brutal murder of her loving husband and the children's loving Daddy. The children are too young and are being taken care of by relatives. And, of course, we don't allow animals in the courthouse, except for guide dogs."

I wondered why he was looking at me when he said that they didn't allow animals in the courthouse.

"We shall prove, ladies and gentlemen, without a shadow of a doubt, that the defendant, Mr. David M. Plopiniski...Poderofsky...*him*, the man sitting right there, did willfully and mercilessly murder this loving husband and Daddy, Mr. Stacy Rickert."

"Why did the defendant do this, you might be saying to yourself?"

I knew I certainly was.

"Well, I'll tell you."

Thank you, I thought. This oughta be good.

"The defendant willfully and mercilessly murdered this loving husband and Daddy, Mr. Stacy Rickert, because, only a short while ago, the defendant was on trial in this very courthouse for the dastardly crime of DUI – Driving Under the Influence. The defendant paid Mr. Rickert to lie on the stand, ladies and gentlemen, yes, commit perjury so that he could help support his lovely wife and his three adoring young children."

At this point I was really surprised he hadn't mentioned the two dogs, one cat, and four goldfish. Oh, yeah. And one hamster. Can't forget the hamster.

"So, Mr. Rickert, that loving, kind, considerate man that he was, agreed to perjure himself so he could support his loving wife, his three young, adorable children, plus his two dogs, one cat, and four goldfish. Oh, yeah. And one hamster. We certainly can't forget about the hamster."

I knew he'd get to them sooner or later.

"So Mr. Rickert went through with the plan and was paid off. But later, Mr. Rickert, being the law-abiding citizen that he was, tried to give the money back to the defendant, and was going to go to the police and confess the whole thing. And that is when the defendant, Mr. David M. Pillaniski, or whatever his name is, did willfully and mercilessly murder, in cold blood, Mr. Stacy Rickert. I thank you, ladies and gentlemen."

I had to hand it to Mignon. He had half the people on the jury totally spellbound.

The other half he put totally to sleep.

Mignon looked around the courtroom, almost like he was lookin' for applause. Only Hot Pants didn't return after the noon recess.

Ain't ya glad ya didn't take me up on the bet?

"Thank you, Mr. Mignon," said the judge. "I think it's about time for our afternoon recess. And I gotta pee again. Court will recess until 2:15."

When we returned to the courtroom, Beanie really surprised me. He was actually there waitin' for us.

It was now Mary's turn to present her opening statements.

"Ladies and gentlemen of the jury," she started, "while the defense certainly agrees with the prosecution that Mr. Rickert was a very loving husband and father, we certainly do not agree with this hogwash that Mr. Mignon has just presented you. Mr. Mignon has more than insinuated that the defendant, Mr. David M. Polpulcionski (thank God *she* got my name right) actually bribed the late Mr. Rickert to perjure himself at Mr. Polpulcionski's DUI trial. And may I add, ladies and gentlemen, that Mr. Polpulcionski, being the law-abiding citizen that he is, and always has been, was found *not guilty* of that crime."

"Ladies and gentlemen, up until the time Mr. Polpulcionski was accused of DUI, he had never even seen the deceased before, and he certainly had no dealings with him after the DUI trial. We, therefore, ladies and gentlemen, will prove conclusively that the defendant, Mr. David M. Polpulcionski is once again *not guilty* of the crime of which he is being accused."

"I thank you for your attention, ladies and gentlemen. I have nothing further at this time, Your Honor."

Mary and I just looked at each other. Apparently Saul hadn't found out anything that could help my case.

Even though I knew I wasn't guilty, I also knew that I was in real deep shit.

"At this time," Beanie began, "since it is getting close to the end of the day, we will recess until tomorrow morning at nine o'clock. May I remind the jury not to discuss the case with anyone or read anything in the papers about it. If anyone should approach you about the case, please notify the court immediately."

"See you all tomorrow."

I just hoped that Saul was out earning his Number One ranking.

Chapter 36: BEANIE AND DEWEY – PART TWO, DAY TWO

When we arrived at the courtroom at 9:00 the following morning, there were two surprises waitin' for us. First of all, Judge Roy B. Osbourne was already there waitin' for us. The second surprise was that he was completely sober.

"Good morning, ladies and gentlemen. I see we're all here, and I hope you all had a wonderful evening."

Was this *really* my old pal Beanie, or was it his nicer twin?

"Is the state ready to present its case, Mr. Mignon?"

"Yes, Your Honor, we most certainly are."

"Well then, Mr. Mignon, kindly call your first witness."

"Thank you, Your Honor. I call Sergeant Walter Hanley."

After Walt...I mean *Sergeant* Hanley was sworn in and took the stand, Mignon started right in.

"Sergeant Hanley, were you familiar with the deceased, Stacy Rickert?"

"Yes sir, I was."

"And how did you know him, Sergeant?"

"I was training him to be a police officer with the East Arthur Police Department."

"And at any time during this training, did you ever have the occasion to meet the defendant, Mr. David Pol...Pol...the *defendant*!" he shouted.

"Your Honor," said Mary, "the defense is willing to stipulate that Sergeant Hanley and Mr. Rickert were the ones who arrested Mr. *Polpulcionski* on the charge of DUI."

She said my last name as if to say *See how easy it is to pronounce, Phil.*

"Thank you, Ms. Payson. Now, Sergeant Hanley, was Mr. Rickert in training with you long?"

"No sir. He resigned before the defendant's DUI trial."

"And could you please tell the court why Mr. Rickert resigned, Sergeant?"

"Objection, Your Honor. The prosecutor is calling for a conclusion from the witness."

"Sustained," said Beanie. But you could tell he wasn't too happy about it.

"Very well. Sergeant Hanley, did Mr. Rickert ever tell you personally why he resigned?"

"Yes sir, he did."

"And exactly what did he say, to the best of your recollection, Sergeant?"

"He said that he was too embarrassed to be a police officer. He said that he made a mistake in taking the money to perjure himself at the defendant's DUI trial."

Apparently Walt wasn't even gonna take a stab at my last name.

"Objection, Your Honor. The transcript from Mr. *Polpulcionski's* DUI trial clearly states that the reason Mr. Rickert resigned was because he didn't want to have anything to do with the way the East Arthur Police Department operated. As a matter of fact, Your Honor, the deceased even apologized to Mr. *Polpulcionski.*"

I was hopin' Mary wouldn't push it too far with my last name. If she screwed it up even once, it could backfire on her.

"And do you have a copy of that transcript, Ms. Payson?" asked the judge.

"No, Your Honor, but we can certainly provide the court with a copy."

"Well, until you do, Ms. Payson, the objection is overruled."

Beanie looked real happy again.

"Thank you, Your Honor," said Mignon. "Now, Sergeant Hanley, did Mr. Rickert say why he took the money to begin with?"

"Yes sir, he did. He said he needed it to help support his lovely wife, three young children, two dogs, one cat, and one hamster."

"Don't forget the four goldfish," said the D.A.

"Oh yeah. I almost forgot. And four goldfish."

"Objection!" shouted Mary. "The prosecution is obviously leading the witness, Your Honor."

"Objection sustained," grumbled Beanie.

It looked like the judge was gonna have an up and down day. From the looks of him, I bet he wished he was hung over again.

"Sergeant Hanley, were you the one who picked up the defendant on the murder charge?"

"Yes sir, I was."

"And did he seem surprised when you told him he was under arrest for murder?"

"No sir, he did not."

"And then what happened, Sergeant?"

"Well, then I took him down to the station, and we sat around talking."

"And what did you talk about, Sergeant?"

"Well, I told him it would be better for him if he confessed, because I knew exactly why he killed Mr. Rickert."

"And what did he say to that?"

"Oh, he gave me some smart answers and told me that *I* was the one who killed Mr. Rickert because he made me look bad at his DUI trial."

"And *did you* kill Mr. Rickert, Sergeant?"

"No, of course not. Why should I? If I went around killin' everybody who made me look bad, they woulda got me by now."

Everyone in the courtroom got a good laugh out of that.

Poor Walt.

"Order in the court," yelled Beanie, bangin' his gavel.

The courtroom quieted down.

"No further questions for the witness at this time, Your Honor. Your witness, Ms. Payson."

"Before you begin with the witness, Ms. Payson, I think this would be a good time to take a short recess," said the judge. "It is now 9:45. If there are no objections, we will recess until 10:00. May I remind the ladies and gentlemen of the jury not to discuss the case with anyone. Court will resume at 10:00."

Before court resumed, Mary told me that she had heard from Saul. Unfortunately, what little he found out, Mary coulda gotten outta Hanley just by askin'.

Court resumed promptly at 10:00, and Judge Osbourne was rarin' to go.

I think I liked the old – and hung over - Beanie a lot better.

"Would Sergeant Hanley please retake the stand?" said the judge. After Hanley was seated, Beanie added, "And remember, you're still under oath."

"Yes, Your Honor."

"Sergeant Hanley," Mary began, "you stated that Mr. Polpulcionski did not seem surprised when you told him he was under arrest for murder. Do you remember that, sir?"

"Yes, I do."

"And did Mr. Polpulcionski say anything as to why he wasn't surprised, Sergeant?"

"Yes, he did."

"And what did he say, Sergeant?"

"He said that he had just received a call on his cell phone that he was going to be arrested for murder."

"And did he say from whom he received the call?"

"Yes. He said it was from a Mr. Nick Rudawski."

"And did he say how Mr. Rudawski knew about this?"

"No, he did not."

"I see. Now, Sergeant, could you please tell the court where the body of Mr. Rickert was discovered?"

"Yes. We found Mr. Rickert's body at the Come Inn and Get It in Queensville."

"I see. And how did you happen to discover it?"

"We received an anonymous tip on our tip hot line."

"And how did you come to arrest Mr. Polpulcionski?"

"Well, after we received the tip to find the body, we also received three different tips that the defendant was seen there that night."

I certainly knew where the Come Inn and Get It was located, but even *I* wouldn't be caught dead in a place like that.

"All *anonymous* tips, Sergeant?"

"Yes, that is correct."

"So then Sergeant, you actually don't have any witnesses that are willing to come forward that can place Mr. Polpulcionski at the scene of the crime the night Mr. Rickert was murdered, do you Sergeant?"

"Well…"

"Could you speak a little louder, please, Sergeant?"

"As far as I know, that is correct."

"Thank you, Sergeant. Your Honor, I move for an immediate dismissal of the case, and for all charges against my client to be dropped."

"Objection, Your Honor!" shouted Mignon. "Even though we don't have any witnesses in the courtroom, we still have three different tips, all stating that Mr…Mr…*the defendant* was at the Come Inn and Get It on the night of the murder. And we certainly know that he had a very good motive for killing Mr. Rickert."

"Motion denied, Ms. Payson. Continue."

Beanie was practically glowing.

"Well then, Sergeant, could you please tell the court what type of clientele frequents the Come Inn and Get It?"

"Objection," said Mignon immediately. "Irrelevant and immaterial."

"Sustained."

Beanie was now on a roll.

"In that case, Sergeant, let me rephrase the question. Isn't it true that most of the people who would go into the Come Inn and Get It wouldn't exactly be your high-class citizens? As a matter of fact, wouldn't most of them be people who would do almost anything for the price of a drink, including making *false, anonymous tips*?"

"Objection, Your Honor!" screamed Mignon.

"I withdraw the question, Your Honor." But Mary had made her point.

"One final question, Sergeant Hanley. Could you please tell us why no employees from the Come Inn and Get It are in court today? Surely one of them would have seen Mr. Polpulcionski if he was there on the night of the murder."

"Uh…yeah…well. Unfortunately, the workers have turned state's evidence against the owners in some charges that have been brought against them, so we now have them in protective custody, and the place has been closed."

"Thank you, Sergeant. No further questions of this witness at this time, Your Honor."

Mary did a great job of putting some doubts in the jury's mind, and makin' Walt look pretty bad on the stand, but I knew I was still a long way from bein' outta the woods. And I almost felt sorry for Walt.

Almost!

"Before we continue," Beanie began, "I see it is almost time for the noon recess. Court is adjourned until one o'clock."

When we returned from the noon recess, a very sober Judge Roy B. Osbourne was already waitin' for us.

"You may call your next witness, Mr. Mignon."

"Your Honor, the prosecution has no further witnesses at this time," said Mignon.

"In that case, you may call your first witness, Ms. Payson."

"Thank you, Your Honor. The defense calls David M. Polpulcionski."

Mary and I both knew that the defendant usually was not called to testify in a murder case, but I was all she had. After I was sworn in, Mary began with her questions.

"Mr. Polpulcionski, could you please tell the court where you were on the night Mr. Rickert was murdered."

"I was at home. Alone."

"So then you have no one who can back up your alibi for that evening?"

"That's correct."

"Did you go into the Come Inn and Get It on the night in question?"

"No. As I said, I was home alone all evening."

"Then, how can you explain three people claiming to see you there that evening?"

"Objection!" yelled Mignon.

"Sustained," answered the judge.

But Mary once again had scored another point with the jury.

"Mr. Polpulcionski, were you at all familiar with the deceased?"

"The only times I saw him were when I was arrested for DUI and during the DUI trial."

"Nothing other than that?"

"Nothing other than that."

"And yet Mr. Mignon would have us believe that you bribed Mr. Rickert to perjure himself at your DUI trial. Did you at any time do that?"

"No, I certainly did not. I never saw Mr. Rickert outside of the courtroom."

"Now, Mr. Polpulcionski, Sergeant Hanley said that you were not surprised when you were arrested for murder. Is that true?"

"Yes, that's true."

"And could you please tell the court why?"

"Well, as Sergeant Hanley stated, right before Hanley arrested me, I got a call on my cell phone from Nick Rudawski, tellin' me that I was gonna be arrested for Rickert's murder." I looked in the back of the courtroom and saw Nick. But not only was he sittin' with Nora, he was also sittin' with Judge Saundra H. Pants. Somethin' was definitely goin' on. I just had no idea what it was.

"Did Mr. Rudawski tell you why you were going to be arrested, or how he knew that?"

"No, he didn't."

"Well, did you ever get a chance to talk to him about it?"

"No, I did not."

"No further questions of the witness at this time, Your Honor."

"Very well," said the judge. "Before you begin your cross-examination, Mr. Mignon, I think this would be a good time to take a fifteen minute recess. Court will resume at 2:15."

While Mary had scored some points with the jury, her case wasn't very strong. Now it was Mignon's turn.

"So, *Mr. Polpulcionski*," he started. He must have caught the surprised look on my face. "I've been practicing, *Mr. Polpulcionski*," he snarled sarcastically.

"You claim you were home alone on the night of the murder?"

"Objection, Your Honor. The witness has already answered that question," said Mary.

"Sustained," said the judge. But everyone in the courtroom could tell he wasn't very happy about it.

"Well then, *Mr. Polpulcionski*, you stated that you didn't bribe Mr. Rickert to perjure himself at your DUI trial, but isn't it true that Julie Crinn could have bribed him?"

"Objection, Your Honor. Mrs. Crinn is not on trail here."

"Objection overruled." Beanie was happy again. "Please answer the question, *Mr. Polpulcionski.* I've been practicing, too," he added.

"Couldya repeat the question, please?" I said. "It's been so long since I heard it, I forgot what it was."

"Isn't it true that you and Mrs. Crinn were lovers, and that Mrs. Crinn would do anything for you?" Mignon shouted, gettin' almost in my face.

I just sat there for a few moments, apparently a little too long for Beanie.

"Well, Mr. Polpulcionski, answer the question, please?"

"Sure, Your Honor. Yes…and no."

"What do you mean *yes and no*, Mr. Polpulcionski?"

"Yeah, we're lovers; and no, she wouldn't do anything for me."

I looked at Julie. She was coverin' her mouth, tryin' not to laugh.

"Let me rephrase the question. Do you have any direct knowledge of Mrs. Crinn bribing the deceased to lie at your DUI trial?"

"No."

"No further questions of this witness at this time, Your Honor."

"You may call your next witness, Ms. Payson."

"I have no other witnesses, Your Honor. The defense rests."

Judge Osbourne looked shocked by this. "Well then, we will begin final argu…"he started.

"Your Honor," came a familiar voice from the back of the courtroom. It was Nick Rudawski. "May I approach the bench, Your Honor?"

Beanie seemed rattled by this. "And just who are you, sir?"

"I'm Nick Rudawski," Your Honor.

"Well, Mr. Rutkowski..."

"That's *Rudawski*," Your Honor.

"Oh, good grief. Just what I need. Another Polack," said Beanie. "Under the circumstances, I think court will adjourn until tomorrow morning at nine o'clock."

Mignon was grinnin' from ear to ear. For the first time, Mary looked like she was in jeopardy of losin' her first case in years, and it was *my* case she was gonna lose.

I had no idea what Nick was up to, and I was really in a pickle. This was no time for Nick to be gherkin around.

Chapter 37: YOUR LAST CHANCE

Well, there you have it, ladies and gentlemen, boys and girls. Every possible clue you could ever possibly imagine to solve the murder of my favorite police impersonator, namely, one Mr. Stacy Rickert. So, I know you've got it figured out by now, but just in case you'd like to review it one more time, let's take a look at the possible suspects.

First of all, we have our murdering lovebirds, Oscar and Teri Smallings. Brother Vincent stated that Oscar wouldn't kill a cop, or even a police impersonator, but they hadn't seen each other in years. Did they do it together, figurin' that they could only be executed once? Did either of them act alone, and if so, why?

Did Sergeant Walter Hanley murder his almost-partner because Stacy made him look bad at my DUI trial?

Did one of the three anonymous winos who phoned in the three anonymous tips bump him off? Or were the three of them in on it together?

Did someone from the now-closed Come Inn and Get It knife Rickert because Rickert had something on one, or all, of them? If so, they were now in protective custody. Good luck gettin' any one of them.

Did someone else involved with the case do it? We've seen possibilities of this throughout the last few weeks? Who could've done it, and why?

What about Nick Rudawski? What was he up to? Was he gonna confess, and why would he murder Rickert? Was he tryin' to protect Nora? How did he know I was about to be arrested for murder when he phoned me? And exactly why did he want to approach the bench?

Could it possibly have been someone who isn't in the book yet? You *know* I just *hate* those kinds of endings, but some writers do get desperate comin' down the home stretch. Do you think I'm that kind of writer?

This brings us to our last two possible suspects.

First of all, Julie Crinn. But if you really think Julie did it, please go back and read the last five chapters again.

Finally, there's me. After all, I *was* arrested for the murder. Did I really bribe Rickert, but then killed him because he tried to back out? I *know* I didn't do it, but then you must know by now that I'm not one to let the truth get in the way of a good story. Am I writin' this from death row, waitin' for my appeal to come up?

So…What do *you* think?

It's your last chance.

Don't let me down.

Hey! I just thoughta somethin'.

Did *you* do it?!

No, you couldn't possibly have killed Rickert.

You didn't even know him.

Did you?

And I'm sure you aren't the kind that would ever go into a place like the Come Inn and Get It.

Are you?

Hmm…

Chapter 38: RICKERT'S KILLER REVEALED – AND I HOPE IT ISN'T YOU

We arrived in the courtroom a few minutes before nine, all ready to go. The problem, as usual, was that Judge Osbourne was nowhere to be found. I kept thinkin' of the old sayin' *Justice delayed is justice denied.* I just hoped it wasn't true, cuz I woulda been the one bein' denied.

"I tried to get in touch with Nick last night, but I couldn't reach him anywhere," Mary said. "Any idea what he's up to?"

"None at all."

We turned around, and there was Nick sitting in the back with Nora, but Judge Pants wasn't with them.

"Well, I guess we'll know soon enough," said Mary.

The jury was there, D.A. Mignon was there, and, of course, I was there with Mary and Stella. We waited…and waited…and waited. Finally, at quarter to ten, Roy Bean Osbourne staggered toward the bench. I would have called him the *Honorable* Roy Bean Osbourne, but that would have been an insult to all the upstanding judges out there.

Both of them!

"Goo' mornin'," slurred the judge. "We will now start with the final armugents to the jury."

"Your Honor!" shouted Nick Rudawski, "may I approach the bench?"

"An' who're you?"

"I'm Nick Rudawski, Your Honor. I asked you yesterday if I could approach the bench."

"Well, Mr…Mr…Oh, God! Another Polack! Tha' was yeserday, an' you may not approach the bench t'day. We will now have the final amudents."

"But Your Honor," started Nick, "I…

"Enough outta you. One more word an' I'll find you in condent of quart," Beanie said, tryin' to bang his gavel.

"Goddammit!" he yelled.

He hit his hand instead.

Nick turned around like he was lookin' for the Lone Ranger or somebody to come and save him, but nobody showed up, so he sat down.

"Now, we will begin the final artulents. Now, we all know how this works. Mish Payshon, you get to go first. Thas so tha' by the time Mr. Migoon is finished sayin' what he has to say, nobody'll remember what you said, Mish Payshon, an' yer client'll lose. Everbody undershtan' that?"

No one said a word.

"Well, Mish Payshon, go 'head. I ain't got all day."

"Yes," said Mary, omitting the *Thank you, Your Honor*."

"Ladies and gentlemen of the jury, my client, David Polpulcionski, has been an honest, hard-working, law-abiding citizen of this community for many years. The prosecution would have you believe that Mr. Polpulcionski murdered Mr. Stacy Rickert because my client bribed Mr. Rickert to perjure himself at Mr. Polpulcionski's DUI trial; and that when Mr. Rickert tried to return the money, Mr. Polpulcionski murdered him in cold blood."

"But, ladies and gentlemen, nothing could be further from the truth. As my client stated under oath, he had no personal contact with the deceased after he was arrested for DUI, and certainly did not bribe him to lie on his behalf."

"Furthermore, my client stated, again under oath, that he was home alone on the night that Mr. Rickert was murdered, and had not gone into the Come Inn and Get It."

"And, I ask you, ladies and gentlemen of the jury, what evidence does the prosecution present in order for you to believe otherwise? They *say* they have three anonymous tips from people who claimed to have seen Mr. Polpulcionski at the Come Inn and Get It on the night of the murder."

"But, I ask you once again, what kind of people were going into the Come Inn and Get It? Honest, hard-working, law-abiding citizens like my client here, David Polpulcionski? No, of course not! These were people who would do anything for little more than the price of a drink. And that includes phoning in *false* anonymous tips."

"Ladies and gentlemen, the prosecution has nothing to go on with its case. I urge you to find my client, Mr. David Polpulcionski *not guilty* of this crime of murder of which he has been accused."

"Ladies and gentlemen, I thank you."

Everyone expected the judge to say something, but apparently he was sound asleep on the bench. The bailiff went over and woke him up.

"Are you done, Mish Payshon?"

Mary remained silent.

"You *are* done," he continued, pointing at me, "you, you, you *Polack* you."

"I she it's almos' ten thutty. We will take a fifteen minute recess. Be back at...at..."

"Ten forty-five," said the bailiff.

"Yeah, ten fory-five," said the judge, tryin' to bang his gavel again.

"Goddammit!" he yelled, hittin' his hand even harder the second time.

When we returned from the recess, the judge was already in the courtroom – technically. He was snorin' away on the bench.

"Wake up, Your Honor," said the bailiff.

"Give Beanie a little kiss."

"Your Honor, wake up!" But it did no good.

"C'mon, honey, give Beanie a little kiss."

The bailiff went over and shook the judge.

"Oh, I like it when you get frisky."

The bailiff was forced to shake Beanie until he finally opened his eyes.

"Where the hell...? Oh!"

"Are you ready wit yer final armugents, Mr. Magoo?" asked the judge.

"May I approach the bench, Your Honor." It was Nick Rudawski again. Who knew what he was up to?

Mary, Stella, and I turned around and saw Nick standing there. Only now he was standing next to Nora and Judge Saundra H. Pants.

"I told you no before, Mr...Mr...*you!*" yelled the judge. "One more time and I'll..."

"I think you should allow Mr. Rudawski to approach the bench, Judge Osbourne," said Judge Pants.

"No," said Judge Osbourne. "Ish my trial an' I'm runnin' it."

"And are you forgetting who the President Judge is for this county, Judge Osbourne?" said Judge Pants.

"No. All right, you can approach the bench."

"Thank you, Your Honor," said Nick.

"Now, whatd'ya want?" said Judge Osbourne. "An' who did you say you were again?"

"My name is Nick Rudawski, Your Honor, and I am a Special Agent of the F.B.I out of Tucson."

So that's what I couldn't figure out.

"Well, bully for you, Mr. Secret Agent. *Secret Agent man, secret agent man, they're givin'...*"

"That will be enough, Judge Osbourne," said Judge Pants. "Please continue, Mr. Rudawski."

"As I was about to say, Your Honor, I know who killed Mr. Rickert, and it wasn't Mr. Polpulcionski."

I was now glad that Nick was gherkin around before. It looked like I would soon be outta the pickle I was in.

"I have a warrant for the arrest of the murderer, Your Honor."

That seemed to sober up Judge Osbourne in a hurry. "Well, that's nice, *Mr. Secret Agent*, only this is a county case, not a federal case, so I'm afraid you're out of your jurisdiction."

"But that's where you're wrong, Your Honor."

"What?!"

"You see, Your Honor, Stacy Rickert was also a Special Agent for the F.B.I. He was investigating alleged federal racketeering against Oscar and Teri Smallings when he was murdered, so that makes this a federal case."

Everyone in the courtroom was totally silent.

"I have here, Your Honor, an arrest warrant for the murder of Stacy Rickert for – the entire courtroom stopped breathing – Roy Bean Osbourne. I'm placing you under arrest for the murder of Stacy Rickert, Your Honor. You have the right to remain silent. Anything you say..."

"I'm well aware of my rights. Please don't insult my intelligence by reading them to me," snapped Judge Osbourne.

"Yes, I killed Stacy Rickert, but it was all because of *her*," pointing at Nora. "I loved her, but then she dumped me for somebody else. At first I thought it was him," he said, pointing at me, "that… that…*other Polack*. But then I found out it was Rickert. I begged Nora to take me back, but she didn't want any part of me."

"Then that night I saw Rickert in the Come Inn and Get It. There were three of us in the place, and I'd already had a few drinks. By the time the guy he was talking to left, I had a few more, and I saw my chance. When his back was turned, I grabbed a knife off the bar and stabbed him and then I left. The bartender was in the back, so he never saw me do it. The next day I called the police tip line from three different phones and left the anonymous tips."

"Bailiff, kindly remove Judge Osbourne from the bench," said Judge Pants, taking his seat.

"Under the circumstances, Your Honor," said D.A. Phil A. Mignon, "I make a motion that all charges against Mr. Ploposkinski be dropped."

At that point, I didn't care how bad he butchered my name.

"No objections," shouted Mary.

"All charges against you, Mr. Polpulcionski, are hereby dismissed. Court is adjourned."

It was time to go back to Julie's and celebrate.

Chapter 39: ALL'S WELL THAT ENDS WELL…or…GOODBYE
FOR NOW

As soon as the trial ended, nine of us went back to Julie's to
celebrate. It was probably the first time that Sandy Pants – she insisted
that everyone call her Sandy – had been flyin' solo in quiet awhile. Or
maybe she was just takin' a break.

After Julie and I took care of the refreshments, everyone started
to congratulate Mary and me, and, of course, Nick Rudawski.

Then the questions began.

"So Nick," I said, "how did you happen to know that Beanie
was in the Come Inn and Get It that night?"

"Oh, that was quite simple, really. Remember when Beanie said
that he waited until Stacy was through talking with someone?"

"Yeah."

"Well, who do you think that someone was? I guess he had so
much to drink that night that he didn't even recognize me in court. The
only good thing about that is that with a good attorney," he said,
looking at Mary, "is that the most he will probably be charged with will
be voluntary manslaughter."

"I'd have to think about that for a few days," said Mary, "and
then only if he came to me. I've had my fill of Judge Roy Bean
Osbourne for quite some time."

"And don't forget, dear," chimed in Nathan Bricks, "we'll be leaving on our honeymoon in ten days."

After everyone congratulated the happy couple, Mary continued, "Yes, we've decided to give it another go, and this time we're going to adopt. That will certainly limit my time in the courtroom for some time."

"Mary," I said, "I guess this is as good a time as any to bring this up. It'll be awhile before I can pay you for your services, but you'll get your money."

"Oh, I know I will," replied Mary. "Saul has finally decided to move to Saskatchewan this coming weekend, so starting next week *you* are my new private investigator. I will have a more-limited practice, but I'll still have plenty of work to keep you busy. I'll just deduct something from your fees every week until you're paid up. Let's see, at what I'll be paying you, that should only take about 87 years, the way I have it figured."

Everyone laughed at that.

Everyone but Mary.

"Oh, and Dewey, I've already made arrangements for you to rent Saul's office. It's in the same building as mine, so be there on Monday morning by nine o'clock."

Julie and I just looked at each other and then at Mary.

"Well, all right. Tuesday then. Mondays are usually pretty slow."

"So Nora," said Stella, "were you really seeing Judge Osbourne?"

"I only went out with him twice, and I really don't know why I saw him the second time. Dewey, remember the time you came to pick me up and I left a note saying that I would be right back?"

"Yeah."

"That's when I went to tell Beanie that it was over, and that I was seeing someone else. I'd met Stacy a little while before that, and we started seeing each other."

"Yeah, I remember that. But I thought Stacy was married and had three kids and all those animals?"

"No, that was all a cover," explained Nick. "The wife was another undercover agent, and we never did bother with any kids. When anyone asked, we always told them they were at their grandparents. The animals we got from pet stores, and we've already found good homes for all of them."

(Just in case you were interested, no animals were harmed in any way during the writing of this book.)

"Stacy and I got along well," Nora continued, "but he told me up front that he could never commit to a relationship, but he would never say why. Now I know. And then Nick came along, and…well…"

"Why don't you tell them, honey?" said Nick.

"Nick and I are moving to Tucson, and we're going to get married – right after, well…"

"Right after I change my last name," Nick picked up. "She said that after dealing with you and me, Dewey, I had to change my last name, or the deal was off."

"So, what are you gonna change it to?" I asked.

"That's what I'm trying to figure out," said Nick.

"Well, what are you interested in?" I asked. "Maybe that would be of some help."

"Surprisingly, Nora and I are both big silent movie buffs. As a matter of fact, once we get to Tucson, I'm going to resign from the F.B.I., and we're going to open a theater that shows nothing but silent films."

"I guess you can do that since you're both billionaires," said Julie.

"Actually," said Nick, "Nora's the billionaire, but I do have some money put aside."

"But I thought Joe left you a billion in his will, too?" asked Julie.

"No. Actually, I'd never even met your husband. We just made up that story about his being my cousin after he was murdered. I knew Stacy was investigating the Smallings and their gang, and after your husband was killed, we knew there had to be some connection. The F.B.I. sent me out to see what I could find out. We couldn't say anything, of course, but we had the lawyer read that phony will to back up my story. You'll be getting my *share* of the inheritance, Julie."

"Well, thank you."

"Oh, and Julie, just so you know, your husband had nothing to do with the illegal activities of the Smallings."

"Well, at least that was *one* thing he wasn't guilty of."

"Nick," I said. "Let's get back to this name thing. So, who is your favorite silent film star?"

"Without a doubt, Charles Chaplin."

"There you have it," I said. "Nick and Nora *Chaplin.*" (What were you expectin'? Hey! You really didn't think I would stoop *that* low, did ya?)

"Well, we really must be going, Dewey," Nick said. "We're flying to Tucson tomorrow morning. *Asta minyana,*" he added, with a silly grin on his face. (What the hell! Why not?)

I had no idea what he meant by that, and it certainly didn't sound Polish to me; but to keep from appearin' real dumb I answered "*Dobja.*"

His silly grin turned into a look of total confusion.

"Well, goodbye, everybody. And good luck to the two of you," Nick said to Julie and me.

"Oh, one more thing before you go, Nick. Why were you and Stacy in the Come Inn and Get It to begin with?"

"Stacy called and said he had to meet an informant there and thought it would be the safest place for us to meet. Little did he know."

"Yeah," I said. "Go figure. Well, the best of luck to you, too. And congratulations once again. Keep in touch, and pay us a visit some time. And again, I really don't know how to thank you for what you did."

"You're welcome," said Nick. "Just doin' my job."

We walked Nick and Nora to their car, but I'm sure it wasn't gonna be for the last time.

When we got back inside, Mary and Nathan were waiting by the door.

"Well, we really should be going, too," said Mary. "But don't forget about Tuesday. Since Saul will be leaving for Saskatchewan, you'll be my number one investigator."

"Hey Sanford," I said. "Yo, Sanford." Still no answer.

"Oh, you can call him Zeke again," said Stella. "I promised that I would give up trying to change him if he promised to come home every night – and also wash his hands before he got there."

"Great to have you back, *Zeke*," I said. "Does this mean you two are living together?"

"Well, for awhile," said Zeke. "We're gettin' married in three months. And Dew, I'd like you to be my best man."

"It would be an honor, Zeke. Congratulations. But, back to what I was gonna ask ya."

"Yeah, Dew, what's that?"

"I wasn't any good in geography. Saskatchewan ain't in this country, is it?"

"I ain't real sure, Dew. Either it's outta the country or it's up around Wilkes-Barre."

Everyone laughed at that. Everyone but me and Zeke.

"Yes, Saskatchewan is out of the country, Dewey," said Mary. "Why do you want to know?"

"Well, since Saul's movin' outta the country, I guess that moves me up to the *357th* best private investigator east of the mighty Manatawny."

Everyone laughed again. This time me and Zeke were included.

"Well, goodbye everyone," said Mary and Nathan.

"I'll see you Tuesday," I said. "And thanks again for everything."

"Well, I guess I'd better be going, too," said Sandy Pants. "I have some unfinished business to attend to."

I was wondering *who* the unfinished business was that she was referring to, but instead I said, "Thanks for coming, and thanks for giving Nick the chance to approach the bench."

"No problem," said Sandy. "Sorry I cut it so close, but I had some business I had to attend to."

I bet she did. I just wondered if Phil hadn't been going out on her if she would have been there at all. I guess the old sayin' was true.

How does it go again? Oh, yeah. *Hell hath no fury like Hot Pants spurned*. That's it, ain't it?

"Oh, and Dewey, please try to stay out of my courtroom unless you're working on a case with Mary."

"I'll do my best, Your Honor."

After Sandy left, the four of us sat around talkin' for awhile, but finally Stella got the idea that Julie and I wanted to be alone.

"Well Zeke," she said, "I guess we should be going, too."

"I guess I'll be seein' ya around the office on Tuesday," I said. "And Zeke, I'll be seeing you, too."

After we walked Stella and Zeke to the door, Julie and I were finally alone. Even though I still had my own apartment, I was spendin' a lot of nights at Julie's, and that night was certainly gonna be one of 'em. And in case you had to ask, Julie's legs *do* go all the way up.

But as I said, I still had my own apartment. We weren't livin' together, at least not yet.

What kind of a cad do you think I am?

Hey, I ain't *that* kind. I finally got to look 'em up, and *that* kind is really somebody who...Oh, never mind. Look it up yourself.

Almost forgot. For those of you who are interested, the last I heard was that Debbie – now played by yet another actress (a kinder, gentler Debbie) was bein' released from the nympho ward for unwed mothers on the condition that she would marry Doctor Fix. Fix, in return, would adopt all the kids that didn't turn out to be his.

What a guy!

So there you have it. My first big adventure.

This is Dewey P., remindin' you once again: *I do, and if you don't on a regular basis, you'll be in big trouble real soon!*

www.ingramcontent.com/pod-product-compliance
Lightning Source LLC
Chambersburg PA
CBHW022146010726
47493CB00002B/360